Apples &

Oranges

Book two in the This & That Series

Brooke Moss

Cover art by: Brooke Moss

Edited by: Meggan Connors, www.megganconnors.com

Published by: Brooke Moss, CHP
ISBN ebook: 978-1-939976-03-1
ISBN print: 978-1-939976-04-8

The author acknowledges the copyrighted or trademarked status and trademark owners of the following wordmarks mentioned in this work of fiction: Givenchy, Guerlain, Michael Kors, BMW, Xbox, Barbie, Elie Tahari, Oakley's Juicy Couture, Levi's, Ray Bans, Hermes, Bon Appetit, Smith and Wesson, Cirque du Soleil, Gucci, Jack Spade, Spanx, Adriano Goldschmeid.

For Monte.

(The sweet apple to my acidic orange. Without you there is no me.)

Chapter One

My mother's latest plastic surgery left her face looking like a potato.

No, really. It was oversized, comparatively speaking (the woman was a size two for crying out loud), and her skin was pulled tight over surgically-enhanced cheekbones and chin. Though the effect was like an allergen test gone bad, my mother, former eighties' nighttime actress Annalise DeLoria, wore the hornet attack aftermath proudly.

My mouth dropped open when I saw her.

"Twenty grand well spent," she announced.

Thirty minutes into lunch, and I was still stupefied by the sight. Her caramel skin looked so uncomfortable, my own face ached just looking at it. And I kept waiting for her head to flop forward, landing face first in her food because of the weight of its man-made parts.

The more Annalise talked—chastising me in Spanish for having the nerve to ask if it was her last procedure since it was lucky number fifteen—the less her lips moved. She looked like a ventriloquist, sitting there calling me a *grosera, mocosa egoísta* over her untouched, undressed spinach salad. Except that her hand wasn't up anyone's ass.

Oh, and she wasn't calling me a *rude, selfish brat* for comedic effect. Oh, no. This was all for the sole purpose of knocking me down a peg or two. After all, I had the audacity to show up for our once-per-year luncheon looking younger, prettier, and more *human* than she did. Never mind that I was thirty years younger. And her daughter.

Nobody outshone Annalise DeLoria. Not ever.

"Well, have you found yourself a man, Marisol?" she asked me through frozen lips.

"I've been dating," I replied cautiously, pushing my smashed red potatoes from one edge of my plate to the other. "Nothing too serious, though."

"You do realize how many calories were in your meal, don't you?" She flared her nostrils at what was left of my salmon filet.

My mother had been dieting for as long as I could remember. One of my earliest memories was of her cussing out my nanny for pouring two percent milk on my cereal. It was no wonder I'd grown up and started my own catering business. Rich, delicious, home-cooked foods at my fingertips every day. Sure, I spent most of my time at the gym working off the foie gras and truffle sauce, but it was worth it. (My super ripped trainer helped, too.) Besides, it was either open a business where I could eat anything I wanted after being forced to diet from the age of seven, or become a hard-core bulimic.

I didn't like throwing up. It screwed up my lipstick and made my breath stink.

Catering it was.

I pushed my plate back, no longer hungry. Being around Annalise did that to me. "So tell me about Don." Maybe asking about my most recent stepfather—the seventh, in case you were wondering—would change the topic. He was a lawyer in L.A. whom she'd met while he handled my fourth stepfather's tax evasion case. They'd been married all of a year, and I was certain she was cheating on him. I didn't have high hopes for the longevity of their relationship.

Annalise waved a manicured hand. "Please. The man barely notices when I'm there."

"Well, he is seventy-three, Mother." I discreetly checked my iPhone for messages, then hid it under my napkin on the table. My business partner, Lexie, was drowning in lobster stuffed mushroom caps, and I needed to get back to work. "I suppose his attention span is only so long anymore."

"Well, he certainly noticed his case last month." She forked a piece of spinach, held it up to her mouth, rethought it, and put it back down. "That's *all* he noticed, if you want the truth."

I shifted in my chair. My mom had never grasped the concept that most people—normal people—actually work for a living. "Well, I'm sure it was a big case if he—"

"Want my advice, my dear?" She put down her fork and steepled her fingers. Her gaze was heavy... or maybe that was just the weight of her giant face. I couldn't be sure.

"Annalise, uh, Mom, I—"

She shushed me with the wave of her hand. "Get yourself a man. An older one who's filthy rich and retired. Who'll worship you, despite your shortcomings." Annalise smiled at a waiter passing the table—a gesture that was almost undecipherable because of her puffed face—then pointed at my head. "One that will ignore your crooked nose. Or your muffin top."

The woman sitting at the table next to us looked at my mom, and embarrassment flushed my skin. I sat up straighter, and willed my cheeks not to turn pink. Conversations like this fostered my obsession with going to the gym seven days a week. Conversations like this reminded me why I avoided my mother like most people avoided the flu. Or crabs. I worked hard for this body, and I'd also paid good money to have this nose.

"Get him into bed before he can get to know you." Annalise paused to sip her zinfandel. "Don't let him see that ill temper of yours. Let him play with the goodies. Get him hooked in bed, then get him to the alter before he asks for a pre-nup."

Now the man next to us was staring. Normally I liked saying things to shock the masses, but when it was my mother, with her ten-carat ring and the latest Givenchy bag, it humiliated me. I felt like the eleven-year-old girl again, being sent off to boarding school because stepdad number three was only

4

fourteen years my senior and didn't like the idea of having a kid hanging around. It made making love on the kitchen counter very awkward.

I'd learned *that* the hard way.

For thirty-two years I'd been on the receiving end of my mother's disapproval. When I got good grades she said I needed to be the prom queen. When I got onto the prom court, she said I needed to title in pageants. When I got on the dean's list in college, she reminded me that by the time she was twenty, she was headlining on a nighttime network drama. When I started my own business, she reminded me that the balance in just *one* of her checking accounts was triple the cost of my portion of the loan.

Being rejected by Annalise was getting really old.

My mother frowned at me. "Oh, Marisol, why are you scowling like that? You know, you'll get wrinkles on your forehead if you do that." Her dark brown eyes scanned my hairline. "I can see you're already getting some."

I touched my skin absently. "I don't want to get married."

"Don't be absurd. Of course you do."

Words shoved themselves to the tip of my tongue and threatened to jump. Dozens of nasty words like *your blouse looks way too young for you*, and *your teeth needed to be whitened again because you look like a pirate*. Insults and jabs much like the ones she spewed my way. I also wanted to say words that reminded my mother she was only saying those things to me so she could hurt me.

Sadly, it was working, but I didn't have to let her see that.

5

With anyone else, I would have come back with guns blazing, weaving a tapestry of insults in both English and Spanish. I would have tossed my long caramel colored hair—which I just had highlighted for this luncheon—and stalked away from the table like a runway model.

But this was my mother. And as I sat there across the table from her, feeling fat and unattractive because of the salmon sitting in my gut like a brick, and the eyes of most of the surrounding patrons on me, I did nothing. I just pressed my lips together and took it.

"The sooner you get married, the sooner you'll get divorced. And that, my dear daughter, is where the money is." Annalise plucked a gold compact out of her purse and reapplied her Guerlain lipstick. "Men will pay more money to get out of a marriage than in. The sooner you get a healthy divorce settlement, the sooner you can stop dipping into the money your father gave you, and you can stop playing that *independent woman* game you like so much."

"Eats and Treats had a great year," I said through clenched teeth. I'd co-owned my business with my best friend, Lexie, for four years now, and each year our numbers went up. We'd even taken on additional help since the birth of her son, and we'd both still managed to take home a salary every week. In the world of small businesses, that was a home run. "We've expanded our workspace and had to turn away a couple of events for this summer."

She shook her head. "What is it you do? Bake cookies or something?"

My molars started to ache from clenching my teeth so hard. "We do sweet and savory, and we provide cooking, waiting, and clean up. We're full service. You saw my business plan."

Yes, Annalise had seen it, but she never once asked me to fly to California to cater one of her many events. When I offered to cater her wedding reception, she turned down the idea, citing that hiring relatives was "gauche."

"I didn't really pay attention." She sighed. "Did you try this wine? It's terrible. Don't they have decent wine in this town? *¡Dios del cielo!*"

Rolling my eyes, I peeked at my phone under the napkin. It was aglow with messages. "Mom, Lexie needs me back at work, I—"

"Why you decided to settle in this one horse town is beyond me." She looked at the neighboring tables with distaste. We were in the nicest restaurant in the city, so the people seated near us were well-dressed and appeared affluent. I assumed Annalise would like that. "Of all the places in the country, Marisol, the *world*, you chose here?"

Unexpected tears jabbed at the backs of my eyes. I wasn't a crier by nature. My friends all said I had a heart of stone, but my mother always managed to bring out the vulnerability in me. I hated that.

"I like it here." My voice cracked, so I tried to cover it up with a cough. The truth was, I settled in Spokane, Washington, for no other reason than the people I'd met since coming here. After overhearing my mother announce she would die of embarrassment if her daughter slummed it in a state college, and being told by my father in Florida that he didn't want any responsibility besides

7

signing the tuition check every semester, I applied to every state college on the west coast. Since I spent most of my high school years making out with the lacrosse team and being a mean girl, most of the colleges in southern California rejected me. On some random act of mercy given by the gods of college acceptance, I got into Eastern Washington University by the skin of my teeth.

"My friends are here," I added, jutting my chin.

I met Lexie and her cousin, Candace, during our freshman year. I was pretty sure they kept me around because I was crass and made them laugh, but they inadvertently filled the giant, gaping black hole left by my family.

When we graduated, I stayed in the area to be near them. Not that I admitted that. No, siree. That meant breaking through my tough exterior to show them what's underneath. Could I have gone to southern California and lived off the trust fund my father had given me? Sure. Hell, I could have moved to Florida and lived like my party animal father for the rest of my life had I wanted to. But I didn't want those things. I guess I wanted to be home, and for whatever reason, this place, surrounded by rolling plains, felt like just that.

"So you'll email." Annalise snorted. "Sell that house of yours and come to L.A. We can go to spas together." She gestured at her face. "Get our yearly maintenance together."

Fat chance, I thought to myself. "I'm not going to L.A. I like where I'm at."

"Oh, please." Laughing like I'd announced plans to become president, she added, "You don't really like it here. You're living here to be difficult. Now come on, the game's over. You've gotten it out of your system. You belong

somewhere more sophisticated. Especially if you're ever going to score a man

worth anything. The men here are so..." Her nostrils flared. I think. "White

trash, if you will."

She shuddered, and the couple next to us grunted. Heat crept up the

sides of my neck. This luncheon needed to be over soon, or I was going to snap.

And by snap, I meant I was going to flip the table over, Jersey Housewife style.

My phone buzzed from underneath my napkin again.

"My *family* is here," I said in a low voice. "And I have to get back to

work."

My mother smiled, though it looked more like a grimace. Her voice

took on a steely quality that made me shiver with fear. I heard that tone plenty of

times growing up. "Oh, please, Marisol. Don't be so dramatic." Annalise paused

for dramatic effect as I picked my purse up off of the floor. "You don't *have* a

family, remember?"

Sucking a deep breath, I tucked my purse in the crook of my elbow.

Annalise always knew how to go for the jugular. All of our lunches ended the

same way. Me with hurt feelings, and her with the hefty ego boost that came

from humiliating her only child.

I stood up and crossed to the other side of the table robotically.

Bending down to kiss her plastic cheek, I whispered, "Have a safe flight home."

Chapter Two

One broken four-inch heel, two sweat marks on a Michael Kors cowl neck blouse, three chipped fingernails, and a broken down BMW 3 Series convertible. Not exactly a fun way to top off my debunked luncheon with my mother.

"*Maldito coche!*" I hissed as I hiked across the busy street.

A woman pushing a stroller in the crosswalk glared at me. "Nice language."

"How was I to know you'd understand?" I snapped. It wasn't my fault she'd heard me calling my car a piece of *you know what.* Besides, who walked their baby around in ninety-degree weather? "Buy a minivan, breeder."

A car honked at me, but I ignored it. The walk sign had long since started flashing red, but I couldn't move any faster, thanks to my busted shoe. I'd left my iPhone under the napkin at the restaurant so I couldn't call for a tow, and the unseasonably warm May weather made my most recent blow-out worthless. Being forced to walk to the nearest auto shop was the icing on my crap cake of a day.

10

I didn't *walk* places. I drove places. Walking was what tree huggers did because they thought car exhaust was the devil. I only walked when I was cooling down on the treadmill after a workout, which usually involved my gorgeous trainer, and in that case, I didn't mind. But in ninety-degree heat with a messed up shoe? *I minded.*

By the time I hobbled into the first garage I'd come across in this sketchy neighborhood—because when do cars ever break down in nice, gated communities with manicured lawns and luxury cars parked in the driveway—I felt like a limp piece of lettuce. My hair was flat, my clothes were wrinkled and soaked, and I was pretty sure I sweated most of my makeup down into a bronze ring at the base of my neck.

Limping past the door of the corrugated metal shop with a red roof, I headed straight for the open double garage doors. There was no time to chitchat with a dimwitted receptionist, and there had to be some grease monkey underneath one of these pieces of crap. I was in a mood. I just spent forty-five minutes across a table from *my mother,* and if that wasn't enough to put someone on edge, I didn't know what would. My stomach dropped as I passed the mirrored glass door. I never went in public looking like this. *Ever.*

"What can I do for ya?"

Jumping, I tripped over a crack in the cement and stumbled into the garage. A kid in his early twenties with a prominent nose and dark, shaggy hair stood before me. His coveralls were oil-stained and greasy, and he peered up at me from underneath the hood of a beat-up truck that looked like it should've been laid to rest a decade ago. He'd clearly be gorgeous one day, once he got the chance to grow into his lovely Mediterranean features, but for now he was sporting the awkwardly cute appearance of someone who knew not the full extent of his capability. I remembered those days.

"Yeah. I need help." I tugged off my other shoe and tossed both of them into a nearby trashcan. The back of my blouse was completely plastered to my skin.

His eyes widened. "Hey-yo. I can help you. What seems to be the problem, pretty lady?" As he stood upright, he whacked his head into the truck hood. He blushed and rubbed his tousled head sheepishly. "Ow. Sorry."

I would've laughed, had I not been on the verge of heat exhaustion.

When his eyes roamed from the top of my head, down to my toes, and back up again, lingering far too long on my cleavage, I sneered and said, "Is it take your son to work day today?"

Years and years ago, I left the seventh grade in May with the body of a pubescent boy, then returned in September with the body of a Playboy model. I inherited my mother's curves and my father's Puerto Rican good looks, and whether I liked it or not, men noticed. Annalise eventually took me shopping, introducing me to the fun of lingerie and four-inch heels. By the time I was sixteen, I'd grown fond of the leering stares, and the way I could control men with the flip of the hair or jut of a hip. Now that I was in my thirties, I used my looks to my advantage for everything from lowered insurance premiums to free mochas.

Hey, you work with what you got, right?

The kid in the coveralls smirked. "Yeah, right. My dad doesn't work here."

I raised an eyebrow. "You're what? Sixteen? Seventeen, kid?"

"Nineteen," he replied with a grin.

"Tempting, big guy." I lifted my dampened hair off of my neck, and his eyebrows rose higher on his forehead. "But really, the sign says family owned and operated. Who runs this place?"

He straightened his shoulders. "Who says I don't? Want a tour?"

The kid was persistent, I had to give him that. But I didn't do the cougar thing. Not with boys *that* young, anyway. The youngest I dated was twenty-two, a full decade younger than me. I'd only done that because Candace declared it inappropriate and morally wrong. And, well, I couldn't let her win that argument, could I? We'd only gone out a few times before I realized I was in competition with the guy's Xbox, and that wasn't gonna fly. I stuck to my own age bracket or older, now.

"I'll pass on that tour." I pulled my wallet out of my handbag, then slid my platinum card out of its worn slot. "But seriously, my car's broken down on Manito Boulevard, and I need a tow."

He laughed. "That sucks."

"Sure does." This kid was getting on my nerves. Pressing my lips together, I glanced at his embroidered nametag. "So, *Trey,* do you think you could find someone to run out there and get it?"

Trey put his hand on the edge of the truck and leaned back casually. It slipped, and he stumbled, then righted himself with a grin. "I might be talked into it."

I tilted my head to the side. "Are you joking?"

Now, normally I enjoy flirting as much as any girl—maybe even more—but today I wasn't interested. Not only was this boy out of my preferred age bracket, but I was also an hour late getting back to work the day before a three hundred guest wedding. This was the last thing I needed.

He shook his head. "No, ma'am."

Aggravation crept up the back of my sticky neck like a spider, so I put my hands on my hips and leaned closer to the kid. He gulped. "Listen up. I've got a dead car holding up traffic out there, and a business partner who will fillet me and serve me up with capers if I don't get my ass back to work. Understand?" He nodded, so I went on. "So how's about you call your tow truck guy and let me borrow a phone, m'kay?"

Trey furrowed his dark eyebrows at me. "You don't have a phone?"

"I left it at a restaurant, okay?" I snapped, wiping my brow. "Seriously, would it kill you guys to air condition this place?"

"Too expensive," growled a low voice from the back of the shop, making Trey stand up straight and tuck his hands into his pockets like a good boy. "There's a recession going on. Or haven't you heard?"

Snarling, I peered around the edge of the truck. "How long have you been over there?"

14

"Long enough." There was a scraping sound as a creeper rolled out from underneath a Honda Civic. "Judging by those fancy shoes you threw away I don't imagine someone like you understands the concept of a recession."

"Excuse me?" I snapped.

"That's my uncle." Trey's voice cracked, and he covered it up with a cough. "We're business partners."

There was a scoff from underneath the Honda. "Hey, Trey, why don't you stop flirting with the woman and tell her whose name is on the lease?"

Whoever it was under that Civic, he needed a throat lozenge. This uncle's voice sounded like he'd gargled with broken glass for a decade or so. With a labored (or was that annoyed?) sigh, a man stood up and ambled towards me.

"Oh my," I said under my breath, dropping my hair and smoothing down the front of my skirt.

This guy was appealing. And by that, I meant *straight shot of heat right to the center of my belly* hot. He was tall, taller than me in a pair of four-inch Jimmy Choo's, which meant around six feet, give or take, and that was enough to make me want to turn a backbend right there on the cracked cement floor.

"You are, Uncle Demo." Trey pronounced the name like *Thee-mo,* the traditional Greek dialect rolling off his tongue like butter.

Oh, they're Greek? Yummy. Good pastries. Handsome men.

Demo sauntered towards me with a scowl. His dark eyes were hooded with thick black eyebrows, and a salt-and-mostly-pepper five o'clock shadow decorated the bottom half of his face. His dark hair, highlighted with silver strands above the ears, was dampened at the nape of his tanned neck and stood in all directions. His coveralls were undone down to his waist, then tied in a knot at his hips, and all that he wore on the top half of his body was a tight white wife beater that practically sang next to his dark olive skin.

Demo, proprietor of Triple D's Garage, was a bonafide Mediterranean stud. Not that I ever dated the work-by-the-sweat-of-his-brow type. My mother called dating men like that "slumming it," but I wouldn't go that far. I just didn't find the rough hands, scarred skin, covered in sweat thing to be hot. No, I usually stuck with doctors, lawyers and executive types. Men who wore suits made out of Italian wool and drove cars as nice as mine or better. Men who spent their days immersed in paperwork and strategy meetings, not axle grease and transmission fluid.

Hey, I'm not stupid. I knew it was shallow, but the apple didn't fall far from the tree, I supposed. Squaring my shoulders, I turned my attention away from the horny kid and onto his buffed up relative. Maybe sticking with the guys in suits was overrated. Candace always said her ophthalmologist husband, Brian, was at his hottest when he mowed the lawn shirtless. Maybe she had a point. Slumming it couldn't be that bad when guys like this were up for grabs.

I've got a Greek wedding to cater this summer. Maybe I can score a recipe for dolmades out of this. Work it, girl.

"Hi, Uncle Demo," I said, sticking out my hand. I added a wink for good measure. "I'm Marisol Vargas."

He pulled a stained grey rag out of his back pocket, and for a second I thought I was going to wipe off his hands before shaking my hand. But then he plucked a wrench off of the bumper of the Honda and started polishing it. "Demetrious Marcos Antonopolous."

"Demetrious... Anan... pop... oh lous?" I grinned cheekily.

"Antonopulous." He said it like I was a moron for being confused by his freakishly complicated surname. Then his brow furrowed even more.

The fire in my belly fizzled. I sure hoped he wasn't in charge of public relations for Triple D's, otherwise they'd be closed by the end of the month. "That's quite a mouthful, Demetrious."

"Demo." His tongue did that rolly-thing that made the name sound delicious. But his mouth was still pulled into a disapproving frown. That scowl was most *un*delicious.

"Uh, okay." I stammered on my words.

"How's that pickup coming?" He turned his frosty glare to his nephew. "Clint will be here for it in twenty. You gonna have it done in time?"

Trey's chest puffed up. "'Course."

"Then why don't you stop ogling the lady and get back to it."

Trey turned back to the truck engine and muttered, "Yes, sir."

Demo's focus landed back on me, and a shiver wriggled its way up my spine. I couldn't be sure if it was from being turned on, or just a reaction to the frigidity he was exuding. "I'll get your car tomorrow."

"Okay, thanks...oh." My shoulders dropped. "Wait. What?"

Demo's dark eyes rolled. Or *almost* rolled, as he seemed to be struggling to keep his disdain at bay. "I said I'd get your car tomorrow."

"But it's in the road." I said dumbly.

"Is it pulled over on the shoulder?" He dropped the wrench into a nearby metal tool box, and it landed with a loud bang.

"Well, yeah, but—"

"Then I'll get it tomorrow. Or tonight, if you're lucky." Tucking the rag back into his back pocket, Demo used his boot to move the creeper underneath his legs. "Leave the keys on the desk and call around noon. Should have an estimate by then."

"Are you joking?" I peered out the garage doors to where a bright blue and white tow truck was parked across the lot. "Why can't you hop into that truck right there and get it?"

Demo started to squat back down onto the creeper. "Busted hose."

"So it doesn't work?" I snapped.

"It will once I get to it."

I started to tap my foot. "Come on. I've got to get back to work."

Demo stood back upright, and leveled me with a steely gaze. "Sorry."

Growling, I pulled my checkbook out of my purse. "All right. Fine. How much will it take to get you to do it?"

"You can put that away, lady."

Jutting my chin out at Demo, I whipped out a pen. "I'll pay you twice what your towing fee is."

"Sorry. Truck's busted." He kicked the creeper again. "I'll...uh...
hurry. I guess."

"You'll hurry *you guess*? Don't you have another truck?" I fished my
platinum card out. "Maybe you don't take checks. How about Mastercard? I'll
pay triple your fee. I've got to get back to work."

Trey released a low whistle. "That's a butt load of money, Demo."

"Shut up, kid," Demo growled. "Listen, I'm sorry, all right? You can't
just throw money around here. It doesn't work like that, lady."

"My name is Marisol." My molars ground together. "And you heard the
boy. It's a *butt load* of money."

Demo shook his head. "You may be able to wave your gold card
around elsewhere, but around here, it won't work. I'll tow your car once the
hose is fixed in the truck. Which will be once I get these *other cars* running."

My hands went to my hips. "Hey, what's your problem?"

He matched my pose, casting a shadow over me. "This is a first-come,
first-served garage. And you're at the back of the line."

I leaned closer to him. He smelled like sweat and gasoline and
something else totally masculine that made my stomach tie itself into a square
knot. "So *move me* to the front of the line."

"Sorry, no." Demo leaned forward as well. We were practically chest to
chest, which would've been exciting, had I not wanted to clock him in the face.
I'd have been intimidated, were I not so pissed.

I never gave up. Ever. When I was a child, my father described me as a "bulldog with a bone," and things hadn't changed much with age. When people said Eats & Treats was too small a company to handle their events, I low-bidded, then over delivered to prove them wrong. Everything I did, I did fearlessly and over-the-top. I learned by watching my father buy and sell commercial real estate in some of America's hottest cities with the ruthlessness of a serial killer and the skill of a fine artist. He used to tell me that taking no for an answer was *never* an option.

I lowered my voice to a deadly decibel. "Yes."

"No."

Though I hated to admit it, I was taken aback. This jerk-off was being rude. Like, *really* rude. I wasn't used to men despising me upon sight. Usually it took a while, after a half dozen dates or so. I'd been called the B word more than my fair share of times, and most of those times I'd actually deserved it.

But never once had I repelled a man the way I was apparently repelling Demo Anton... Antop... Ann...

Whatever the hell his name was.

Time for a change in my approach. Taking a deep breath, I let my shoulders drop, and forced my scowl to melt into a smile. My narrowed eyes morphed into the heavy lidded gaze I used more often than I cared to admit, and I touched a fingertip to Demo's chest.

Oh my. That's firm.

Wait. Focus, Marisol.

"Listen," I purred. "Can't we come to an agreement? Why don't you let your nephew take over the Honda, and you can slap a new hose into the tow truck for me?"

His honey brown eyes widened. "What?"

"Then after we get my car, you can run me to my job, and get back in time to fix my Beemer before I'm even ready for our dinner." Batting my eyelash extensions, I let my palm rest on Demo's chest, soaking up his warmth.

"Dinner?" he growled.

"Uh huh." Smiling, I tossed my hair. Just a little. "Where are you taking me?" I felt a thump underneath my palm and did a mental fist pump. *Worked like a charm. Like always.*

Demo's hand caught my wrist, making me gasp.

Okay, that was kinda hot. Maybe Annalise was wrong about blue-collar men.

Then he guided it—not so gently—back down to my side. "You honestly think I'm going to fall for that?"

Heat washed over my face. "I... well, yeah." I didn't even have a smart-mouthed response for Demo. This was new territory for me.

Trey laughed, and the engine he was working on muffled the sound. "I would have."

Snorting, I hissed, "Then *you* should've offered to fix the tow truck before Dudley Do-right got involved."

Demo raked a hand through his hair, making it stand on end. "Look, lady—"

"Marisol," I barked. Rude bastard. I'd said my name at least three times already.

"Look, *Marisol*, you're fourth in line." He backed away from me, and scooped up a rusted tool off of the ground. "I'll get your car as soon as I can, then I'll call you with an estimate. If you don't like what I can do, you're free to take your business somewhere else."

"But Demo, there aren't any garages for, like, seven miles." Trey raised his head and banged it on the truck hood. Again. "Ow. Damn."

"Then that's something she might need to consider."

I looked down at my feet and grimaced. They were already black on the bottom, and my pedicure was shot. And thanks to this peculiar little mid-spring heat wave, I'd tested the capability of my deodorant enough for one day. Plus, if I didn't get back to Eats & Treats soon, Lexie would serve my backside on a platter with beluga and water crackers at tomorrow's wedding.

Releasing a long, guttural sigh, I rolled my eyes at Demo-the-mechanic. "Fine. Have it your way."

One of his eyebrows tugged upward. "You sure 'bout that, your majesty?"

My hands clenched into fists involuntarily. I hated being at this jerk's mercy. "I don't really have another choice, do I?"

"Well then, like I said, leave your keys on the desk with your number." Demo turned away from me, and I spotted the edge of a huge tattoo that sat between his shoulder blades. It looked like Greek lettering, and I couldn't make out what the symbol was, but was surprised it wasn't something random and tacky. Guys like this usually had ink of the silver naked lady holding a bong or the Tasmanian Devil covered in blood. Tacky crap like that. This Demo character had kitsch written all over him.

"Got it. And don't think we're doing that dinner anymore, big guy. You lost your shot." Striding past Trey, who was watching us with pointed interest from underneath his alcove of engine, I slammed my keys down onto the filthy metal desk sitting near the office door. Then I bent at the waist making sure he had a perfect view of my backside while I scribbled my number onto a dusty scrap of paper with a chewed up pencil.

"I'll try to deal with the disappointment." He squatted back down on the creeper.

"Right," I said through gritted teeth, turning towards the open garage doors to leave. "Now to find a payphone. There's no way I'm using that *culo limpie's* phone right now." I added that last part under my breath as I padded towards the sunlight, in search of a payphone.

"What does my being an asshole have anything to do with you needing a payphone?" Demo called from behind me.

I froze and shot a lethal glare over my shoulder. For the first time since emerging from under that Honda, Demo Anton...ant...on...pop....*whatever his last name was*, smiled as he lay half covered by the dented blue metal.

"You speak Spanish?" I snarled.

"Yup. Greek, too." His smile faded. "Surprised, Princess?"

A plethora of snarky responses came to mind, but I decided to go for the jugular this time. "No. You can learn anything in prison. I'll bet you made some lovely license plates, too. Maybe even the one on my Beemer."

He rolled himself back under the Honda, and out of sight. "Οκύλα."

Smirking, I took off across the hot pavement in my bare feet, his laughter ringing out behind me. If he thought I didn't know he'd just called me a bitch in Greek, he was more stupid than I pegged him to be.

Like I said, I'd been called that plenty of times before.

Chapter Three

"I think he's gay." I threw a handful of shelled peas into the bowl with more strength than I anticipated, and they rolled back out the other side.

"Easy there, turbo." Lexie looked at me with raised eyebrows.

When I'd marched into work three hours later than promised, she'd been ready to live up to her redheaded reputation. I could practically smell the curse words in the air. But one look at my blackened feet and sweat-soaked blouse, and her anger quickly melted into amusement. Apparently riding a city bus back to work without shoes or my blessed iPhone was punishment enough, and she'd promptly handed me a water bottle. Now we were working into the evening to get ready for an event the next day.

"You know, just because a man doesn't roll over and let you scratch his belly the minute you look at him doesn't make him gay," Candace said, picking up the stray peas.

I raised an eyebrow. "It wasn't his belly I was planning on scratching."

She was usually the voice of reason between the three of us, mostly because she was the mother of three kids and constantly broke up fights between the little buggers. But she had the whole cooperation thing down pat, compared to Lexie and me. You see, Lexie had only been married to Fletcher about a year, and she and her husband had a blended family with two kids. The closest I'd ever been to an altar was standing in as my mother's maid-of-honor in her fourth wedding.

Or was that her sixth? Oh, well. It didn't really matter.

Usually at the first sign of contention in a relationship, I was out the door, a habit Candace had been trying to break me of for years. Especially when I dated Lexie's husband, Fletcher. Yeah. I dated *Doctor* Fletcher Haybee before Lexie married him. It sounds weirder than it actually was. The man wouldn't lay a hand on me, because he was so obsessed with my waif-like friend, and by the time we broke up, I was so sexually frustrated, I would've made out with a bum.

I didn't. But I could have.

Lexie plopped another basket of fresh sugar snap peas in front of me. "Maybe he just wasn't interested."

"That never happens." I pointed an empty pod at her. When she smiled innocently at me over her shoulder, I added, "Until Fletcher came along. Damn him."

She giggled. "He threw off your mojo."

Tossing a handful of pods over my head, I groaned dramatically. I was good at dramatic. "He did! Don't you understand how frustrating that is?"

It wasn't that I thought I was the most attractive woman in the world. Far from it. If I thought I was beautiful, I wouldn't go see my dermatologist every month, and I wouldn't have injected fat from my butt into my lips three years ago. I wouldn't pay up the nose for hair extensions dyed the perfect shade of caramel to match my eyes, or fork out what most spend on their mortgage for a handbag that I may or may not sleep with at night. No. I didn't do those things because I felt good about myself. I did them because every time I looked in the mirror, all I saw was my Grandma Rosia's nose and my father's downturned mouth—and surgery could only fix the nose so much. I saw cellulite on my thighs and eyebrows that needed weekly waxing because they're being pulled together like magnets. When I laughed, I sounded like a braying donkey, and when I spoke, I had a low tone that I once heard referred to as a "blow job voice."

I wanted it to be a compliment, but honestly, I was pretty sure it wasn't.

I feigned confidence to cover up that I wasn't sure I really liked myself at all. I bought designer clothes and drove a now useless Beemer to prove that I was every bit as glamorous and desirable as my mother, and every bit as successful and independent as my father.

Losing Fletcher to Lexie hadn't ruined my mojo. The truth was, I'd never really had it in the first place.

"Maybe you should go out with his nephew," Candace suggested, pushing out a stool and sitting down next to me. "Whatever his name was. You said he was cute in a gawky kind of way."

"It was Trey." I blew a strand of hair back from my eyes. "And he *was* cute. But he was also nineteen."

"Whatever." Lexie laughed. "You always say you're looking for a cougar opportunity."

Rolling my eyes, I dropped another handful of peas into the bowl. "Please. It's called a *cougartunity*. And nineteen is too young for my blood."

Candace shook her head. "My ears doth deceive me."

I snarled down at my hands. "It shouldn't even matter that he doesn't want me. I don't want him, either."

"But he was hot." Lexie popped a pea in her mouth. I shot her a look, so she added, "I mean, that's what you said. And usually when a guy is attractive, you're all over that like white on rice."

"Hot doesn't really begin to cover it." I used a pea pod to feign fanning myself. "Seriously, you guys. Demo had the whole rough-around-the-edges thing happening."

"Dee-mo?" Lexie scrunched up her nose. "What kind of name is that?"

"Greek, right?" Candace looked at me for confirmation.

Nodding, I tugged open another pod. "It's short for Demetrious. And I can't for the life of me remember his last name, since it had about forty-two syllables."

"Antonopulous," Candace said triumphantly.

I gaped at her. "How did you know that?"

She tossed a handful of peas into the bowl triumphantly. "Triple D's garage, right?"

"You were stalking me today." I smiled despite myself. "You watched me walk around with no shoes, sweating like a sumo wrestler running laps. What kind of a friend are you?"

"Shut up. I did not." Candace laughed, tucking her long blonde hair behind her ears. "One of Brian's patients recommended that place, so he took our minivan there last year. He met Demo once or twice."

My stomach twirled. What the crap was that about? I didn't even know the guy, much less like him, and I was whirling like a top at the mention of his name. This was embarrassing. "Oh, yeah? What did you think?"

Lexie's eyes widened. "You like him."

"I do not." I shoved a pea pod into my mouth. "He and I were not exactly simpatico. Complete opposites. Like apples and oranges, we were."

"Yes, you do." She snickered. "Your voice cracked. Besides apples and oranges are both fruit."

"Apples are sweet, and oranges are acidic. Totally different. And my voice cracked because that Demo character's got the keys to my car," I lied. "So, Candace, as you were saying…"

She and Lexie exchanged a look. "Well," she said. "Brian told me he was a bit gruff."

Snorting, I reached for the fresh ears of corn I had to shuck. "That's an understatement."

"But he does excellent work." Candace reached for a corn. "The van purrs like a kitten now. And Demo does work on trade when people can't afford him. Brian said he once put in a new transmission for a veteran just for serving our country."

One of my eyebrows pricked upward. So there was a nice guy underneath Demo's hard, crusty exterior. Too bad he was such an ass, because it was impossible for anyone to know there was a nice guy in there.

"He sounds pretty great, Mar." Lexie folded some crème fraiche into the shelled peas. "Maybe you should consider asking him out."

I pressed a hand to my chest. "*Me* ask *him* out? You've got to be kidding me."

"Marisol doesn't ask men out." Candace ripped a leaf off of an ear. "They always ask her, remember?"

"Oh, that's right." Lexie grinned at me. "No wonder you're so bent out of shape."

"I'm not bent out of shape." Sighing, I dragged my hand down my face, leaving streaks of mascara on my palm. "I'm just... just... okay, fine. I'm bent out of shape."

"Aha! I knew it!" Lexie slapped her hand down on the stainless steel table. "You like him."

Candace gasped. "Do you really?"

"No. *No*, I do not." I plucked up a few strands of corn silk. "He's a jerk. A big one. I can think of a few obscenities that describe Demo Antonopolous perfectly. But I won't say them in present company." I nodded my head in the direction of the playpen that was set up in the corner of the kitchen, where Lexie's baby was snoring away.

"You're getting soft." Candace yanked another leaf. "Ever since Lexie had Ian, you've stopped swearing so much."

Rolling my eyes, I folded my arms across my chest. "Go to hell. I have not."

"Yes, you have." Lexie nodded. "The other day you spelled out *penis head*."

"She did?" Candace put her arm around me and squeezed me tight. "Oh, Marisol, I'm so proud of you."

Cringing, I wriggled out of her grip. "Okay, okay. Come on. You know how I feel about affection and all that." She giggled and let go, so I smoothed my hair down casually. "What I'm trying to say is, I don't like Demo. But he's nice to look at. And he could be cruising all over Spokane right now in my car."

Lexie stopped stirring. "I thought your car was broken down?"

"It is." I shook my head. "You're missing the point."

"Well, get to it," laughed Candace.

"My point is," I said. "Demo acts like a total bastard, and I'm pretty sure he's got a Tasmanian devil tattoo on his back hidden beneath some Greek lettering, which knocks him further up on the douche scale. But he's also gorgeous. And I loves me a gorgeous man, am I right, or am I right?"

"Right," they both said in unison.

"You're sort of known for your impeccable taste in men," Candace pointed out. "You tend to stalk any prey wearing an Armani suit, and you don't stop until you've torn him to shreds."

"Which begs me to ask…" Lexie added some fresh chives to her mixture. "Isn't this mechanic a little bit…" She bit her lip and winced. "You know, below your standards?"

"What's that supposed to mean?" I snapped.

"Calm down." Candace touched my shoulder. "What Lex is trying to say is, didn't you once tell us that Annalise taught you not to date below a certain standard?"

Lexie nodded. "Which is why you wouldn't go out with the garbage man when he asked."

"He was pretty fine, too," Candace agreed.

Embarrassment pressed down on my shoulders, and I had to force myself to stay sitting up straight. I didn't want to show my friends I was embarrassed by my behavior. I worked hard to appear cocky all the time.

"Maybe I'm trying to change that." When both Candace and Lexie looked at me curiously, I added, "About myself. I'm trying to stop snubbing people because of my mother's stupid rules. Where have her rules gotten her?"

"Good point," Lexie said at the same time Candace blurted, "Kudos to you, Mar."

"Gee, thanks," I muttered.

Lexie tossed a pea in my direction. "It's good to see you broadening your horizons. There's a whole world of blue collar men you're missing out on."

"I'm not saying I'm going to start at the top of the list and work my way down." I pinched the bridge of my nose. I'd been in a funk all day, beginning when I sat down with my mother at the restaurant and cresting when Demo-the-mechanic rejected my advances. It didn't matter that I'd only been trying to score faster towing. Now that I knew he didn't want me, I wanted him. How screwed up was that?

"Want to go out with the guy who cleaned our gutters last spring?" Candace asked, popping a pea into her mouth. "He was cute. In a parolee sort of way."

"Ooooh, an ex-con." Lexie's eyes lit up. "That's a good starting point."

"Is that all you guys think of me?" My eyes bounced between both of their faces a few times. "That I'm just your slutty friend who is going to hump her way through the garbage men and landscapers in town?"

They blinked at me. "Um." Lexie swallowed a mouthful of crème fraiche, a smile ticking the corners of her mouth. "No?"

I tore some corn silk off of an ear. "That sounded convincing."

Candace bumped shoulders with me. "Come on. Let your old, married friends live vicariously through you. It's not every day we get to seduce men with the use of our prowess, like you."

"Just once I'd like to be able to talk Fletcher into bed in Spanish," Lexie announced, wistfully staring off into space.

33

"It doesn't work." I smirked at her, despite myself. "I tried, remember?"

"It sure didn't." Candace snorted. "Brian tries to talk dirty to me in Mandarin, but it always sounds like he's cussing me out."

Lexie and I dissolved into giggles.

"Wait, wait, wait." I shook my head. "You guys are going off on tangents, and I have a point to all this."

"Well, get to it!" Laughed Lexie. "You lost me way back at the Tasmanian devil tattoo."

I took a deep breath, then released it slowly. "I don't like being a snob like my mother."

"Good," they both said in unison.

"And I don't like being rejected." I blew my hair back again. "So maybe I just need to get this Demo character off my chest. You know, scratch an itch and all that."

"You mean you *do* want to go out with him?" Lexie pointed a finger at Candace. "I told you."

"Fine." Candace reached into her pocket, and produced a dollar bill. When she saw me gaping, she added, "I just didn't think you'd admit it."

"I'm gonna take it a step farther. I think Mar wants more than just to slum it," Lexie announced decidedly, pushing her glasses up. "I think she wants domesticity. The house, the husband, the minivan, the two-point-five kids and a golden retriever."

"Don't get carried away," I interrupted.

"Can it, Vargas." Candace nodded at Lexie. My friends conspired against me, as usual. It was like this when they tried to convince me to stop tanning, too. "All this time with baby Ian, and she's decided that procreation isn't as vulgar as she originally thought."

Lexie snapped her fingers. "So she *is* going soft."

"I never thought this day would come." Candace waved her hands in front of her face, as if she were trying to avoid tears. "Our girl's all grown up."

My cheeks heated, so I hid behind a veil of my hair. They were right. Or *partially right*. After watching their husbands hold their chairs for them, and listening to the tinkling sound of their kids laughing when Lex and Can made goofy faces and offered peanut butter and jelly sandwiches without the crust… I was starting to think I was missing out on something.

Before Lexie and Fletcher unified their family, I was a serial dater. And until recently I saw no reason to change that. But nowadays I was surrounded by happy couples and happy families, and everywhere I looked everyone was happy, happy, happy. It was sickening. But I kind of wanted it, too.

And it wasn't like I was going to find it with Demo-the-mechanic. Oh, no. He was nothing more than what I called him: an itch that needed to be scratched. But secretly, deep down under my coiffed exterior, I longed for someone to curl up with while wearing sweats and eating peanut butter straight out of the jar. I just wasn't ready to admit it to the world. Or my best friends.

"You're looking pretty contemplative, Mar." Candace stopped what she was doing and watched me closely. "Seriously. Are you thinking about asking Demo out?

I shrugged. "Maybe."

A distraction. That's what I needed. Something to take my mind off my twisted perspective on marriage and relationships. Something to take my mind off the overjoyed lovebirds in my adoptive family. And seducing the hot guy who rejected me was just the ticket. An ego boost would make me feel better. Normal.

"You're contemplating actually dating the Tasmanian devil tattoo guy?" Lexie's eyes widened. "Like, for more than a week?"

Candace elbowed her. "Be nice."

"Okay, a month?" she corrected.

"Whatever." I wrinkled my nose at my friends. "Having babies *is* gross. And I'm not dating the mechanic because I've got some sort of domestic fever. I'm dating the mechanic because he's hot. And *nobody* rejects me. Nobody."

They exchanged a glance.

"There's the Marisol we know and love," Candace said wryly.

Lexie sighed. "I had such high hopes. I would have made a poppy seed cake with a lemon buttercream frosting for the reception."

My stomach growled. She did know my favorites. I pushed myself back from the table. "Oh, give it up. Both of you."

Pressing the feelings of loneliness and inadequacy that had been following me around like smog for the past few weeks—okay, the past few *months*—deep in the back recesses of my mind, I gestured at the playpen. "Lex, take your baby home and get your freak on with the good doctor."

"Wait, I still need to get this fresh pea mixture into the pastry shells." She looked longingly at the playpen. "Fletcher's been on call, so we haven't seen each other in days. I miss him."

Jealousy tugged at my heart, but I covered it up with an exaggerated eye roll. "Ugh. Please. I can finish this. Just go. And you." I pointed to Candace. "You don't even work here. Enough with the helping us out for free. Go home and mug on your hubby, and I'll cut you a check for your time tomorrow."

"Are you sure?" she asked.

I nodded. "Of course. Now get out of here, would you? Your happy marriage and family talk is giving me a stomachache. Besides, as soon as you leave, I'm opening up a bottle of that merlot we have for tomorrow's event."

Lexie narrowed her eyes at me. "Ha ha. Real funny." It was common knowledge that she'd gotten pregnant after indulging in a bottle of merlot all alone. "How will you get home?"

Candace dropped her car keys onto the table. "Take my car. Lexie can drop me off, then I'll pick it back up in the morning."

"Thanks," I said with a wave. "You guys are the best."

"We know," Lexie said as they made their way towards the door.

I watched as they packed up their things and left into the setting sun, back to their noisy, chaotic homes. The only things that waited for me at home were Thai leftovers and a bitchy Siamese cat. No noise. No mess. Just the quiet stillness of a single woman's home filled with matching furniture that offered style over comfort. Nobody would be there to welcome me. Nobody would care whether I showed up or not, except Cocinero, who would eventually get tired of licking his own balls and want some tuna.

Grabbing a rubber spatula, I sat down at the table and started turning the pea mixture again. Grunting at myself for being so pathetic, I caught a glimpse of myself in a nearby stainless steel bowl. My hair frizzed into a halo around my face, and most of my makeup gathered underneath my lower lashes in some sort of Emo look I was entirely too old for. I looked like hell.

"You'd better get yourself together," I said to my reflection. "Especially if you're going to seduce Demo-the-mechanic tomorrow."

Chapter Four

Sure enough, my cat was itching for some serious food when I got home. Sadly, when I got him as a kitten ten months earlier, I started the habit of holding Cocinero on my lap while he ate. Now, almost a year later, he refused to consume a morsel of food without being cuddled and adored as he chewed.

Nobody knew how spoiled Cocinero really was. *Nobody*. I would've died had Lexie or Candace found out I catered to my pet this way. They already made fun of me for buying the damn thing after Fletcher and I broke up. (I'd spent much of my time with Fletcher complaining about how annoying his giant moose-dog-hybrid was.) I could practically hear them explaining that Cocinero was an amalgam of all the babies I wanted.

Screw Candace and the *one* psychology class she'd taken—she always made assumptions like that. When I bought Eats & Treats with Lexie, Candace said I tried to put down roots because I never had roots with my parents. When I started spending Christmas mornings with her and Brian and the kids, she decided that I did it to make up for the lack of holiday memories from my childhood.

Well… maybe she had a point. A little one.

"Slow down," I said to the white puffball in my lap, my voice high and squeaky. "You'll get the hiccups."

Cocinero looked up at me with his shiny black eyes and blinked.

"Yeah, yeah," I replied. "I love you, too."

There was a time, way before I moved to the inland northwest to escape the madness that was living in the same city as Annalise, when I owned a cat name Freedom. She'd been my treasured pet until I went to college, and my mother's pool boy accidentally knocked her into the pool, where she drowned. But that was beside the point.

Freedom was a gift from my father, given to me on the day he left. I was seven years old, and I still remembered every detail of the experience. My therapist once told me I remembered everything about that day because it was a traumatic experience, but I like to say it was because I was gifted with a photographic memory. Frankly, the therapist was right, though I've never admitted that to anyone.

"Marisol, come inside. Now," my nanny, Hanna, scolded me from the front porch. She, too, was mad at my dad. Not just because he loaded up his Jaguar convertible with suitcases without offering me so much as an explanation, but because in leaving my mother, he was also leaving her. She'd had big plans on being the new Mrs. Vargas.

Too bad for Hanna. My father had bigger plans. And those plans didn't include his self-obsessed wife, the nanny he'd been boinking for a year, or his daughter.

"No!" I bellowed—I was a screamer, a trait nobody who knew me enjoyed—running down the stairs to the circle drive in front of our palatial house. My father was just starting the engine on his dark green car. "Daddy, wait!"

He either didn't hear over the sound of purring motor, or he was ignoring me. He slid his aviator sunglasses onto his tanned face with the casual ease of a man leaving to play golf with his buddies. Except that he was abandoning his family for a life of less responsibility and more excitement in Fort Lauderdale, Florida.

The car started to roll forward, and I pawed at the shiny green metal with my hands. "No! Daddy, no!" I cried, stumbling in my bare feet. The cement was hot in the southern California sun, and it burned my soles. "Wait!"

He hit the brakes, and the jaguar screeched to a halt. "Marisol? What the hell are you doing?"

"We haven't played with the kitty yet." I wiped my nose with the back of my hand, and limped to the driver's side. "You said we'd play with her. You promised."

My father took his sunglasses off and rubbed his eyes tiredly. "No. I said you *could play with her. You, Marisol. I've got to go"*

41

He hadn't said so, but I knew he was leaving for good. "Take me with you," I begged. "I'll bring the kitty, and we can all go on vacation."

"I'm not going on vacation." His mouth pulled into a line. "And you're not coming with me."

Tears rolled down my face, and my nose was running. But I didn't care. "Why not?"

"Because your place is here with your mother." He glanced in the rear view mirror. "She needs you. She's sad."

My mother wasn't home. She'd gone to a spa for the weekend with her friend, and I'd heard her telling Hanna she'd never been happier. "She's not sad, Daddy. But she'll be mad when she comes home and finds out you left."

Even at seven years old, I'd been acutely aware that my mother had better things to do than raise a child. Especially one who'd given her stretch marks that had to be surgically corrected. That's why Hanna was there to take care of me.

"Come back inside," I pleaded, tugging on the door handle. It was locked. "We can play with the kitty, and then you and Hanna can go swimming in the hot tub again. I'll be a good girl, and go watch TV."

My dad winced. "I don't want to swim with Hanna anymore."

I looked over my shoulder at my nanny, who was glowering at him with her arms folded across her chest. "Then you can give her the day off, Daddy. Come back inside. We still need to name the kitty. I vote Puffy. Or Sparkles. What do you want to call her?"

He laughed, and for a millisecond, I thought things were looking up.

"Freedom." He slid the glasses back onto his face. "I want to call her Freedom."

"That's a silly name, Daddy." I smiled, even though I could feel something bad looming. "Can you come inside now? P-please?"

He shook his head. "No, baby. Not this time."

"Can I go with you?" My voice got higher. "I can pack super fast."

"They don't let kids come to Fort Lauderdale, Marisol." His voice was low, resigned. And I knew his mind was made up. "It's a grown up city."

I thought about what it would be like when Mom got home, and it was just her and me in the giant house. She would be annoyed with me, so much more so than she already was. We were only together when we had company over, and I needed to come down in a pretty dress for everyone to see. At least when my dad was around, he noticed me. Sure, most of the time, it was to tell me not to leave my toys around, or that I needed to be quiet because I was giving him a splitting headache. But being noticed and getting hollered at was way better than being ignored.

"I don't want to be alone." It was all I could think of to say. "If you leave, nobody will talk to me."

"Go let Hanna take care of you. She'll make you some chocolate milk." Dad threw a glance in his rearview mirror. "I gave her a big, fat bonus check, so she's not going anywhere."

"Daddy, I—"

43

"I gotta go, Marisol." He put the Jaguar in gear. "Back away from the car."

"Please don't go." I wept, snot creeping out of my nose. "Please don't leave me."

He grimaced at me. "Pull yourself together. Your face is a mess."

"I love you, Daddy." As soon as the words left my mouth, I felt embarrassed. We didn't talk like that in our family. Mushiness only existed on television shows like the one mom used to be on. Squaring my shoulders, I said it again. "I said, I love you, Daddy."

He sighed. It was a long, drawn-out, irritated sigh almost drowned out by the purring car engine. I waited for him to say it back. For my dad to tell me that he loved me too, and that he would send for me as soon as he got settled in Florida. Maybe even a kiss or a hug, to top things off.

But...Carlos Vargas didn't do emotion.

"Go tell Hanna to wipe your face, Marisol. Nobody wants to look at an ugly little girl with snot on her face."

And with that, he peeled away, spitting a hot burst of exhaust out of the tailpipe, and leaving me standing in the sun alone.

I stood there crying for what felt like forever. Hanna didn't come to get me, or wipe my face, or make me chocolate milk like my dad had promised. I stood there until my mother's car rolled into the driveway, and she emerged looking refreshed and shiny from her time at the spa. She'd taken me by the hand and walked me into the house, through the living room, and into the oversized kitchen, where I'd promptly been passed off on Imogene, the cook.

Hanna gave her notice later that night, and I'd gotten a new nanny, Sara, the

next day.

Freedom and I spent all of our time together after that, clear until I ran

off to college in Washington state, where I'd not been allowed pets in university

housing. By that time, Freedom was arthritic and barely mobile, which is why

she'd drowned when she'd been pushed into the pool with the end of a ladder.

I'd cried for days.

Cocinero took his last bite of food, then wriggled out of my arms,

jerking me out of my thoughts. My eyes were blurry as I followed him to the

French doors that led out into the backyard. I hated thinking about my dad.

Every time I did, I wound up like this. Weepy, morose, and utterly pathetic.

"Let's go potty," I told the cat as he sat, bored, next to the glass-paned

door.

As soon as the door cracked open, Cocinero squeezed through and

sauntered off into the darkness. My backyard, like the rest of my house, had

been decorated to perfection. The patio furniture was covered in a black and

white damask print that coordinated perfectly with the white rocks in the fire pit.

The pergola above my head was painted a crisp white, then threaded with gauzy

black fabric that swayed perfectly in the wind. I paid over fifty dollars a yard for

the stuff, which was kind of stupid considering the window of warm-weather opportunities to utilize this outdoor oasis was especially small in this part of Washington. But I had to have the best.

If I learned nothing else from my mother over the years, I managed to cling to that little nugget. Which was why my house was adorned with white leather couches, Waterford crystal sculptures, silk wallpaper, and shaggy cashmere rugs that were so un-kid-friendly, Candace had to make her three kids wait in the car when she came over.

Sure, I lived alone. And sure, sometimes being alone with my thoughts made me feel so isolated, I could climb the walls. But doggone it... my house looked like a picture out of Interior Decorators Monthly. And that there was a fact.

Cocinero bounced around the river rocks that bordered my lawn, undoubtedly taking his time to find the proper place for taking a crap, when my home phone rang inside the house.

I glanced at my watch. It was almost ten o'clock. Nobody called me this late, except for the occasional booty call. But I wasn't currently involved with anyone, a fact that irritated me almost as much as the fact that my cat insisted on taking an hour to take a dump every night. A booty call sounded nice right about now.

"Probably Lexie," I murmured to myself, slapping across the hardwood floors with my bare feet—which were still repulsive from my little adventure earlier. She was probably up feeding the baby, and fretting about the quiches. She was infamous for adding an ingredient at the last minute that transformed dishes from good to great, and unfortunately that inspiration only seemed to happen long after we'd stopped cooking for the night.

I plucked up receiver, and answered without looking at the number. "Lexie, this is the worst booty call I've ever gotten. You know I haven't swung that way since that one kegger in college."

There was silence on the other end.

"Lex?" Pulling the phone away from my ear, I looked at the tiny screen. "Oh, um. Sorry. Who is this?"

"Is this Marisol Vargas?" The deep, gravelly voice on the other end sent a whirl of excitement shooting up my spine.

Demo-the-mechanic. I'd left him my home number back at the shop, since my iPhone was still missing. Note to self: replace cell tomorrow.

Well, well. Maybe it was a booty call after all.

Not interested, my ass, I snickered to myself. "This is she," I purred. "And let me guess. This is Demo... Demo... uh..."

Dang that crazy last name of his. It was blowing my sexy cover all to pieces.

"Antonopolous," he replied.

"Right." I pressed my lips together and reminded myself to keep my temper in check. "So why are you calling me so late? A little lonely in the garage at night?"

"I towed your car after we closed," Demo said simply.

My eyebrows rose high on my forehead. He'd done something nice for me. Maybe there was hope after all. "Oh. Well, thank you."

"Since it was after hours, I'll have to charge time and a half."

My eyebrows dropped back to their normal spot. "Of course."

"You made it sound like money wasn't your primary concern," Demo explained in a flat voice.

"It's not," I hissed. "Do you always work this late at night?"

"I knew you wanted it back quickly," he answered simply. "So I brought it back and took a look."

I leaned against my kitchen countertop and waited for the bad news. The booty call scenario fizzled right before my eyes. "So what's the verdict?"

I heard him shifting some papers, and then the clang of something landing on the metal desk. "You've got a bad alternator."

"The car's only a year old!" I blurted.

"It happens. Got a buddy across town who works with BMWs all the time. He says your make and model are infamous for alternator problems."

"Can I get his number?" Grabbing a pen and paper out of my nearby mail stack, I readied myself to write. "Maybe he'll be able to fix it."

"Oh, I can fix your car." Demo's voice took on a defensive edge. "I'll have it ready by ten tomorrow morning."

"You can?"

"I can."

"You've got the right parts, and everything?" I didn't know much, but I knew enough to know that BMW parts weren't usually sitting on the shelves in most Spokane mom and pop auto shops. That was the reason why I usually took it to the specialty shop at the dealership for maintenance.

"Got a buddy who owns a parts store."

"My, you certainly have a lot of buddies. He let you into his shop to get the part this late at night?"

"*She* opens at six am. It's in stock."

A random spark of jealousy blinked inside my chest. I really needed to get a grip on myself. "Well, I underestimated you, Mr. Antonopolous."

Yes! Got his last name right. Score one for me.

"Seems to be a habit," he grunted.

I grit my teeth together. "And you're telling me that you're going to fix my Beemer first thing in the morning?"

"Yup."

"For time and a half, right?"

"The tow was more," Demo growled. "The labor will be standard cost. Unless you'd like to pay more, Princess."

Seeing red, I pushed myself away from the counter. "Hey, who do you think—"

"Sorry. Listen. You want me to work on your car?" he interrupted. "I've got a client who needs new sparkplugs in his delivery van real bad. I can do that first, if you like."

"Just one moment." I put the phone down on the countertop and kicked the back of my couch a few times, leaving black footprints. "*Estúpido, grosero culo limpie!*"

I thought I heard a chuckle when I picked the receiver back up and said, "I would love it if you fixed my car first thing tomorrow."

When Demo spoke again, there was a smile in his voice. "You know I speak Spanish, right?"

I scrunched my face up and slapped a palm to my forehead. Whoops. I'd focused so much on his bulging biceps and surly attitude, that I'd forgotten that detail. "Yes," I lied. "Yes, I do."

"Well, it's settled then. See you at ten."

"Right." I felt like punching a hole in something. Anything.

He hung up before I could say another word.

Chapter Five

I went to Triple D's the next morning dressed for success.

Not catering success, per say, but man-eating success. Form-fitting pencil pants; a red, sleeveless Elie Tahari blouse; and five-inch, red platform pumps topped off my look. As soon as Demo saw me emerge from the cab, he stood up and watched with pointed interest as I click-click-clicked into the garage. Sure, I was going to have to don a smock when I got to work, but all that mattered was I marched up to Demo with legs—and confidence—for miles.

That is, until he opened his mouth.

"Good morning, Demo," I said, putting a hand on my hip and smiling. I wore lipstick in the exact same shade of deep red as my blouse and shoes, and every time I wore it I got compliments. I waited for him to respond, positive that *Operation Seduce Demo-the-mechanic* was in full swing.

He drew a long breath, then took his time to release it while he held my gaze, steady and strong. "I wondered when you'd show up."

"I—" My hand dropped from my hip. "What?"

Demo jerked his head to the right. "Car's ready."

"Good." I swallowed a snotty retort and hiked my purse further up my arm. Why in the world was I trying so hard to make this guy want me when he was so clearly disinterested? "What do I owe you?"

Demo ambled over to the metal desk, and tugged a grease-stained sheet of printer paper out from under a disassembled auto part. "The tow, plus parts and labor came to four hundred sixty-three and seventy-two cents."

I walked around the circumference of my car, stopping to wipe at a piece of dust that disguised itself as a scratch. I could feel his eyes on me, but I didn't hurry. Once I circled the whole car, I opened the driver's side door and looked at the mileage.

"Looks like you drove it for a while. What gives?" I asked nonchalantly.

Demo faced me. "I drove it out a few miles down Highway 27and back once the new alternator was in to make sure it was running right."

"Huh." I slammed the car door. "Seems a bit excessive."

He folded his arms across his chest. He'd not yet put on his coveralls, so his thin grey tee shirt did little to hide those delicious muscles. "You seem a bit nitpicky."

Matching his pose, I let the smile drop off of my face. "You seem a bit overly sensitive."

He took a step closer to me. "Well, you seem a bit rude."

"Well, you seem a bit bipolar." I took a step closer to him. We were only about a foot apart now, and I could feel electricity popping and crackling between our chests. I couldn't tell if it was because we wanted each other... or because we wanted to throttle each other. Maybe both.

A line appeared between Demo's dark eyebrows. "Bipolar? That's the best you got?"

"Seriously!" I threw my hands up. "You work on my car at the crack of dawn to be nice, and then you treat me like garbage when I come to pick it up! I came in here in the hopes of making peace with you, but your mood swings are shifting like a hyperactive pendulum!"

He glared down at me. "You think coming in here dressed to the nines is going to make me give you some sort of discount or something?"

"I don't need a damn discount." Tugging my purse open, I produced my credit card. Again. "Four hundred sixty-two dollars. Take it."

Demo snatched the card out of my hand. "And seventy-two cents."

"*Fastidioso*," I muttered under my breath.

He leaned in close. There was that aroma again. Why oh why did it smell so good to me? "For the hundredth time, I know what you're saying. And I'm *not* annoying."

"Good." I met his steely gaze with my own. "And *yes,* you are."

For a second, I thought he was going to laugh. I mean, we probably looked pretty ridiculous. Chest to chest, leaning into each other like two dogs ready to fight. If I walked in on the scene, I would assume we were seconds away from killing each other... or making out. But from where I stood now, making out was nowhere on the horizon.

I wasn't sure whether to be happy or sad about that. On one hand, Demo looked beyond *delicioso* this morning. His dark hair was every bit as messy as it'd been yesterday, but not yet soaked with sweat around the neckline. And his dark eyes positively shone as he razzed me, goading me into yet another argument.

But on the other hand, Demo was a serious jerk. He was moody and surly, and obsessed with knocking the wind out of my sails at every opportunity. Why he hated me as much as he did, I didn't know. But I no longer wanted to change it. Sure, making Demo Antonopolous want me would've been a fun accomplishment—one to put down in my diary, if I had one, I'm sure of it—but it wasn't worth standing in the filthy garage arguing anymore.

We stared at each other with a venomous current buzzing between our bodies. Neither one of us willing to look away first. Neither one of us willing to admit we were behaving like idiots. I heard the sound of a car pulling up in the small parking lot outside, but still we stood there, unmoving.

Finally, at the sound of a car door shutting, Demo blinked. "On your Visa?" he asked mildly.

"Please." I replied, my tone icy. Screw this crap. It wasn't worth it.

He went into the office, leaving the door open behind him. There were dozens of framed pictures hanging on the wall, and stacks and stacks of paperwork everywhere. Each of the frames was different, each bearing a different family portrait. Some were faded and discolored, and the clothes the people wore looked dated. Others were bright and new, and the clothes in those pictures were trendier. The resounding detail in each of the shots was that they all had the same dark eyes and wild black hair as Demo. The Antonopulous genes ran strong with this clan, and in each of the pictures, their smiles were wide and joyous.

I wanted to ask if those were all pictures of his family. How big was the Antonopulous family tree? How many generations had worked in Three D's? Who pissed in his Cheerios that morning, making him grumpier than everyone in the pictures?

But instead, I stood there with my arms folded.

My stubborn streak was legendary.

"Oh, yeah, You'll have to come back," Demo called, tearing a receipt off of the credit card machine, and lumbering back towards me.

"I what?" I laughed. "You've got to be kidding."

He looked about as cranky as I felt. "I looked it up. Your BMW has two recalls out."

"Oh, right." I waved a hand dismissively. I remembered getting a letter in the mail from the dealership a month or two ago—or maybe more—about that. "Okay. I'll make an appointment with the dealership."

"I ordered the parts through my friend." He put the receipt down on the corner of the metal desk and fished a pen out of one of the drawers. It was plastic and chewed on, just like the one I used the other day. "They'll be here in a week or so."

Shaking my head, I took the pen and scrawled out my signature. "Not necessary. It's free if I go through the dealership."

"They're only free within a year of the recall," Demo explained. "After that, you have to pay for labor."

I shoved the receipt at him. "Then I'll pay them for labor. I'll pay whatever—"

He rolled his eyes and tossed it onto the desk. "I know. But for what it's worth, though, I charge half of what they charge. *Half.* You won't find that anywhere else in town."

I watched Demo for a beat. The garage itself had seen better days. The doors were rusted, and the sign out front had begun to crack and curl around the edges. It was clear he needed the business, especially if Candace was right and he fixed cars for trade.

"Demetrious, are you groveling?" a little voice scolded from behind my back.

Demo looked over my shoulder, and his surly expression melted away. "Good morning, Yiayia."

I turned around and was met with a tiny old woman who stood eye level with my chest. A perfect helmet of white hair covered her head, and the handbag hanging from her elbow was at least half the size of her little body. On her wrinkled face, she wore a pair of thick glasses adorned with a blue and white beaded chain.

"Morning, Demo. Who's this?" she asked.

"A customer." He nodded at me. "She was just leaving."

Trey sauntered into the garage, carrying an oversized tray of fresh baklava. "Geez, Yiayia, do you think you made enough this morning?" He chuckled, before stopping when he saw me. "Oh, hey. Marisol, right?"

I nodded. "Yes. Hi, Trey."

"She remembered my name," he said to Demo with a grin.

"Congratulations," growled his uncle.

"Ugh. So grumpy." The old woman swung her giant black purse at Demo, swiping him on the hip. "He's always grumpy. Even when he was a kid. Grumpy."

I laughed despite myself. "I'm glad it's not just me."

"No way. Uncle Demo's always in a mood." Trey lifted the corner of the plastic wrap on the tray. "Baklava? My yiayia makes the best around. It has won contests at our church. She makes treats every morning for our customers."

"Thank you." The smell was heavenly. I plucked one from the tray, knowing my trainer would punish me for it later. But once I took a bite, and the rich, heavy sweetness filled my mouth, I knew it would be worth it. "This is incredible."

The old woman beamed. "Thank you, dear." Her tiny, wrinkled hand slapped the side of Demo's arm. "Well, aren't you going to introduce me to your girlfriend, Demetrious?"

"Oh, I'm not his girlfriend," I said at the same time Demo said, "She's not my girlfriend."

She winked at me. "But you will be."

"Like I said, Marisol was just leaving." Demo plucked my keys off of a hook above the desk and handed them to me. "Have a good one."

Her little hand smacked his arm a second time.

"Ow, Yiayia," Demo said, rubbing his arm. "Easy."

Giggling, I shared a smile with Trey. It was nice to see someone of Demo's stature getting his ass kicked by an old lady.

"Be polite, young man," she ordered. "Introduce me."

Demo drug a hand down is face. "All right. Yiayia, this is Marisol Vargas. I replaced her alternator this morning."

"I'll bet you did," Trey snickered. When his Yiayia smacked the back of his head, he added, "Ow. Sorry."

Demo looked at me. "Marisol, this is my grandmother, Thea Antonopolous."

I shook her bony hand. "It's nice to meet you, Mrs. Antonopolous."

"Oh, please." She grinned. "That's too formal."

"Very well, then, *Thea*." I popped the rest of the baklava into my mouth and chewed it slowly. Seriously… so good.

"Call me Yiayia," she ordered.

I shook my head. "Oh, I couldn't. I barely know you—"

"Well, you know me now. My grandson just introduced you." She patted my hand kindly. "Tell me, Marisol. Do you have a grandmother?"

I blinked at her. Nobody had ever asked me that before. "I, uh, don't. Actually. My father's parents are deceased, and I've never met my mother's parents." I felt Demo's eyes boring into the side of my head, but ignored it.

Her cool hands squeezed mine. It felt like she was made out of crepe paper. "Well, then you can call me Yiayia. That's Greek for grandma, you know."

"Oh, I don't think—"

She frowned. "Every girl deserves a grandma."

Unexpected tears pricked at the backs of my eyes. "Yes, ma'am."

"Okay, well, that was nice." Demo took my elbow in a firm but gentle grasp. "Marisol has to go now."

"Aw, I just met her." Yiayia's grip on my hands tightened. "Don't be such a stick in the mud, Demetrious. Let me get to know the lady a little more."

"Yiayia's been trying to get Uncle Demo married for years," Trey told me. "All her other grandchildren are married by now, and he's the only one still not making babies. She's got expectations, you know."

"Trey." Demo shot his nephew an icy glare. "Yiayia, she just came to get her car so she could get back to work. She's probably in a hurry, aren't you, Marisol?"

"Hush it," Yiayia snapped, gesturing to the baklava Trey was still holding. "Eat something, Demetrious. You're acting like a goat."

Demo released my elbow and jerked his hand through his hair, standing it on end. I waited for him to retort, but he said nothing.

59

I hated to admit it, but part of me wanted to stay. This Yiayia character could shut Demo up in one sentence, and for that, I had endless admiration for her. And besides that, the woman's baklava could have easily substituted sex in my life for a very, very long time. It was if God himself had made it.

I wanted the recipe.

"So tell me, Marisol," Yiayia said, looping her arm through mine and guiding me into the office, where she settled herself on a stool. I heard Trey sniggering out in the garage, and Demo telling him to shut up. "Are you married?"

I settled across the desk from her. "No, ma'am. Never even been close."

"My Demetrious hasn't been married, either." She nodded her head in his direction. When I followed her line of sight, Demo was bent under the hood of a yellow Toyota, shaking his head at me as he cranked a wrench back and forth. "He got close once, but she ripped his heart out, the little tramp." I choked on a piece of baklava, and she smiled proudly. "You like those? They're my mother's recipe. Best Baklava at the North Spokane Greek Orthodox church bake sale five years running."

"Yes, they're incredible." I looked around for a napkin, but alas… we were in an auto garage, and there were none to be found. I settled for the back of my hand. "Do you only bake? Or do your skills include savory treats, too?"

She pressed a crimped hand to her chest. "Oh, my yes. I cook everything. I learned to cook in Papagos. That's where my family was from. My parents ran a café."

Oh, this just got better and better. "No kidding?" I squeaked. "I'm a caterer."

"Aha, you see?" She shook a finger at me. "I knew there was something about you I liked. What is your specialty?"

I thought for a moment, and heard Demo scoff from under the hood. "Come on, Yiayia. Look at those fancy clothes. Does really she look like she can cook?" he called.

"Hush!" She scolded. "Please excuse my grandson. When he's around a pretty girl, he gets nervous and puts his foot in his mouth."

"Yiayia," warned Demo.

"Demetrious Marcos Antonopolous," she barked.

Offering him a haughty glance, I giggled. "Is this your family on the wall, Yiayia?"

She nodded proudly. "Yes. My husband and myself. Our children. Their children. Their children's children. Every generation clear down to Little Demetrious' generation."

"Little Demetrious?" The urge to crack up was getting stronger. "Is that what you call Demo?"

Yiayia shook her head. "No, I meant Trey. His full name is Demetrious Bakas, and his mother is Demo's third sister. We call him Trey for short."

"His third sister?" I croaked, sitting on my hands to avoid grabbing another baklava. "Out of how many?"

"Six children in that branch of the family tree." Yiayia beamed up at the wall. "His sister, Leni, is Trey's mother. She's this one right here." She tapped a picture above her head. "And his other siblings are Niko, Agalia, Dion, Athena, and Cyrene."

"Do you visit Demo and Trey at work often?" I asked.

She jutted her chin out at me. "Oh, I'm not visiting. I work here."

"You work here?" My mouth dropped open. "At your... I mean, even though..." My voice petered out. I didn't know what to say. I was pretty sure Yiayia was in her early *hundreds*. There had to be a law against making your grandmother work in a dirty auto shop.

"You mean even though I'm old?" She grinned. "Eh, I'm not so old. I'm eighty-seven years young."

"Well, I hope your grandson pays you well."

Yiayia nodded. "I've been answering phones here since 1943. My husband started the garage with ninety-three dollars in his pocket and having never driven a car before. Oh, he was always good at tinkering with things, and he learned fast enough. That was the original Demetrious. Then our oldest son took over. He was obsessed with cars, and brought them home from the junkyard to rebuild. That was the second Demetrious. When he died of cancer three years ago, *his* son took over. That's the one who's pouting under the hood of the Toyota over there."

"Not pouting, Yiayia." I could hear a smile in Demo's voice.

She shook her head. "Silly boy. Now he's training his nephew, and the fourth Demetrious, so that he'll be able to take over the garage someday."

"Will you change the name to Four D's?" I asked.

"Well, I don't know," she shrugged her stooped shoulders. "Suppose that's up to Demo. But who knows what goes on in that boy's head."

Demo groaned. "Come on, Yiayia. Stop monopolizing the lady's time. She's got to get to work."

"Yes, yes. I'm sure she does." Yiayia patted my hand, then picked up another baklava. "Here. Take one for the road."

My brain screamed *no, no, no!* But my stomach growled for some more. I was going to spend *a lot* of time on the elliptical this week, that much was certain. "Thank you," I said, taking it from her. "It was lovely to visit with you, Yiayia."

"The pleasure was all mine," she said. "Bring your fancy car back to us anytime. We'll beat anyone else's price. I guarantee it."

"Of that I have no doubt."

"Or just come back to see me," she offered, winking. "Or to see Demo."

"You got it." I stood up and propped my purse on my elbow. "Say, before I go, can I ask you a question?"

"Of course, my dear." She sat up straighter on her stool. "Shoot."

"Don't let her ask you for a discount, Yiayia." Demo growled in the garage. "She's got money."

"Oooh, burn!" Trey laughed.

Ouch. Shooting Demo a venomous glare, I shifted so that my back was to both of the D's. "I have a wedding coming up this summer. A Greek wedding, in fact."

"In the Greek Orthodox Church downtown?" Her eyes lit up. "Such a lovely church. All of my children were married there. And some of my grandchildren." She sent a pointed glance over my shoulder at Demo. "I wonder if I know the family. Where's the reception, dear?"

"The Montvale Hotel."

"Oh, they must have some money to spend." Her white eyebrows pinched together when she smiled. "Greek receptions can get pretty rowdy. Marisol. I hope you make them pay for extra plates."

Laughing, I tucked my hair behind my ears. I'd forgotten about the plate breaking tradition. Thank goodness for Yiayia. "My partner and I have been asked to cook a full buffet complete with authentic Greek dishes."

"That sounds lovely." She sighed contentedly. "Nothing celebrates the start of a life together like some pilafi kritis and dolmas."

"Good! That's what I was hoping you'd say." I clapped my hands together. "Because I've been trying some recipes, and haven't gotten the grape leaves right—"

Demo appeared in the office doorway. "Yiayia doesn't share recipes."

"Is that so?" I offered him a haughty glance. "So, Yiayia, what do you think? Can you help me?"

I waited for her reply, watching as her eyes—the same shade of dark chocolate as Demo's—bounced back and forth between her grandson and me. Five seconds meandered into ten, and the only sound was Trey singing Nicki Minaj in the garage. After long enough to be officially awkward, Yiayia's crinkled face brightened, and she clasped her hands together.

Score. Smiling smugly at Demo, I leaned in close to Yiayia. I didn't want to miss a detail. I wondered what made the recipe perfect? Extra coriander? Maybe some anise?

"Demo's right," she said finally.

"Oh, thank—" I did a double take. "Say what?"

Yiayia tilted her head at me. "I don't share my recipes with anyone who isn't family."

"Oh." My shoulders drooped, deflated. I could practically hear Demo grinning next to me, but didn't look up at him to check. "Not even for dolmades?"

"But don't you worry." She pointed an arthritic finger at me. "It'll happen soon enough. And when you're family, I'll give you the recipe."

Chapter Six

I carefully placed a sprig of fresh dill on top of the last lobster-stuffed mushroom on the tray and stood back to admire my work. It looked pretty damn good, if I did say so myself, but I relied on Lexie's taste test to confirm it. I'd eaten four pieces of homemade baklava with Yiayia, and judging by its rich goodness, they were about two hundred and twenty calories apiece.

Now, usually I enjoyed a good butt kicking by my hot trainer, but the one I had coming was going to be rough.

"Hey, Mar, are those 'shrooms about ready?" Lexie called, coming into the kitchen with an empty tray propped on her shoulder. "These small business owners are ruthless. I went through all those shrimp canapés in less than three minutes."

"Yikes." I pushed the mushrooms towards her. "I hope the fact that they're all starving isn't an indication of how their businesses are doing."

"Hey, we're a small business, and we're doing all right." Lexie popped one of the mushrooms into her mouth, then washed her hands in a nearby sink. "Don't be a snob."

My cheeks heated, as I realized who I sounded like. For years I'd thrown out comments and digs, all in an attempt to appear funny and confident, when in actuality I sounded like I poured pretention into my coffee in the morning.

"You're right." I wiped my hands on a towel. "I'm sorry."

Lexie stopped what she was doing, and her eyes widened. "I, uh, okay."

We stared at each other for a beat, unsure what to say next. Apologies weren't my forte, and I never dealt them out easily. Finally, I waved my hand. "Argh. Don't make such a big deal out of it, or I'll never say it again." I plucked some breadbaskets off the counter. "Come on. Let's get these people fed, before I break down and eat all these appetizers myself."

"Whatever you say." A smile teased the corners of Lexie's mouth. We pushed through the swinging door into the bed and breakfast dining room where the Manito Small Business Association was holding their latest meet and greet.

We got this event for the first time this year, after a tight bidding war with two much larger catering companies. I liked to brag that the fact I wore a low cut sweater to the tasting was the reason, but the truth was, Lexie's cedar-smoked salmon pate had driven it home.

We entered the dining room. "So tell me," she said through the corner of her mouth. A woman approached, plucking a mushroom from the tray, and Lexie waited until she meandered off before she finished her thought. "Are you gonna get the recipe for dolmades, or what? You said you hit it off with the grandma today."

"I certainly did." I smiled widely as a man grabbed a roll out of one of the baskets. "She asked me to call her Yiayia."

Lexie giggled. "What does that mean? You're not calling her a bad name in Spanish, are you?"

"That was Greek." I handed a roll and a napkin to an old man passing by. "It means Grandma. And I have not yet scored the recipe. But don't worry. I will."

"Is there seafood in those mushrooms?" a man with a beard asked Lexie.

"Yes, sir. Pacific lobster." She pointed to one of the other waitresses we'd hired for the evening. "There are cheese-stuffed mushrooms just over that way."

"Thank you," he said, setting off on his mission.

Lexie turned to me. "So how come you didn't get the recipe?"

I shrugged, feigning nonchalance. My conversation with Yiayia had stuck with me for most of the day, and I replayed it about a thousand times. She clearly assumed Demo and I were going to wind up together, thus making me family and someday worthy of her recipes. But then again, some senior citizens thought their dead relatives were in the room. My guess was that as sharp as Yiayia was, she didn't see the deep-rooted distaste her grandson and I had for each other.

Apparently she hadn't picked up on the fact that I'd gone to Triple D's to make him want me... only so I could drop him on his face later, too. Thank goodness.

I sighed. "She said she only gives her recipes to family."

Lexie snorted. "So when's the big day?"

"Don't get carried away," I warned her with a scowl. "But don't you worry, either." I nodded at a woman who was biting into her roll. "I'll get it."

Lexie chuckled. "I can Google another recipe—"

"No!" I yelped, making an old man with a mushroom jump. "Sorry, sir." When he walked away, I dropped my voice to a whisper. "You don't understand, this woman's baking is amazing. The baklava made my toes curl."

"You said that about *my* baklava," she hissed.

"Well, this is even better." I widened my eyes at her. "It was better than sex, Lexie."

One of her auburn eyebrows rose. "That's a bold statement, coming from you."

It was true. I spent the bulk of my adulthood—thus far—with a fairly liberal sense of sexuality. When done properly, and safely, sex could be a lot of fun. And in an attempt to reject my mother's warped sense of marriage and its fiscal benefits, I supported myself financially and scoffed at any use of the "R" word (relationship.) I used sex as a really cool way to pass the time and cure boredom. No commitments, no strings, just safe, consensual humping amongst friends. It was a win/win, right?

Wrong. Needless to say, my friends—both of whom were happily married with kids—were mortified by my lackadaisical attitude about the horizontal boom-boom. They seemed to think I'd been so scarred by my mother's seven marriages and my father's inability to commit to, well, *anything* that I was completely disconnected from what mattered most in life.

Marriage. Home. Family. Whatever.

"Orgasmic baklava?" Lexie sucked in a sharp breath. "That's something I'd like to try someday."

"Well, you will, if I have anything to say about it." I muttered as a woman took two rolls, then scurried away like a rat. "I'm working on this problem and intend to fix it sooner rather than later."

"So you *are* marrying the mechanic?"

"No. But I will date him."

Lexie rolled her eyes back at me. "Okay, yesterday you were going to date him just so you could dump him. Now you're going to date him for his grandmother's recipes?"

"Yes," I said. "Don't say I never did anything for our business."

Lexie shook her head and laughed. "This is a new low even for you, Mar."

I lowered my voice as a group of people passed. "Oh, don't make it sound so dirty. I'm not going to sleep with him for the recipes. Though it *is* tempting. He's really quite beautiful, in a greasy, gritty, *he-might-punch-me-in-the-face* sort of way." I jutted out my hip and laughed.

70

"Ugh." Lexie wrinkled her nose. "You have such a way with words."

I smoothed down the front of my apron. "Thank you."

"So you're not going to sleep with him?"

"No."

"Even though he's kind of hot?"

"Yes."

"And you're Marisol, queen of hooking up with gorgeous men."

Giving her a pointed look, I thrust the basket of rolls into another person's face. "Fresh sourdough rolls with brie centers. Made this morning."

A woman with a giant nose ring squealed with delight. "Oh, my! Sounds delicious. Thank you."

"I told you the brie center was genius," I whispered to Lexie. As soon as nose ring lady walked away, I added, "Scoring those recipes will be worth abstaining from sex with Demo-the-mechanic. Because his grandmother's baklava recipe alone could make his prowess in the bedroom seem wanting."

My friend's eyes widened as she scanned the room. "Um, are you sure about that?"

I plucked a mushroom off of her tray, and popped it into my mouth. "Positive," I said around my mouthful. "Knocking the dickhead off of his high horse will be an added bonus." When I finished chewing, I swallowed and blinked at Lexie. Her face had gotten almost as red as her hair. "What's up with you?"

"Well, I don't know about Demo the dickhead," she said lowly, her eyes bugging out of her head. "But you've got a tasty pastry staring at you over there. And oh… oh, my."

"What? Who?" Brushing crumbs off of the front of my shirt, I looked over my shoulder. Sweat instantly pricked at my hairline. "Holy crap! It's *him*."

There, at the far end of the room talking to a group of men, was Demo—watching me with a half-annoyed, half-amused expression. He looked a little out of place, with a plaid shirt tucked into a pair of pressed cargo khakis. He wore scuffed church shoes, and his wild brown hair had been gelled into submission. Everyone else in the room was wearing their best. Suits, dresses, slacks, ties. But not Demo Antonopolous. With his scruffy five o'clock shadow and grease stained fingernails, he looked like he'd stumbled into the wrong party on his way to a Nascar event.

He kinda looked like hell. The sad part was? He looked *good* that way.

"Damn…" It came out half groan, half whimper, and I regretted saying it the second it came out my mouth. A fire had started deep down low in my belly.

Lexie choked on a snicker. "No time like the present to put this plan into effect, Mar."

"Shut up," I snapped. She just grinned at me, the cocky little brat. "Fine. It's time for my ten-minute break anyway."

"I couldn't agree more." She handed the nearly empty mushroom tray to me and grabbed the baskets. "Go give him some mushrooms. A way to a man's heart is through his—"

"Yeah, yeah, yeah. Whatever. I tried that with your husband and he still rejected me."

Her cheeks pinked when she smiled like a lovesick tween. "Okay, then. Good luck."

Tugging the elastic out of my hair, I shook it so that it tumbled down over my shoulders, and prayed there wasn't a health inspector at the meeting tonight. Then, after hoisting the tray up onto my shoulder, I sauntered my way across the room, swaying my hips like a hula dancer. I was pretty sure I appeared to be strutting around like a cat in heat, but I could tell by the way Demo's jaw dropped that it was warranting the desired effect.

"Good evening, gentlemen," I purred, swirling the tray off of my shoulder and holding it under their noses. "Want to try some of my lobster-stuffed white mushroom caps? From what I've been told, they'll melt in your mouth."

All of the men in the semi-circle dove into the mushrooms like they'd been in a Turkish prison, but Demo stared at me, his brows pinched together. "What are you doing here?" he asked.

I blinked at him. "I'm the caterer. Why don't you try a mushroom?"

"No thanks." A waiter passed by with a bacon wrapped shrimp, so he grabbed one and popped it in his mouth.

Anger bubbled in my chest. *Nobody* rejected my food. "Are you

kidding me?"

Lexie whisked past my back with the breadbaskets. "Tsk, tsk, Marisol,"

she whispered.

Dammit. Taking a deep breath, I tried to cool down. *Remember the*

recipes.

"How are the shrimp?" I asked casually.

He swallowed. "Good."

"Oh, wonderful. Because I made those, too." Topping my sentence off

with a wink, I put a hand on my hip and smiled at the row of men standing

before me, chewing like cattle. "Well, boys, have you tried the cedar-smoked

salmon pâté?"

"Pâté?" One guy who looked like he'd been over served by at least two

drinks, maybe more, wrinkled his face. "Isn't that fish eggs?"

He breathed on me, and I held my breath until the fog cleared. Make

that four drinks.

"No, that's caviar." I touched his arm to steady him as he swayed in

place. "Pâté is a meat paste served on toast. It sounds peculiar, but it's really

quite good. You should all try it." The men nodded, and made their way toward

the food tables across the room. All except Demo and drunk guy, who was

staring down the front of my shirt. "Especially you, cowboy," I added, releasing

his arm. "You need some food in your stomach."

"Right. Got it." He hiccupped. "Salmon paste. I'm on it."

74

Demo and I watched him stumble away. "That's Greg Thomason," he said wryly. "He owns the magazine stand in the park."

"I see." Holding out the tray, I offered, "Change your mind about that mushroom?"

His eyes rolled down to the mushrooms, then back up to my face. "You're not going to stop until I eat one, are you?"

I shook my head. "No, sir."

Demo grabbed one and jammed it into his mouth. He chewed it furiously, never losing eye contact with me. Once it went down his gullet, he blinked. "There. You happy now?"

"Maybe." I narrowed my eyes. "Did you like it?"

"A little."

"You're only saying that to be a jerk."

"No, I'm not."

"Yes, you are."

"No."

"Yes."

"No!"

"Yes!"

"All right, knock it off, you two." Lexie took the now empty mushroom tray away from me as she passed by again.

"Okay, let's call a truce." I cleared my throat. "Why don't we start over?"

Demo's eyebrows pinched together. "What?" he asked, as if this was the dumbest idea he'd ever heard.

Hell, maybe it was. Maybe he didn't hear too many ideas.

"Hush." I stuck out my hand. "Hi. My name's Marisol Vargas."

"Knock it off." He shook his head. "You're so weird. We're total opposites, you know that? Like apples and oranges."

I sighed. "I said the same thing yesterday."

"Then why are you doing this?" He raised an eyebrow at me.

My hand dropped. "Because I'm coming back to Triple D's as soon as those recalled parts come in. We may as well be friends, since you're my mechanic now."

His expression softened, just a touch. "You're not going to the dealership?"

I let my shoulders rise and drop. "Nah. You'll do the work for cheaper, anyway."

"Money is no object to you, remember?" He took a pull off his beer and watched me process his words.

I sucked in a sharp breath. "If I didn't know better, I'd think you enjoy ticking me off."

"It's a safe bet." One side of Demo's mouth tugged upward, and he took another drink. "Well, for what it's worth, thanks for the business. We can use it."

"You're welcome."

76

He leaned forward and bumped my arm with his elbow. "And thank you for indulging my Yiayia today. She loves talking to the customers."

My face heated when our bodies touched. *Why did my face heat? What's wrong with me?*

"Oh, uh, you're welcome," I said. "It was my pleasure, though. Really. I had fun listening to her stories. She said your father died a few years ago. I'm very sorry."

Demo looked down. "You didn't do it."

Yikes, not the response I was expecting. I pressed my lips together, refusing to lose my temper. Again. "No, but it's never easy to lose a parent."

"Nope." Demo looked me up and down. "Can I ask you a question?"

Now we were getting somewhere. I smiled and tossed my hair. "Sure."

"What's a girl like you working as a caterer for?" he asked. "You don't seem the type."

Part of me wanted to call him something offensive in Spanish, but the other part of me understood where Demo was coming from. I got comments like that all the time—most of all from Annalise.

But, when I looked up at him, and felt a rush of... honesty. Well, that was strange. "When I was a kid, my mother was obsessed with weight. She tried every diet and procedure under the sun to keep her figure. She's had four tummy tucks, and the woman's never been over a size four." Demo shook his head, and I explained, "That's very small. So when I was about five or six, she decided that I was getting too chubby, so she put me on a diet, too."

His dark eyes widened. "She put you on a diet when you were five?"

"Uh huh." I shook my head. "Slim Fast was the first one. My parents called it chocolate milk, but I wasn't stupid. Then I did the grapefruit diet. Then the cabbage soup diet, that one was my least favorite. We went through them all. By the time I was a teenager, I was obsessed with food. But I had to sneak it. The chef snuck me plates of food when my mother wasn't looking, and I became a closet foodie." I laughed at my own joke, but after a beat or two, I realized Demo wasn't laughing with me. "What?"

His frown returned. "You had a chef?"

Ignoring his question, I went on. "When I went off to school, I had no idea what my major would be, but then I stumbled upon the culinary arts class one afternoon as they were all learning how to dice onions. The whole hallway reeked, and there were tears running down my face, but I knew I'd found where I was supposed to be. My degree is a Bachelor's of Culinary Arts, and I get to cook every day. Plus, it really torqued my mom off. It was a classic two birds with one stone scenario."

"I see." Demo smiled—just the briefest flash of happiness on an otherwise cantankerous face—and it was one of the most glorious things I'd ever seen.

He. Was. Gorgeous.

I opened my mouth, then closed it. Then opened it again. What was my deal? Never once in the existence of *men* had I ever been at a loss for words around a guy. The only time I ever got this goofy around a man was when I was crazy about him. And there was no way in hell I was crazy about Demo Antonopolous.

He reached out and plucked a breadcrumb out of the hair next to my cheek. I was surrounded by the scent of Triple D's garage, mingled with soap and something so undeniably musky and male, it made me want to pee my pants.

Aw, hell. Maybe I was a little bit crazy about him. But it was only because his Yiayia held the key to preparing the world's best Greek delicacies for the biggest event Eats & Treats had ever booked. Oh, yeah… and also because Demo was hella hot. But whatever.

He took a step closer, his shadow looming over me. "So tell me, Marisol."

"Yeah?" My voice came out way breathier than could ever be considered cool.

"Are you trying to seduce me…" Demo's voice was deep and gravelly, and sent my stomach into a spin cycle. I opened my mouth to respond, but he cut me off. "Just to score my Yiayia's recipes?"

"What? No!" I cleared my throat and stepped back from him. "Come on. Don't be stupid. I've got my own recipes. *Cómo te atreves a acusarme de eso?*"

"I'm not accusing you of anything," he said, polishing off his beer. "Just asking a question."

"A pretty rude one," I yelped. *And freakishly accurate, too.*

"You know what I think?" He pointed his bottle at me. "I think you *are* trying to score the recipes. And I also think you speak Spanish when you're ticked off, because you think you can get away with saying things that nobody else can understand."

My hands flew to my hips. "Now, listen here—"

A phone rang in Demo's pocket—the theme song to the old eighties TV show, *Magnum PI*, so fitting—and he put up a hand to shush me. Anger bubbled in my chest again. Who the hell did this *mechanic* think he was?

He looked down at the screen on his phone and winced. "I have to take this."

I grit my teeth together. "You need—"

He put his hand up again, rendering me speechless. "This is Demo," he said, turning away from me. "Yeah… yeah… uh huh. Well now really isn't the time… I'm at a party. What do you mean with who? Some small business thing… Um, no… I said, *no.*" Demo glanced at me over his shoulder and shrugged. "Listen, I'll call you later… no, I do care. I… oh, really?"

I tapped him on the shoulder. "Excuse me? Were we not in the middle of a conversation?"

"Just a second," Demo said into the phone before turning back to face me. He handed me his empty beer bottle. "Here. And, uh, thanks for the mushroom."

I stood there, seething, as he took his phone out the exit, leaving me standing alone. Like a fool. Apparently, I'd been dismissed.

Demo-the-mechanic had just taken a *booty call* right in front of me.

Chapter Seven

"Just go. I'm fine." Hoisting the overstuffed garbage bag over my shoulder, I gave Lexie a gentle push toward her car.

Fletcher had called—three times—because the baby refused to take a bottle, and now she was on the verge of tears. "Are you sure?" she whimpered, unlocking her door. "There's still so much clean up to do, and we already let the wait staff go."

"It's no big deal. I just have to pack up the stuff and mop the kitchen floor." I gestured at her blouse. "Seriously. Go before your boobs do that freaky leaking thing again. I can't unsee that, you know."

Lexie rolled her eyes. "All right. Just be sure to track down that Janis lady. She still owes us three hundred dollars."

"Three hundred dollars. Got it." I saluted her and patted the top of the car as she fired up the engine. "Get out of here before my nice streak wears off."

She rolled out of the Bed & Breakfast parking lot, leaving me in the darkness with the stinky garbage bag. Sighing, I trudged toward the trash bins at the back of the property. My feet were aching so badly I felt like cutting them

82

off and walking on stumps for the rest of the night. And it was a good thing the party was over, because if I listened to one more person talk about the injustices of health care requirements for small business owners, I would put my head in an oven.

"Come on," I grumbled, setting down the bag and trying to lift the bin lid, which was apparently made out of lead. I shoved it up a few times, only to have it slam back down with a bang. "Stupid, worthless, piece of steaming—"

"Need a little help?"

"Oh!" I jumped, knocking over the trash bag at my feet. It was Greg Thomason, who hadn't passed out yet, which was a miracle judging by the way he was shuffling toward me in a jagged line. I lost sight of him after Demo took his booty call, and assumed he caught a cab home to sleep off his wild night with all the neighborhood bookstore and café owners. "Hey there, Greg. You're still standing?"

He held out his arms, swaying. "Still here. Waiting for my cab, actually."

"Good call on the cab," I said, picking the garbage bag back up. "You're a little wobbly."

He gestured to the inn. "My friend, Bernie, took my keys. He owns Blinkie's Flower Shop."

Nodding, I tried—and failed—to open the lid again. "Oh, yeah. I've been in there. Excellent Ecuadorian roses."

"Right you are, pretty lady!" Greg pointed at me and grinned crookedly. I half expected him to drool out the side of his mouth. Oh wait, he just did.

"Ugh," I grunted as I tried to throw the bag and open the lid at the same time. "Seriously. It's like this thing is made for six-foot-tall bodybuilders only."

Greg giggled and snorted. "I'm six-foot-two. My ex-girlfriend said my feet are like skis."

"Well, that wasn't very nice, was it?" When I glanced at him, he looked like he was going to cry. Searching for the much-needed cab, I added, "Foolish girl didn't even know how good she had it, did she?"

His lopsided smile returned. "She sure didn't! She doesn't appreciate me like you do, huh, Caterer Lady?"

I tried to stand on the garbage bag so I could reach the lid more easily, but stumbled. "That's right. And my name's Marisol."

"Marisol... Marisol... Marisol. I like that name." Greg came closer, and the light from a nearby streetlamp lit his face. There was a red, square mark on his cheek. He would've been attractive had he not looked like he'd hit the floor of the restroom at some point this evening. "Hey... you're havin' a hard time, aren't you?"

"You're perceptive."

He tilted his head. "Huh?"

Smiling, I stepped off the bag. "Actually, I'm glad you're here."

"I'll bet you are." Greg went to lean against the dumpster, and missed, stumbling. "Whoopsie."

"Whoa." I caught his elbow and helped him right himself. "You all right? Feeling sick, big guy?"

His voice dropped an octave or two. "Feeling randy."

"Feeling randy?" I let go of his elbow. "Now you're speaking Austin Powers? Oh, this is rich. Come on, help me get this bin open, and I'll wait for your cab with you, okay?"

Greg's eyebrows went up. "You're coming home with me?"

I snorted. "Not tonight. You, my friend, need to go home and get some sleep."

He grabbed the lid and swung it open with one toss, his reddened eyes locked on mine. "Don't want sleep."

My smile hardened. "It doesn't matter what you want, Greg. That's what you need."

He leaned in close, his breath heavy with the smell of locally brewed beer. "I *need* some fun tonight, Mary."

"Marisol," I told him through grit teeth.

Greg hiccupped. "Whatever."

"Well, that's too bad. Because all you're going to be getting tonight is sleep." I shoved the garbage bag toward Greg. "Help me hoist this into the bin?"

"Sure, I can." He ran a hand down the length of my arm before taking hold of the bag. "Is it me, or is there something between us, Mary?"

Releasing a nervous laugh, I helped him shove the bag up the side of the bin, and over the edge. "The only thing between us right now is the stench of rancid food."

Greg wiped his hands on his pants. "I don't want anything between us. 'Cept skin." He sniggered and touched my cheek. "What'dya say?"

His hand smelled like garbage and I cringed. "Not a chance. Let's go call that cab company again." This poor guy needed to go home and hit the mattress, stat. He would feel like a colossal douche in the morning. *If* he even remembered.

"Why are you playing hard to get?" Greg slurred.

I stepped away from him. "I'm not playing. I really am hard to get." Actually, I usually wasn't, but that was beside the point. I turned over a leaf Plus, sloppy drunks with tile marks on their faces weren't my style.

He tilted sideways, and burped. "That's… stupid."

I gestured toward the inn. "You're looking a little green around the gills, buddy. Why don't you let me make you some coffee inside? I've got a Colombian roast that will—"

"Shut up." Greg's hand came down on my forearm with a slap. It was with more force than I was expecting, and I gasped. As soon as I stopped talking, his demeanor softened. "Come on. Let's walk down to Benny's for a nightcap."

Jerking my arm away, I clenched my teeth together. This guy was ticking me off now. "No, thank you. I have plans."

"Oh, come on." He raked a hand down his face, making his eyes even redder. "You don't have plans. Give it up."

I drew a deep breath, then released it slowly. "Go home and get some sleep."

"Tease," he spat down at me, his red face glowing in the dim light.

"Gotta go, Greg." Forcing a tight smile, I sidestepped his arm and headed toward the kitchen door. I didn't scare around men easily—you can't remain single and independent into your thirties and not know how to watch out for yourself—but I was rattled. We were back far enough from the street that there weren't any other people within earshot, the dinner guests were long gone, and the last of my staff had left. It figured.

"Aw… come back," he groaned.

"No, thank you," I yelled over my shoulder. I would throttle the bartenders the small business bureau hired for the night. They apparently had no idea when to stop serving someone.

"Hey, bitch!" Greg's voice cut into the night, and his heavy footsteps thudded on the pavement. "I'm talking to you."

Picking up my pace, I touched my pocket for my new iPhone. Lexie and Fletcher only lived a few blocks away from the inn, and Fletcher wouldn't mind coming down here to scare away a persistent drunk. It was rare, but official: Drunk Greg was freaking me out.

And true to form, I left the damn thing in the kitchen. I would have my iPhone surgically connected to my hand first thing tomorrow.

Greg grabbed my shoulder, jerking me backwards. "I *said* I was talking to you," he snarled into my ear.

"You need to get your hands off of me." I twirled around and shoved him in the chest. When he stumbled backward, I yelled, "Go home and sober up, before I call the cops."

Greg's expression morphed from confused, to belligerent, to livid in the span of a half a second. "Call the cops? Call the…" he grabbed my upper arms. Hard. "Who do you think you are?"

"Let go!" I yelped when he gave me a shake.

"Hey! Get your hands off her!"

I heard the deep, gravelly voice before I saw Demo out of the corner of my eye. He barreled toward us with his fists clenched at his side, ready to swing.

"Who the…" Greg looked from me, to Demo, then back again. "You sleeping with Antonopolous?"

"I'm not sleeping with *anybody*," I growled, wriggling out of his grip. There were red marks above my elbows that would be bruises by morning. Super.

Demo was nose to nose with Greg in an instant. "You like roughing up women?"

"Roughing up? What? What the hell are you talking about?" Greg stumbled backward, but Demo followed. "We were just talking."

"Talking?" Demo's chest pressed against Greg's, and I was pretty sure his biceps were vibrating. "You expect me to believe that?"

88

Greg laughed, and it came out high pitched and hysterical. "Tell him, Mary. Tell him we were talking."

"Her name is Marisol," Demo growled.

I rolled my eyes. "Don't dig your hole any deeper, Greg. We weren't talking."

A cab rolled into the parking lot, stopping right beside the testosterone faceoff. A cabbie with a backward Mariners cap emerged. "Hey. Everything all right out here? Somebody call a cab?"

I gave Greg's shoulder a shove. It was easier not to be scared with Demo here, in all of his puffed up glory. "Yes, sir. Our friend here needs to go home."

"Come ooon, Demo, you know mmme." Greg's voice cracked as he backed away from the hulk of muscle that was my mechanic. "We were jusht hhhaving some fun…"

"Grabbing a woman like that's not fun." Demo opened and closed his fists a few times. I could see his pulse in the side of his neck. "Never let me catch you acting like that again, or I'll put you in the ground. Understand?"

Greg's hands went out defensively. "Hey. Whoa. Whatever, man."

Demo pulled a ten-dollar bill out of his pocket and handed it to the cabbie. "Get him home, and watch him walk in."

"Yes, sir," the driver said, sliding back into the driver's seat.

Greg fiddled with the door handle a few times before getting it open. "No harm in trying. Boy's got a right to get laid once in a while."

I cursed under my breath. This guy was a piece of work.

"Sit down and shut up." Demo gave him a shove, making Greg flop like a doll.

Greg's head hit the door when he flopped into the seat. "Ow, dammit. Bros before ho's, right, buddy?"

"Go home," Demo ordered. The car door slammed, and Greg rested his forehead against the window, promptly falling asleep.

Demo and I watched in silence as the cab pulled away. I couldn't believe that just happened. In all my years of working and dating, I'd never felt *afraid* before. Maybe Candace was right when she suggested a self-defense class a few years ago. I scoffed at the idea then, but now I wish I'd considered it. It would've felt *increíble* to ram my knee so far into Greg's balls that they popped out his ear canals.

I realized how hard my heart thudded in my chest. I pressed my palm to my chest and gulped in a breath of warm night air. I needed to get a grip. It was just a drunk moron. It didn't mean anything. I wasn't in any *real* danger. Right?

As soon as the cab's taillights disappeared, Demo turned to me, and put a hand on my shoulder. "You all right?"

"Fine. I'm fine." I stepped away from his touch, and fanned myself. Pesky tears poked at the backs of my eyes again, and I wasn't about to let them fall in front of Demo-the-mechanic. "He was hammered. I could've taken care of myself."

He shook his head. "Greg was out of line."

I waved off Demo's words. "You didn't need to do anything. I can handle things." But my voice shook.

"You're welcome." Demo said softly.

Dammit, he felt sorry for me.

"I…" My voice cracked, and I cleared my throat. "I didn't need…"

Okay. Between me, myself, and I, that situation was scary. The way Greg's moods vacillated between sloppy, goofy drunk and ticked off. The way he'd grabbed me. *Twice.* What if Demo hadn't come out of nowhere like that? Would I have been able to fend that creep off?

My eyes filled up and spilled over. "Okay. All right. I'm sorry." I covered my face with my hands. "*Thank you.* I appreciate your help, Demo."

He wrapped his arms around me, tentatively at first, but we melted together quickly enough. Pressing my face into the worn cotton of his shirt, I cried for a good two or three—maybe five—minutes. His scent, minty soap and the faintest hint of gasoline, danced through my nose. My shoulders shook as I wept for the first time in more years than I could count, but for some peculiar reason, I didn't care. It was that odd rush of honesty I seemed to feel every time Demo was around. There was no BS-ing this guy, and as much as I hated it… I loved it, too. It felt good to cry. Maybe I needed it.

"Shhh, it's okay now," Demo whispered, his callused hands rubbing a circle between my shoulder blades.

His touch left a trail of tingles on my skin that I didn't care to admit to anyone.

91

"I just…" I hiccupped. "I… I…"

"Don't talk," Demo instructed, resting his chin on the top of my head. He tightened his arms around me, and I soaked up the warmth his body exuded. And man, oh, man. Demo put off some heat. There was something incredibly comforting about being held by someone as strong and unwavering as Demo Antonopolous. It was like being hugged by a redwood tree.

"I'm sorry," I sputtered. "I don't usually do this. I'm usually much more collected, and, um…" I didn't finish my sentence because Demo tilted his head so that his face was down by my temple, and he sniffed my hair.

Sniffed it.

"Do you have a ride home?" he whispered.

When I pulled back and looked up at Demo, his dark eyes reflected my own face back at me. Instead of his telltale scowl, the corners of his mouth pointed upward, just the tiniest bit. "I can drive myself," I said hoarsely. "My car's right over there."

He tucked a strand of my hair behind my ear. "You're still shaking. You should let me run you home."

I wanted Demo to kiss me. *Badly.*

I wanted to know if his face was as rough as it looked, or if he was a gentle giant underneath the tough guy with a massive chip on his shoulder exterior. I wanted to know what he tasted like. And what his lips on my lips felt like, or what his lips felt like on my skin…

I gulped. "I'm fine?"

Well that didn't sound convincing at all.

Demo's thumb brushed the skin below one of my eyes, wiping away the remnant of one of my tears. The air between us sparked. "It's okay to let someone take care of you, you know."

For a second, I actually considered it. Toyed around with the idea of dropping my Miss Independence façade, and playing the part of the damsel in distress. But the sound of approaching heels clicking on the cement broke apart our moment.

"Who the *hell* is that, Demo?"

"Stacia." Demo's hands dropped, and he took a step away from me.

Wiping my eyes, I turned around, finding myself face to face with a very ticked off blonde who was on the fast track to melanoma with her tanning bed-bronzed skin. In her strapless salmon-colored dress, this Stacia person was dressed for a party, or simply to impress Demo, who appeared half sheepish, half bored as he rocked back on his heels and shoved his hands in his pockets.

She sneered at me. "Who is this whore?"

My mouth dropped open. "I, uh, excuse me?" Okay, so Demo's call from earlier wasn't just a booty call. It'd been a booty call *from his girlfriend.* It was all coming together for me now. "Girlfriend?" I hissed at Demo.

He shrugged. "It's not like that."

"What are you telling her?" Stacia shrieked, her dangly earrings dancing around her face.

Glaring at Demo over my shoulder, I put my hand out. "Hi. I'm Marisol Vargas."

"I don't care who you are," Stacia shoved past me, and thumped Demo on the chest. "Who is she? What are you doing with your arms around that tramp?"

He gritted his teeth; the nice guy from just moments ago was long gone. "You're misunderstanding—"

"*Misunderstanding?*" she bellowed.

My face, still wet from tears, scalded. "Okay, I'm out of here."

"Marisol, wait." Demo reached for me, but I moved too fast for him.

I'd been grabbed by one too many men tonight. All I wanted was to finish my work, collect my three hundred dollars, and go home. Sure, Cocinero expected me to sit and pet him while he ate, but at least he didn't make me feel useless and stupid. Well, not much, anyway.

"Goodnight, Demo." I slammed the kitchen door behind me.

Chapter Eight

I didn't hear a peep from Demo for a week, and hadn't really expected to. After all, he was busy with his blonde girlfriend, who clearly had trust issues, and I wasn't going to get the recipes—or a kiss—from Demo any time soon. Which was fine by me.

Sort of.

Okay, so I was frustrated about it. I made two batches of baklava and one batch of dolmades that all turned out sub-par. I had no idea how to make authentic Greek delicacies, and not being capable of doing something never happened to me. Usually all it took was a test run and maybe some tweaking, and my food was good to go. But this time around? Argh. Not even close. Not for the amount of money these people were paying us.

And, adding to my list of frustrations, not only would I *not* be getting those much-needed recipes, but there would be no smooch-smoochy—or *more*—with Demo. While I hated to admit it, there was something about the way it felt resting against his chest that night. Happy, warm, *safe*. I could only imagine what being full-on seduced by *His Royal Crankiness* would be like. If my imagination had anything to say about it, pretty damn good. Not that I would ever find out.

Harrumph.

And then… exactly seven days and eight hours after what Lexie and Candace were now referring to as *the incident*, I got a very terse voicemail from none other than Demo:

"Uh…yeah. This is Triple D's calling. Your parts arrived, and I can fit the work in sometime this afternoon. I've got a pretty packed week, so if you don't bring it in, you'll wind up waiting another week or so, and I know how you feel about waiting. So… you know. Bring it on in."

That man seriously needed to brush up his phone skills. Demo couldn't have sounded less interested in me, or my business, and I didn't imagine he'd given our little moment in the dark another thought.

Which is why I didn't even bother to dress nicely when I took my Beemer to Triple D's. I'd been frosting cupcakes to the soundtrack of Lexie's fussy baby's screams since six that morning. I wore old jeans and a tank top splattered in blue food coloring. I didn't care whether I saw Demo or not. I just wanted to drop my car off and throw a wave in Yiayia's direction.

"Wait here," I told Candace, who offered me a ride back to work in her gross old minivan. The sound of some Barbie DVD played in the backseat, and all of her kids—even her son—stared at the screen hanging from the ceiling with slack jaws. "I don't think your little ankle biters will mind."

96

"Where's the hottie?" Candace leaned over the top of her steering wheel. "Can I meet him?"

"You sure as hell cannot meet him," I scolded. "Just wait here. I'll be right back."

"Go jump him!" She laughed. "Have another *incident,* and make him forget all about the blonde."

"Whatever," I hissed. "I'm going in, dropping my keys, and then we're out of here. Be ready."

She stifled a giggle. "Got it."

As I approached the garage doors, Trey wiped his hands on a greasy rag and called, "Welcome back, Marisol!"

"Thank goodness it's you." I stalked across the cracked parking lot to give him my keys. "Your uncle called me. You've some replacement parts for my car."

"Right-o." Trey jerked his chin in the direction of some nearby boxes. "Came in this morning. You gonna wait for us to be finished? Yiayia's in the office and loves company."

My heart tugged. My entire life I wondered what it was like to have a grandma, and now I was irrationally attached to some old lady I met once. But in my defense, Yiayia was really sweet. And that baklava was crazy good. "Sorry, no. Not today, Trey. I've got to get back to work."

He flexed a wiry arm. "Don't you want to see these guns in action?"

"Nope. My ride is waiting."

He peered around my shoulder. "The blonde in the van? She's hot."

I shook my head. "You think every woman's hot."

"Fair enough." He shrugged and looked at my shirt. "You been killing Smurfs, or something?"

I brushed at the tank, but it did nothing. "No. I've got a sweet sixteen party to cater tonight, and the color scheme is blue, bluer, and bluest."

"And you didn't bring us some?" Trey shook his head, a smile teasing his mouth. "Man, and my yiayia gave you baklava and everything."

"Sorry, kid." I held out my keys. "I've got to get back, anyway."

"Your loss. She made kourabiethes, too."

I pressed my lips together. I had a weakness for the shortbread cookies covered in confectioners' sugar and almonds since discovering them at an Orthodox Church bazaar a few years ago. I gained five pounds after sitting alone in my house with them for a weekend, and vowed never to indulge in kourabiethes again. Leave it to Yiayia's cooking to knock me off the wagon.

I chewed my lip. Surely one wouldn't hurt. "Well, I—"

"Well, if it isn't her Highness." Demo emerged from the office, polishing what looked to be a radiator cap—but really, what did I know—with a towel. "Decided to grace us with your presence?"

Irritation stung like a bug bite, but the way Demo looked in his coveralls, open just enough to show some very manly-looking chest hair and what appeared to be another tattoo, made up for it. Seriously. Had I known mechanics could look this good, I'd have bought a lemon years ago.

98

"You left a message." I wrapped my arms around myself, suddenly self-conscious. Girlfriend or not, I wasn't usually seen in public without a full face of makeup and a couture outfit. Annalise taught me the value of a pretty lady long before she instilled values like honesty or chastity.

Wait. She never got around to either of those. At least I developed *one* of them on my own.

"'Bout time you showed up." He set the cap down, and tossed the towel at Trey. "I don't know if I can fit you in anymore."

"I couldn't get away from work until now." I threw my arms out. "What did you expect?"

Seriously. Why in the world was I so attracted to such a colossal dickhead?

Oh, right. Because he was so nice to look at. And underneath all of those whiskers and grease stains, he was kind of a nice guy. Though he kept that personality trait under tight wraps, didn't he?

"Lay off, Uncle Demo," Trey called from under the hood of a Volkswagen. "She was working on cupcakes."

"Cupcakes? Sounds intense." Demo held out his hand to me. "I need your keys."

"Keys, *please.*" I held out the keys, hovering them above his palm. "And yes, I was making cupcakes. Not all of us wind up with oil under our fingernails when we work."

He eyeballed my tank top, a smile tickling the corner of his lips. "Just frosting, Princess?"

"Stop calling me that." I snapped, putting my keys back in my pocket. "What is your problem?"

Trey stood upright and leaned against the bumper of the Volkswagen. "Here we go again…"

"Shut up, Trey." Demo took a step closer to me. "By the way, *Marisol*, you're welcome for rescuing your butt the other night."

I sucked in a sharp breath. If I had a nickel for how many times I'd replayed my encounter with Greg, I'd have a hundred dollars by now, and every time I thought about the moment he grabbed me, I shuddered.

"Thank you," I said quickly. I returned his annoyed expression with an equally aggravated glare. "I would have thanked you that night, but your girlfriend seemed pretty ticked off to see me."

"Who?" Demo frowned.

Balling my fists at my sides, I stalked toward the garage doors. "I've got to go."

"She isn't my girlfriend," Demo called, stopping me in my tracks.

I turned around. "Clearly she thinks differently."

"*She* is named Stacia," he said. "And she thinks differently about lots of things."

"Seriously, do you speak in riddles all the time, or just do it to irritate off?" Storming back over to the Volkswagen, I slapped my hand down on the metal. "You know you could have told me you had a girlfriend."

"For the second time, Stacia's not my girlfriend." Demo tugged on a wrench and grunted. "I mean, why that's any of your business, I don't know. But she's not."

Trey caught my eye and snickered.

"Get to work," I snapped at him.

"Hey." Demo's glare went from me to his nephew. "Get to work."

Trey scuttled off to the back of the shop, and I leaned close to Demo. "If you told me you were seeing someone, or that someone thought she was seeing you, I wouldn't have tried so hard to hit on you."

Demo chuckled. "You've been hitting on me all this time?"

"Well, *yeah*." I groaned. "I mean, when we weren't fighting."

He smiled mildly. "We're always fighting."

"That's for damn sure." I swatted at a hair that escaped from my ponytail. "What I'm trying to say is, had I known you were involved with someone—"

"We're *not* involved."

"I would have backed off," I finished. "I wouldn't have hugged you like that, you know?"

Demo gave the wrench another yank. "And all this time I thought you were after me for my yiayia's recipes."

My stomach clenched. *He is* way *more perceptive than I gave him credit for.*

"So now that we've got that girlfriend garbage cleared up," he looked at me, the faintest shadow of amusement on his whiskered face. "Are you going to try hitting on me again?"

I met his smile with one of my own. "Try? Demo, if I hit on you, there's no luck about it. You won't know what hit you."

"That so?" He leaned on his elbows, bringing his face closer to mine. The same whirl in my chest that I felt that night at the inn returned. "Then I guess it's a real bummer that it still won't work."

My skin flushed. "Uh huh, and... wait, what?"

Pushing himself off the Volkswagen, Demo stood upright, towering over me. "Too high maintenance."

"Oh, yeah?" I looked him dead in the eye. He didn't intimidate me. I could slip back into bitch mode, just as easily as he could slip into arrogant tool mode. If he wanted to pretend that there hadn't been some sort of cosmic connection between us that night, that was fine by me. "What's your type, then? Loose? Alcoholic bar fly? Chain smoker? Meth dealer? Sorry I don't fit the bill."

"You're gorgeous and confident." Demo scoffed. "Not to mention conceited, flashy, kinda pretentious, entitled, maybe even a little bratty." He glanced up at me, and wrinkled his face. "I mean... no offense, or anything."

My head jerked back. His words stung like a smack. Not because I was insulted, but because I'd been called every one of those things. More than once. Not that I would admit it to him. "Those are mighty big words for a guy like you."

His dark eyes narrowed. "This is exactly why I didn't want to date you before, and I still don't."

"Has anybody told you that you're a dick?" I asked him, my voice shaking.

"A time or two, yes." He grit his teeth together. "Has anybody told you that you're an over-confident little show pony?"

"You sure didn't mind cuddling up with the show pony the other night." I thumped Demo's chest with my finger. "That is, until your girlfriend showed up."

His face was starting to turn red. "She's *not* my girlfriend."

The office door swung open and the matriarch of Triple D's appeared in the doorway. "Demetrious Marcos Antonopolous. Are you abusing this young lady?"

"Abusing? Really?" Demo closed his eyes and took a deep breath. "No, Yiaya."

She leaned over so she could see me around Demo's shoulder. "Hello there, Marisol. How are you?"

I waved at Yiayia, and my heart tugged. There was something about that old broad that made me want to put on fuzzy PJs and sit down with some

103

cocoa to listen to stories of the days of yore. "Hi, Yiayia. I'm fine, thank you. How are you?"

"Just great, dear." She smiled, her wrinkly face scrunching up. "Is my grandson giving you a hard time?"

I looked up at Demo, who fixed his gaze on something across the shop. By the disconnected look on his face, he might've gone away to his happy place, and it only irritated me more. I wanted to cuss him out. I wanted to bring my knee up to collide with his man parts with a satisfying whack. I wanted to leave Triple D's in a blaze of melodramatic glory, then ride off in Candace's minivan…

Oh, crap. Candace was still waiting for me.

"No, he and I were just talking," I told Yiayia. "But I have to run now. My friend is waiting, and I have to get back to work."

"Back to the cupcakes?" Demo asked, his voice low enough that his grandmother couldn't hear.

"Shut up, grease monkey," I whispered, my voice shaking.

Demo shook his head. "I was just gonna say we like cupcakes around here. In case you made extra."

I whipped my hand up, poking him in the chest again. "You think I'm going to bring you treats when you're acting like such a jerk?"

Yiayia appeared between us. Man, she moved fast for having gone to high school with *Abraham Lincoln*. "You know what you both need?" Both Demo and I looked down at her, perplexed. "A date," she said proudly.

"Good luck with that, Yiayia," Trey called from across the garage. "They can't stand each other."

"Can it, kid," Demo groaned.

Yiayia threw her head of white helmet hair back and cackled. "That's what they think."

I shook my head. "Actually, he's right. We can't even talk for five minutes without arguing, and—"

She took hold of both of our chins at the same time. Her grip was alarming for a woman her age. "When I met my husband, he told me I was the last woman on earth he'd ever take to the altar." Yiayia's gaze landed on her grandson's face. "We were married eleven weeks later."

Demo and I stepped back from in unison. "Don't think it's gonna happen," he announced at the same time I said, "Thanks, but no thanks."

Her eyes, which were the same shade of dark chocolate as Demo's, bored into mine with the intensity of a newly refurbished engine. "You'll mark my words, Marisol. He'll ask. I promise you that."

Digging in my pockets, I produced my keys. "Hey, Trey!"

"Huh?" He poked his head around the far end of the Volkswagen.

I looked at Demo, whose lips twitched in return. Tossing the keys at the lanky teenager, I headed for the doors. "Call me when the Beemer's ready."

Chapter Nine

Maybe it was the fact that I was on my second glass of pinot, or maybe it was just that I was home alone on a Friday night… but I was in a weird mood.

I almost never went into a weekend without a date. For years, I attributed that to how lovely and desirable I was. But what really drove me to go out with someone—anyone—every weekend without fail, was really… my father.

He only called five times in the three years since peeling out of the driveway. When he finally asked my mom to let me fly to Florida for a week to see him, I built up the visit in my head. I expected trips to the beach, evenings watching the circus, picnics, carnivals, and maybe even a ride in a hot air balloon. He'd never done things like that with me before, but I heard all sorts of exciting stories from friends with divorced parents, and fully expected my own father to pull out the stops trying to buy my affections.

I was wrong.

We spent the first five days with Penelope, the sixty-year-old woman he hired to clean his house. My dad left for work before I rolled out of bed in the morning, then returned late in the night, half-drunk from the client dinners he hosted. I spent most of my visit paddling around in the pool while Penelope drank coffee in a lawn chair.

"Well, well, well. Look at my pececito."

I gasped, and paddled to the side where my dad waited with his briefcase. It was only two in the afternoon, and he was home already. He'd come home to spend time with me! I was ecstatic, kicking like a fool to reach the tiles.

"Ack!" Penelope cried, shielding herself from the drops of water. "Not so hard, not so hard, Marisol."

"Mom put me in swimming classes four days a week," I told my dad, pool water running in rivulets down my face. "My instructor says I'm her second best student. I am your little fish, Dad. I'm ten times better than a fish. I can hold my breath for thirty-seven seconds."

"Impressive, kiddo." He looked at his watch and winced. "Ouch. Gotta run, baby. Tell Penelope to take you to Ernest's for dinner. They make great burgers."

Scowling, I drifted away from the wall a few inches. Mom didn't even allow me to eat burgers. He'd have known that, had he stuck around. "Are you coming?" I asked.

"Sorry, no can do." He shook his head, and ran a hand through his brown hair. I got my thick locks from him, and his was starting to thin on top. At that moment, I was glad. He deserved to go bald. *"I've got a date tonight, kiddo."*

"A date?" I treaded water. *"Can I go, too?"*

My dad laughed. *"On my date?"*

"Yeah. I'll be good. I won't talk, or anything."

He started to walk towards the house. *"Forget it. It's Friday night, Marisol."*

"But I haven't seen you all week, and I fly home on Sunday!" I whined.

"You just saw me." He kept walking. *"Come on. Don't be a child about this."*

Anger flushed my skin, despite the cool water. *"I'm not a child. I'm almost a teenager."*

He looked at me over his shoulder. *"Then act like it, Marisol."*

"I'm bored." I scowled at him, paddling in place. I wanted to go home, but my mom would be mad if I showed up out of nowhere two days early. *"Not like you care."*

My dad looked up at the sky and groaned. He tugged his shades out of his suit pocket roughly. *"This was a mistake."*

My blood boiled, and I swam to the side of the pool. *"This visit? Or me?"*

"Don't be so dramatic." Dad frowned from behind his sunglasses. I could tell by the wrinkle between his eyebrows. "I flew you here, didn't I?"

Penelope put her coffee cup down and smiled sadly at me. "Why don't we go inside and pick out a movie, Marisol?"

"No." I pulled myself out of the pool, and stomped over to where Dad stood. He jumped away from the water dripping off of me. "I want to hang out with you, Dad. Just one night, that's all."

He grimaced. "It's the weekend, Marisol." Dad over-exaggerated his syllables like he thought I didn't understand the concept of a weekend. Believe me, my mom had made the importance of a Friday or Saturday night very clear. "I can't just cancel. Look at you. You're practically grown up now. You shouldn't be playing in a pool all day."

"Shut up." I pouted, suddenly feeling self-conscious in my bathing suit. I was starting to get a womanly figure, and some of my friends had even started their periods. I waited for my dad to scold me for telling him to shut up, but he just looked out at the sand and blue water beyond the edge of his patio and sighed.

"I'm gonna give you a little piece of advice, Marisol." He put his hands on his hips and strolled towards the beach. I followed, leaving wet footprints as I walked. His steps stopped just short of the sand. "The people who count in this world—the people who stand out—are the ones who are out there. Being seen in the hottest restaurants, and the best clubs. Showing up with the hottest woman..." He glanced at me. "...or man as your date."

A warm wind swayed the palm trees over our heads, and I waited for Dad to say he was bringing me out on his date. So I could be seen too.

"Never let a weekend go by without a date, Marisol." He pointed his finger like this was the best advice he'd ever bestow upon me. "Always be seen. Always be on the go. Always have something to do on your weekends… and nobody will forget about you." Patting my head, Dad walked past me, and ducked into the house without another word.

My shoulders dropped. He was leaving me again.

Penelope put a towel around my shoulders. "Come on. Let's dry off and go to Ernest's."

Wriggling out of her grip, I threw the towel on the wet patio tiles. I didn't want to spend another night eating with my dad's housekeeper. I wanted to go home. Sure, my mom would be mad that I'd come home early and interrupted her time with her boyfriend, but I didn't care. I wasn't ever going to be forgotten by my dad again.

Cocinero's horrendous yowling interrupted my thoughts, chasing away memories of my father like a fog, and I looked around at my still-empty house. I guess I'd given up on trying to ensure I wasn't forgotten by anyone. It was too much effort. Who wanted to spend their time on meaningless date after date, when there were twelve hundred thread -count sheets and a pissy Siamese cat waiting at home?

Throwing back my head and downing the rest of my pinot, I turned off the lights in my kitchen and headed for the stairs. I was pretty sure I recorded *Avatar* the other night. That would be a good way to spend my evening… me, the big blue alien dude, and Cocinero.

Once again, my thoughts were interrupted by my cat's yowling and hissing. When I came around the corner into the foyer, he clawed at the bottom of the front door like there was a chunk of Pacific cod waiting on the other side.

"Stop that," I scolded him, scooping the ball of white fluff off of the floor and cuddling him to my chest. He wiggled out of my grip, landing on the wood floor and resuming his clawing. "Ugh. Come on, Cocinero, I don't have time for this tonight."

There was a muted thump outside, and the meowing started again.

"Who's here this time of night?" I asked my cat. Peering out a nearby window, I saw nothing but the giant, yellow rhododendron bush I had my gardener plant last year. The thing had tripled in size, blocking my entire view of the driveway, just like Candace had warned. Now every time she came over, she pointed to it and rolled her eyes.

As usual, I chose beauty over function. It was the same with my Juicy Couture pencil skirt. And my Beemer. And my five-inch nude spiked heel pumps. This was a really embarrassing pattern with me.

I heard the sound of a car door shutting and scooped Cocinero back up. Straining to see through the mustard yellow blossoms, I came up short. "Who's out there, sweetie? Do we have company?"

Cocinero quieted, and we both stood in the darkness, listening. It was probably my neighbor. She was in her sixties and spent most of her weekend nights square dancing with a club downtown. Usually two or three times a summer, she brought her fellow square dancers back to her house for late night drinks after a show. I'd never seen Agnes bust a move on the dance floor, but word on the street said she wasn't half bad. I was all for anything that kept a widowed sixty-year old woman out having fun until eleven at night.

I guess it gave me hope for my own golden years. But whatever.

"Must be Agnes, Cocinero. She and her friends must be whooping it up after a gig." I pressed a kiss to his soft head. "Let's you and me go upstairs and get in bed."

There was another thump, followed by a deep groan. This time it came from just outside the front door.

"What the…?" I froze in place. Cocinero meowed lowly, then burrowed deep underneath my arm. "You're a terrible body guard." Tip-toeing back over to the door, I pressed my ear to the wood. I could hear some scraping, and some indecipherable muttering.

My blood ran cold. What if Greg found out where I lived? It wasn't difficult. I knew enough people from the party, he could have asked someone where to find me. What if when he woke up the next morning, instead of feeling stupid for behaving like a belligerent tool, he decided he was mad?

My fingers shook as I checked the locks on the door. Each was in place, thank God. "Don't be scared, don't worry," I whispered to Cocinero, knowing I was saying it more for myself. "Everything's fine. Mommy's got her gun."

I glanced at the chair in the corner of the foyer where I usually tossed my purse. *Aw, hell.* Sure enough, I'd taken it up to my bedroom when I changed my clothes.

I wasn't even sure how to shoot the damn thing. Why, oh why, had I declined the opportunity to go shooting with Candace and Brian last year? I scoffed at them, calling them conservative barbarians, but now I kicked myself. There was another scuffling sound, and I peeked through the window, squinting to see beyond the rhododendrons.

Sure enough, there on my flagstone front walk, was a pair of legs. The feet, clad in dark boots, were kicking furiously to free themselves from the garden hose they were tangled in.

Gasping, I jumped back from the window, and practically threw my cat into a nearby chair. "Call the cops, call the cops, call the cops!" I hissed at myself, scrambling through the darkened first floor to where my phone was…

NOT plugged in.

"Son of a… what is *wrong* with me!?" I scanned the counters, opening and closing drawers. Sweat pricked my forehead. I left the damn iPhone in my purse. Which was… I don't know where. "I swear upon everything good and holy on this earth, I am going to duct tape it to the side of my fracking head!"

For someone who prided herself on independence, I was embarrassingly scatterbrained lately.

Cocinero hissed in the foyer, and I knocked over my empty wine glass. It landed in the sink with a shatter. "Shhhh!" I told myself. For all I knew, Drunk Greg was outside with a chip on his shoulder, and I was beckoning him in. "Home phone. Home phone. Where… is… the… home phone?"

Cocinero yowled in the foyer, and it was followed by a swift knock on the door. Yelping, I dove for the door and flipped open the control panel on my alarm system. I'd never pushed the panic button before. Well, there was that one time when I pushed it because I thought I saw a mouse in my kitchen, but I learned very quickly that the panic button was *not* used for those kinds of emergencies. Although, the fireman who came was quite hot. But that's a story for a different time.

Another knock rang out, and my heart leapt into my throat. Gads, was this enough of an emergency to push the button? A potentially drunk and disgruntled guy I rejected and subsequently inflamed?

"Marisol!" The voice was low, angry, and very close to the door. That much was clear, despite being muffled by the wood. I nearly peed my pants, and my hand came down on the red panic button with a decisive slam.

The house filled with the ear piercing sound of an alarm, and I slapped my hands on my ears. Cocinero jumped off of the chair to dart from one end of the house to the other several times, his fur turning into a white blur.

"You're not helping!" I yelled, barely hearing my voice over the alarm. I pounded on the door with all my strength. "HEY BUDDY! YOU'D BETTER GET OUT OF HERE, BEFORE THE COPS SHOW UP!"

Though I could barely make out his words, I thought I heard a holler coming from the other side. "OH, COME ON, PRINCESS. THE *ALARM?*"

Wait. What? Did I recognize that voice? That low, gravelly pitch? That edge of irritation in the tone? It was hard to hear over the screech of the alarm. I peered through the window, but only saw darkness, part of the garden hose, and those damned yellow flowers.

"DEMO? IS THAT YOU? I—" Groaning, I punched in the code to stop the alarm. Once it stopped, a deafening quiet filled my house. Breathing a sigh of relief, I leaned against the door. "Demo, why are you on my porch?"

I heard him sigh. "You are seriously high strung."

Shaking my head, I flipped off the door. "There was a man on my porch in the middle of the night. What did you expect? I could have *shot* you."

"Doubtful. But it's only ten," he called. "That's not the middle of the night."

"Shut up," I whispered.

"How long until the cops come?"

As if on command, a tinny voice filled the foyer. "*Good evening, Ms. Vargas. I see you hit the panic button. Are you in need of assistance?*"

So that's *what I paid an extra forty bucks every month for,* I thought.

"Um…" I said into the speaker on the wall. Snickering to myself, I added, "Maybe." It would serve Demo right to get handcuffed and frisked by a cop. Besides, it might be kinda sexy.

"Oh, come on, Marisol. You gotta be kidding," the growly voice said from the other side of the door.

The tinny voice returned, this time more insistent. *"Ms. Vargas, are you in need of assistance? Should we connect you with emergency services?"*

"No." I rubbed my eyes, and scooped Cocinero off of the floor. "I'm fine, thank you. It was a mistake."

"You can say that again," he muttered.

"Helllllooooooo?" Agnes came in through the kitchen, making me jump a foot off of the floor.

"Holy hell!" I yelled. "How did you get in?"

She held up a flowered keychain. In her other hand she held a cast iron skillet. "I used the key you gave me. Are you okay? Did you see another mouse?"

I stared at the pan. "Why did you bring that?"

"Oh, this?" She held it up and examined it. Her breath smelled like Irish cream. "I grabbed it in case you needed me to fight off an assailant. Are you sure you're all right, dear?"

Releasing a long breath, I leaned against the wall. "I'm fine, I just—"

Static crackled through the speaker. *"Pardon me, ma'am. Are you in need of assistance?"*

"I'm fine. It was a misunderstanding. I'm sorry." The tinny voice thanked me, then with a beep disappeared. I turned to Agnes. "It's my mechanic. Er, a friend. I didn't mean to scare you."

"Mechanic?" Agnes cuddled Cocinero to her ample bosom, which was pushed up and locked into place by her square dance costume.

"Friend. Or, well, I don't know… just…" Tucking the stray strands of hair hanging loose from my ponytail behind my ears, I unlocked the door and swung it open.

Sure enough, there in the darkness stood Demo, with my black garden soaker hose wrapped around one of his legs and a seriously pissed off scowl on his face.

"You sure he's your friend?" Agnes whispered, once again right behind me. "Looks a little bit angry."

"He's always angry," I whispered back, before shaking my head at Demo. "What are you doing here so late? What is wrong with you? Are you stalking me now?"

He scoffed. "Of course you think I'm stalking you."

I threw out my hands. "You're on my front porch in the middle of the night!"

"I already told you, it's not the middle of the night."

"Yes, it is."

"Two or three in the morning is the middle of the night," he countered.

"No, it's not. That's a good morning."

The corner of his lips ticked up. "Okay. Maybe one. But definitely not ten at night."

"You're a moron."

"You're a brat."

Agnes flicked on the porch light, and stepped between us. One of her hands went on each of our shoulders. "You two are so cute."

Demo and I both gaped at her. "We can't stand each other," I said lamely.

She shook her head, grinning. "You can't fool me. That there's a lovers' quarrel."

"No," Demo said, scrubbing a hand across his five o'clock shadow. "It's not."

"Please." She wagged a red-nailed finger in Demo's face. "I know two people who are mad about each other. You should've seen my Albert and me. We were at each other's throats nearly every day. Then at night, we were at each other in another way, if you know what I mean." Agnes jabbed Demo in the ribs with her elbow.

"Ow." He rubbed his side, then held out my car keys. "Look, I'm only here to give you these."

"My car is here?" I peered out the door, and around the massive rhodie bush. The shining back bumper of my Beemer gleamed in the darkness. "You already finished it?"

"Yeah, it wasn't so hard." Demo waved a hand. "Figured you'd need it tomorrow, so I thought I'd leave it here. You know…" He shrugged and his words trailed off.

"As a surprise?" Agnes fed him. "That's so romantic."

He scoffed. "Please."

I was taken aback. Every time I made up my mind about Demo, he surprised me with a random kind gesture that was more Prince Charming than giant douche bag. "Thank you," I said quickly. "Very much."

Demo nodded. "Yup." He looked around awkwardly. "Listen, Marisol, you need to take better care of yourself. You should leave your porch light on, so burglars won't think the house is empty."

I scrunched up my face. "Were you worried about me?"

He didn't answer and instead turned to Agnes. "And you, lady, you're not going to defend anyone armed only with a skillet. What if I had a gun?"

Agnes grinned and jutted out her hip, as if she were some sixties' sex kitten. "Oo, is it a big one?" She jabbed a thumb in my direction. "Besides, she's the one with a gun."

"It's in my purse," I whispered.

Agnes frowned. "Where's your purse, dear?"

"I'm not entirely sure." I shrugged.

Demo's eyes narrowed before he turned back to Agnes.

"A skillet isn't a defense against a weapon," Demo continued as if neither of us had spoken. "Next time, you call the cops. Let them sort it out."

"Yes, sir." I saluted him, and looked around for someone in a waiting car. "How are you getting home?"

His shoulders rose and dropped in a noncommittal shrug. "I'll walk. There's a bus stop down the road, outside the subdivision."

119

Agned beamed. "That was very chivalrous."

Demo ignored her and shook my keys. "I was gonna leave them under the mat, but then I tripped on your damned soaker hose."

Snorting, I took the keys from Demo. "A little clumsy, are we?"

"Well, if you had your porch light on, I would've seen it," Demo snarled, bending down to unwind the hose from around his boots. "It's *black*, and it's dark out."

I tried to help his feet get untangled. "I didn't know I was having company, so I didn't know I needed to leave the light on."

"Your porch light should always be on."

"Oh, brother. Don't start with that again." I rolled my eyes and tossed the hose into the flower garden. "I'm safe enough. You heard the alarm system."

"You know, he's right, dear." Agnes patted my shoulder. "I always leave my porch light on at night. It's just good sense, Marisol."

Demo smiled. "Told you."

"Shut up," I snapped. That smile was gorgeous. And impossible to ignore. My own personal kryptonite.

Agnes sighed and threw her arms around both of our shoulders. My face crunched against her starchy puffed sleeves. "You two bring back memories."

"Of death by suffocation?" Demo's voice was muffled by a mouthful of lace.

120

"Of my Albert." She rested her head against mine. "He always told me to leave the downstairs sink dripping at night in the winter. And, of course, I was stubborn, and I refused. And do you know what happened?"

I had to crane my head to see beyond the sleeve. "What?"

She squeezed us harder. "The darn pipes froze during the ice storm of ninety-six! Gah! Can you believe it?"

"Not at all," I said at the same time Demo uttered, "Nope."

"Why don't you do yourselves a favor and kiss?" She loosened her grip on our necks, and grinned as we stood upright.

"Um, excuse me?" I folded my arms across my chest, suddenly uncomfortable.

Demo stared down at me, his expression indecipherable.

"C'mon. Make your old neighbor happy." She bounced in place, making her petticoats swish. "Kiss and make up."

Dead silence fell. I considered telling Demo to take a flying leap and to take my neighbor with him. But I resisted. Mostly because Agnes was a good neighbor. She gave me homemade huckleberry syrup—an Inland Northwest delicacy—every Christmas, and when her son came for visits in the winter, he always shoveled my driveway. They're good people.

And the possibility of kissing Demo? Holy mother of deliciousness. He stood on my porch with a pair of ripped black jeans and a white V-neck tee shirt so thin it was practically translucent. And his face? Oh, heavens... that five o'clock shadow was impressive. I secretly hoped he *never* shaved again. Even if it was just a kiss for Agnes's sake, I didn't care. It would be worth it. For experimental purposes only, of course.

"Uh, I better go." Demo turned to leave.

My heart dropped.

"Oh, no you don't." Agnes linked her arm in his and tugged him back into place. Then she hiccupped. Or burped. I wasn't sure which. "Come on. Don't leave mad. Kiss and makeup."

Silence filled my foyer, and Cocinero started clawing at Demo's bootlace. Five seconds passed. Then ten. Then fifteen.

"Listen, Agnes—"

"Shut up." Demo shook off Agnes's grip and closed the space between our bodies. His rough hands cupped my face, tangling in my hair and nearly tugging it from my ponytail. I didn't have time to think, or breathe, or blink, because he tilted my head to the side and crushed his mouth down on mine like he was going to war the next day.

Spots of light flashed behind my closed lids, and we landed against the doorjamb with a dull thud. Demo's lips were like satin and sandpaper all rolled in one, and when they nudged my mouth open, I might have accidentally released a little moan. One of his hands went to the small of my back, tucking me against his body so snugly it took my breath away, and when his tongue tickled the inside of my lower lip, my knees turned into jelly and I had to grasp the front of Demo's shirt to stay upright.

He pulled away just enough to nip at my lower lip, releasing a swarm of butterflies in my stomach that threatened to knock me right onto the tile floor, then dove in for more. The kiss was like nothing I'd felt before. It was equal parts achingly romantic and utterly desperate. I raked my hands up his chest, to his neck—where I felt his pulse thudding underneath the tanned skin—and then up to his messy hair, which I grasped with white knuckles. I never wanted this kiss to end. I wanted it to go on for the rest of the night, until the paperboy threw the Spokane Gazette at our feet.

When Demo's lips finally pulled apart from mine, he ran the pad of his callused thumb across my swollen lower lip, causing a shiver to two-step down my spine. His eyes were heavy lidded as he gazed down at me, mouth parted, breath halted. He looked perplexed. And maybe sort of surprised. And... well, *seriously turned on.*

As was I.

"I... uh..." Demo didn't finish his thought. Instead, he just stared at me. The air between us was electric, sparking and popping like downed power lines.

I nodded. "Uh huh. Do you wanna—"

Agnes popped up between us again, making Demo stumble backwards. "Wasn't that nice, you two?"

We nodded once in unison. There was nothing to say. The kiss had been the equivalent of bringing gasoline to a brush fire, and judging by the way Demo looked like he'd been kicked in the side of the head... he thought so, too.

Blinking, I tore my eyes away from him. "Thank you for coming over, Agnes. I'm sorry I scared you."

She pressed a kiss to my cheek. "Not at all, dear. I'm just glad you weren't cut into pieces. I don't do the sight of blood at all."

I chuckled, ignoring the heat pouring off Demo's body. I would've felt it half a block away. He wanted me. And holy Hannah, I wanted him, too. "Me, too."

"Now, I'm going home before my dance troupe drinks all the coffee." She winked at me. "I hate it when that happens. Enjoy your night, you two."

I glanced at Demo. *Oh I intend to.*

I wasn't letting him get away. He was coming inside so I could see how much damage gasoline and a brush fire could do.

"Well, goodnight, kids." She giggled, stepping off of my porch.

"Goodnight," I called, before pointing at Demo. "You."

He pointed to his chest. "Me?"

"Yes, you." My voice was hoarse. I guess extreme horniness did that to a person. "Come inside."

Demo's eyebrows rose high on his forehead, and he put his arm around Agnes's shoulders. "Why don't I walk you to your door?"

My stomach dropped. "What? No. I can drive you home."

Please say yes. Please say yes. Please say yes.

"No." Demo held up a hand. "I mean, no thank you. I'll be fine."

I opened my mouth. Then closed it. What just happened? Had he not felt that spark between us? What was his problem?

And before I could protest, Demo and Agnes disappeared down my front walk.

Chapter Ten

"Marisol, every time you come here, you get prettier. Do you know that?" Yiayia beamed at me as I entered the Triple D's office with a tray of homemade caramel toffee latte cupcakes.

"I made these for you," I told her, setting the tray down on the desk before her. "You know I'm trying to win you over with food, right?"

She picked up a cupcake and took a lick of the frosting. "Well you're doing a good job of it."

"Does that mean I can have the recipe for you dolmades?"

Yiayia patted my cheek. "Not even close. You've got to be a part of the family first."

I made out with your grandson last night, and contemplated what it would be like to lick this caramel sauce off of his abs. Does that count?

"Fine," I squeaked. "I consider it a challenge."

She winked one of her crinkly eyelids. "I'm sure you do."

"Okay, no recipe today." I sat down across the desk from her and relaxed. "So, is Demo around? I didn't see him under any cars out there."

"No." Yiayia shook her head. "He's out picking up a tow clear on the north side of town. Why?" Her eyes widened. "Were you hoping to see him?"

My face heated. Something about this old broad chiseled through my cool exterior, and poked at my inner self-conscious geek. "No." I said it too quickly, and I knew it. Yiayia's smirk confirmed she picked up on it. "What I meant was, I just wanted to pay him for his work on my car."

"Oh, well I can help with that, dear." She opened a file drawer and tugged out a manila folder with my name on it.

"No computer system?" I asked.

"No need." Yiayia replied, tapping her temple. "Got all the client info right up here."

I raised my eyebrows at her. "That doesn't worry Demo? You know, in case..." Insert awkward pause here. I mean, come on, the poor lady wasn't going to live forever! "You miss work, or something?"

"You mean in case I die?" she deadpanned.

I cracked up. "Well, I wasn't going to say it."

"Why not? All of my kids and grandkids do." She let her bony shoulders rise and drop. "No need to worry. I've got at least another five years before I kick the bucket."

"How do you know?"

Again, she shrugged. "A psychic told me in 1974."

"She told you when you were going to die?" I croaked.

"*He*, and yes. He told me exactly how and when I would kick the bucket."

We sat quietly. The only sounds in the office were the traffic going by outside and Yiayia's chewing. Finally, I threw my hands up. "I can't take it anymore. How are you going to die?"

She put down her half-eaten cupcake. "I thought you'd never ask. It will be fast and almost painless but quite dramatic. I'm going to have a massive heart attack in the European grocery on Selman avenue."

I gasped. "That's horrible!"

"No, it's not," she quipped. "I love that place. The owner gives me a discount because he thinks I'm cute."

I cracked up. "He does?"

"Uh huh," Yiayia said proudly, plucking up her cupcake. "He's been after me since my Demetrious died, God rest his soul." She blew a kiss to the ceiling.

"Wow. Go you!" I brushed some crumbs off of the front of my black shift mini dress. I'd worn it one other time, and wound up in the back seat of a local congressman's limo afterward, so I secretly hoped for similar results when Demo saw me in it. Of course, he foiled that plan by *working*. "Why don't you date him?"

She made a face. "He's Russian. I mean, not that there's anything wrong with that. I just can't see myself with anyone but my husband. And especially a non-Greek."

"Oh, I see." Picking at my manicure, I thought about how to propose my next question. "So… does that rule hold firm for your whole Greek community?"

"No. Not anymore." Yiayia waved a hand. "Nowadays, people date whomever they choose. Three of my children married non-Greeks. Though they eventually joined the church, so we got them in the end." She winked at me. "It's almost twice as many with grandchildren. Times are different now. People are a lot more accepting than they were when I was growing up."

"That's good." When Yiayia's eyes twinkled, I added, "I mean, you know, for your grandkids, and all."

"Uh huh." She tilted her head at me. "What is your heritage, dear?"

I swallowed a mouthful of frosting. "My father is Puerto Rican, and my mother is half English and half Cuban. My mother lives in California, and my father lives in Florida. I rarely see them."

What was up with me when I was around this woman? I was becoming the queen of the overshare.

"Are you and Demo dating, Marisol?" she asked boldly.

No. But I've made a few porno movies in my head about him. Does that count?

"No." I blinked at her a few times, hoping to prove my nonchalance.

Yiayia narrowed her eyes. "Are you sure? Be honest with me, young lady."

"No, ma'am." I tucked my hair behind my ears and looked away from her probing stare. "Our relationship is purely professional. There's nothing going on between us. In fact, I'm pretty sure your grandson hates me."

And until he pressed me against that doorjamb, I thought the feeling might be mutual… now all I can think about is how desperately I want to get him into a hot tub.

I glanced at a candid shot of Demo, Yiayia, and some other scattered family members. Demo's smile was wide and unabashed, and the picture appeared to have been taken years ago, so his hair was dark and cropped close to his head. His bare arm was slung over his grandmother's shoulders, and his muscles were flexed and defined.

Aw hell, I'd settle for a deep puddle, for pete's sake.

"You'd be surprised with Demetrious." Yiayia polished off her cupcake, and folded the wrapper neatly. "Often times, when he acts like he hates someone, it usually means he likes them a whole lot."

My heart skipped a beat. I'd gone to bed a mature woman last night, and woken up a lovesick tween that morning. Go figure. "Well, then he must *really* like me."

Yiayia took another cupcake. "That's what I thought, too."

Excitement whirled through my gut. Maybe I would get that recipe after all. That was what was important, right?

The memory of Demo's lips crushing mine, and his hands tangling in my hair flashed in my mind. The excitement in my stomach quickly caught flame. Okay, so maybe I cared about more than just the recipe. So sue me.

"Can I ask a personal question, Yiayia?" I asked, grabbing my own cupcake, and tasting the frosting.

"You don't strike me as the kind of girl who beats around the bush, Marisol."

Snorting, I shook my head. "That would be accurate."

"Then shoot," she said.

I took a deep breath. "Why is Demo so grumpy?"

"Oh, you noticed that?" She chuckled.

I gave her a sideways glance. "It's hard not to."

"His father was always gruff, too." Yiayia thoughtfully chewed her bite. "I suppose Demo was always fairly stoic. When he was a kid, he took sports very seriously and had a tendency to beat himself up when his team lost." I looked up at a group of pictures in the far corner of the room, where a row of Antonopolouses were lined up in wrestling uniforms.

I craned my head to see it more closely, but Yiayia interrupted my examination. "He really changed for the worse when Belinda left him, I suppose."

"Belinda?" When she looked at me, I casually added, "Just curious."

131

"You don't know the story of Belinda White?" She tsked and licked frosting off of her fingers. "That girl did a real number on my grandson. The little tramp. I'm surprised he hasn't told you."

"Apparently you're under the impression that Demo and I are friends." I tossed my hair. "We're actually not compatible. At all."

Until we're making out.

She stared at me for a moment, then waved my words away. "Oh, don't be silly. Of course you are. Opposites make the best pairs, dontcha know?"

Something inside me stirred, and for a split second, I felt hysterically happy. Weird. "Okay, enough about that. Why don't you tell me what happened with that bitch Belinda?"

Yiayia snorted. "I like you, Marisol."

"I like you, too." My heart swelled. The feeling was uncomfortable, so I jammed another bite of cupcake in my gullet. This wasn't *my* grandma. I shouldn't feel this way about Yiayia. My grandmother was somewhere in California, probably sipping a strong drink and surrounded by men decades younger than she.

Wait, that was what I should've been doing. What the hell was up with this new side of me? Cupcakes and old ladies? I was losing my touch!

"Belinda was Demo's high school sweetheart." Yiayia dropped her voice low even though nobody else was in the garage. "They went to all of their dances together, all of their proms. She's in all of his high school pictures, and he even bought her a promise ring when they were seventeen."

132

"A promise ring?" I snorted, but quickly shut up when she narrowed her eyes at me. "Sorry."

"It was very sweet. You seem like a girl who needs a little sweetness in her life."

Well, she had me there.

Yiayia adjusted her glasses. "You see, in our family, you grow up, you get married, you buy a house, then you have a family. There is no greater joy than in that family. Is your family close, Marisol?"

"Not exactly."

"All my grandson ever wanted was to have a wife and children to support. He wanted to be just like his father, who worked every day of his life to support *his* wife and children. It was very noble."

I shifted in my seat. This was such a departure from my own family. I only saw my parents every two years or so, and even then the visits were long enough to eat an uncomfortable meal, then bail so I could go home to a fresh mojito to decompress. I overheard my father telling a friend that getting married and having a kid was his "worst mistake," and I based my own attachment phobia on that overheard conversation for years.

"After graduation, Demo proposed. Belinda said yes, and our families planned the wedding of the year. Her grandmother and I were on the Bible auxiliary together at the church, so we were friends. We started making her dress from the fabric of both of our dresses. It was beautiful. And Demo's parents took a second mortgage and rented the biggest ballroom at the Spokane River Inn for the reception. It cost them a fortune."

"Pretty swanky." Lexie and I had catered a few events there, and they were nothing short of posh, to say the least. It seems the Antonopolous family had pulled out all the stops. "So what went wrong?"

"I'll tell you." Yiayia leaned forward conspiratorially. "It was the night of the rehearsal dinner. We were all in the church, watching while all the groomsmen and bridesmaids lined up, when all of the sudden, Demo's best friend, Allan, grabbed him by the collar and punched him right in the face. Right there at the altar!" My mouth dropped, and she just nodded. "I know. Well, Demo wasn't expecting it, so he went down like a ton of bricks, blood coming out of his nose, and when he asked what the H-E-double-hockey-sticks was wrong, guess what Allan said?"

"What?"

"He said that he'd always loved Belinda, and that she loved him right back." Yiayia wrung her hands. "Allan said he couldn't sit by and watch Demo take away the woman he'd loved since tenth grade. So we all sat there, waiting for someone to say something. Waiting for Belinda to send Allan away, or just *something,* you know?"

"What did Demo do?" I envisioned a younger version of Demetrious Antonopolous beating the hell out of one of his groomsmen while all of his relatives looked on. It looked pretty hot, if I did say so myself. But then, I'd always had a good imagination.

She sat back in her seat. "He stood back up, wiped his nose on his sleeve, and asked Belinda if it was true. We all waited. Waited for her to deny it. I mean, nobody thought that she was having an affair. We all thought that Allan had some sort of unrequited crush on her or something. But then she admitted it. She looked right at Demo, in front of their whole wedding party and both of their families, and admitted that she'd been fooling around with Allan for a year. She said she was in love with him, too. And that she didn't want to marry Demo, but hadn't been sure how to tell him."

"Holy crap." I didn't know what else to say. That was pretty harsh. I'd never gotten close enough to an altar to be left at it, but to get punched in the face—and the heart—by your best friend and fiancée? Wow. My heart tugged, and I rubbed at it absently. Since when did I feel spontaneous bursts of tenderness? "What happened next?"

"So Demo did what Demo *usually* does," Yiayia said sadly. "He beat the crap out of Allan right there in the church and broke his nose and collar bone. Belinda started to cry and told Demo she hoped he rotted in hell. Allan pressed charges, the police came, and Demo spent the night in jail before they came to their senses and realized my Demo was not the 'primary physical aggressor,' as they put it. The church banished him for six months, and during that time, the priest who was at the rehearsal dinner married Allan and Belinda. Their wedding was on the anniversary of Demo and Belinda's first date."

"Ouch." I sat back in my chair and stared up at the pictures on the wall. In most of the pictures, Yiayia's grandchildren were posing with the respective

135

spouses and children, smiling brightly for the camera. In all the pictures of Demo, he was either alone, or with siblings. If those pictures—and his surly attitude—were any indication, Demo was a wounded soul.

"All my grandson's done since his wedding was called off is chase women," Yiayia lamented. "Date them for a month, or a week, or just a night. He says he's not the marrying kind, but I know better. He wants love, but won't give himself the chance to find it. Honestly, I don't think Demo believes he deserves love."

My heart started to thrum in my chest. Pounding against my chest wall like a hammer, and taking my breath away. Demo sounded like me. "I can relate," I mumbled. And it was the truth. I could relate all too well.

"That's why you two are perfect for each other." Her wrinkled face folded into a grin. "Two restless souls with great chemistry. It's a win-win."

"Yiayia!" My face scalded, making it even harder to catch my breath. A year ago, before Lexie and Fletcher got married, and I started considering settling down—*shudder*—I would have used Demo's wounded soul as an excuse to get into his very lovely fitting Levi's. I mean, come on. The guy was gorgeous. Plus, I was still on the hunt for Yiayia's dolmades recipe. Oh, and did I mention he was sexy?

Oh, I did? All right, then.

But now? Now that my two best friends were all gaga eyed over their handsome husbands, and raising perfect little babies with dimples and curls, and all of that adorable nonsense I usually hated… but now found completely endearing and lovely…

Now I felt inclined to actually *date* Demo. I wanted to spend some time with him. Get to know him. Talk to him. Figure him out. Make him laugh so that his glorious smile would come out to play. Meet all of his Greek relatives and listen to them yell at each other in their native tongue over a table covered in luscious, fattening food. And, yes, get him into my bed. Eventually.

Hell, I was going soft, not *dead.*

I gasped, and slapped my hand over my mouth. *Holy mother of heaven, did I actually* care *about him? What the crap was happening to me? What was next? Scrapbooking and handmade aprons? Baby booties and child proof locks on my liquor cabinet?*

Kill me. Just kill me.

Yiayia looked at me closely. "You okay, kiddo?"

"Yes, ma'am." I pushed myself out of the chair. I had to get out of here. The more time I spent with this old lady, the more I lost my grip on reality. On the nice, comfortable, sex-kitten-without-any-commitments reality I created for myself. "I should run. I just remembered something I have to finish up at work."

"You look spooked," she commented.

I am, I thought. This was too uncomfortable. I was actually starting to itch, and not in a *go to the doctor and get an ointment* kind of way. In an *I feel something for this guy and we've only kissed one time* way. This was too much

137

to handle. I needed air. And a drink. And maybe even a weekend with a delicious man with an accent that I would never see again. In no particular order.

"No, I'm fine," I squeaked, grabbing my purse and hoisting it onto my shoulder. "I've got so much to do and not much time to do it."

She watched me with a smile teasing the corners of her mouth. She looked like Demo when she did that. Dang it. "Like what?"

"I…uh…" I swiped at my brow. Good grief, was I sweating now? "I need to stop at the market. We need a flank steak, at least thirty pounds of new potatoes, fresh mint, three containers of mascarpone, a dozen duck eggs, and I have to locate some Bitto cheese."

Her silver eyebrows rose high on her forehead. "You going in the electric chair tonight?"

Laughing despite myself, I finally took a breath. "No, ma'am."

"I knew it!" Yiayia's finger thumped on the desktop. "You like Demetrious."

"No." I swallowed down the emotions tickling the back of my throat. "I'm sorry to disappoint you. But I only come here to see you."

She looked unconvinced. "Sure you did."

"And to score your recipes," I added.

"Dream on, kid." Yiayia pointed at my chair. "Sit back down, young lady. You've got feelings for my grandson."

"No, I—"

"And he has feelings for you, too." She grinned proudly and tapped her temple. "You see? It's a sense. I can practically smell relationships."

The sound of click-clacking heels halted in the doorway. "Demo has feelings for who, Yiayia?"

Yiayia's shoulders dropped, and her smile faded away. "That's Mrs. Antonopolous to you. Hello, Stacia."

Demo's booty call from the other night adjusted the plate of chocolate chip cookies she was carrying and waggled her hot pink fingernails. "Hi, Yiayia."

"Are you deaf?" Yiayia snapped.

Stifling my laughter, I reached out and patted her wrinkled hand. "I have to run. Can you tell me what my total for the work on my car came to?" I could feel Stacia shooting daggers at the side of my head with her eyes, but ignored it.

Yiayia shuffled through the pile of invoices atop the desk. "Um… looks like it's paid in full."

"That can't be," I said, pulling out my credit card. "I owe for the labor, at least."

"So I brought y'all cookies," Stacia announced, pushing my cupcakes aside and plopping down her tray of cookies. I flared my nostrils at them. I could smell store-bought baked goods from a mile away. Poor schmuck. "Is my Demo around?"

"It's marked paid in full." Yiayia ignored her, then flipped the paper around so I could see the signature at the bottom of the page. "Signed by none other than my infatuated grandson, Demo."

Stacia sucked in a sharp breath. "*Infatuated?*"

That fluttery, low-oxygen feeling returned. "Well, thanks," I squeaked.

"Don't thank *me*," Yiayia said in a suggestive tone. "Come back and thank my grandson with a date."

Stacia's hand went to her hip. "Hey. I'm right here."

"I know, dear," Yiayia told her, before winking at me. "But my grandson doesn't like you. He likes *her*."

Chapter Eleven

"You know I hate complimenting you, Marisol. But this potato salad rocks."

When I looked up from the salmon on the grill, Candace's husband, Brian, stood before me with a plate heaped so high I wondered how he managed to hold it with one hand. "Aw, Bri. You're finally admitting that I am superior in a kitchen to you? I never thought I'd see the day."

He rolled his eyes and slid his Ray Bans off of the top of his head and back onto his face. "Whatever. Don't push it."

Ever since the day Candace introduced me to Brian after a football game at college, we competed over who had the ethnic cooking in the bag. He was half Chinese, and his tiny powerhouse of a mother taught him everything there was to know about making homemade Cantonese egg foo young and water chestnut cakes. I tried to deflate his ego by perfecting homemade flan and green chile con carne, but unfortunately Brian was not easy to intimidate. We spent the better part of the last ten years poking fun of each other, throwing insults over family dinners, and trying to trip each other.

We understood one another, and I considered Brian to be a brother. That is, if I had a brother who was an annoyingly self-confident Asian American optometrist.

"Honey, leave her alone. She's the one cooking today." Candace put her arm around her husband and grinned cheekily at me. "Thanks, Mar. You know I would have done it."

"Yeah, yeah." I turned a salmon steak and took a whiff of the fresh mint I marinated it in. "We all know that's not true." I was in charge of cooking our barbeque every Memorial Day, and she knew it. The responsibility became mine after an unfortunate turkey-vs.-deep fryer mishap. And I didn't mind—even though I griped enough for three premenstrual teenage girls—because standing behind the grill always seemed like the place for the one single gal in the group.

Lexie pulled a loaf of bread from one of the picnic baskets. "Hey, kids! Wanna go feed the ducks?" A chorus of cheers rose from our group, and she grinned at me. "Do you mind, Marisol? Ian's asleep in the stroller, and we'll be right back."

Shrugging, I flipped a salmon steak. "Sure. He's not going to need the boob anytime soon, right?"

Fletcher walked by and looped his arm around Lexie's shoulders. "As always, Marisol, you've got a way with words."

"Ha!" I yelled, a smile tickling the corners of my mouth. "You wouldn't know. You dumped me for her, remember?"

Lexie leaned against her husband. "Don't worry. Your time is coming. I can feel it. I'm thinking the theme will be…*My Big Fat Greek*—"

I pointed my spatula at her. "Don't even finish that thought."

"What? You said he was a great kisser." Candace popped a chip in her mouth and watched while I dramatically rolled my eyes.

"It was just a kiss," I groaned. "It meant nothing."

"That's the Marisol we know and love," Brian teased, ducking just far enough away from me to avoid the swing of my spatula. "Kidding. I'm kidding."

"I wouldn't call a kiss that makes your eyes roll back in your head, followed by some free auto maintenance, *just* a kiss." Lexie grinned at me smartly. What a brat.

Fletcher chimed in. "Sounds serious."

"Trading make out sessions for work on your car?" Brian tossed a grape in the air and caught it in his mouth. "Keepin' it classy, eh?"

"Shut up," I hissed. "I didn't *ask* for it to be free."

"Down boy. Heel." Candace patted her husband on the arm. Our sibling rivalry act bugged her, and she was forever on our cases to treat each other better. "Marisol got free auto work because the hot Greek mechanic dude likes her."

"And even though Marisol is pretending to only like him to get a dolmades recipe." Lexie narrowed her eyes at me. "Did you get it yet?" When I shook my head no, she went on. "The truth is, she likes him. Like, a lot."

"No, I do not." My heart squeezed in protest, and I ignored it.

"I don't believe you." Lexie said. "Not for one second. I think you're going soft."

I opened my mouth to argue, but Candace cut me off. "I agree. I think you're starting to want a taste of the family life."

"Now, don't get ahead of yourself," I grumbled. "I'm not in a hurry to start changing diapers, or anything. But…"

After a few seconds passed, everyone leaned forward. "But?" Fletcher asked.

"I don't know." I turned another salmon steak. "It was a good kiss. That's all I'm saying. It made me think about things a little bit."

"Like love and marriage and baby in a baby carriage?" Brian teased.

Again, Candace swatted his arm. "Shush."

"Well, look at you guys!" I blurted. "You've all got kids and spouses, and I'm always by myself."

"You used to say that giving up your independence would be like chewing off your own leg," Lexie said.

"I know." I bit my lip. "But, sometimes the idea of settling down sounds kind of nice. I mean, ever since you squeezed out little Ian, and you and Fletcher got married, I've been noticing how empty my house is every night."

Candace pointed at Lexie. "I told you she'd come around."

"Sucker bet." Lexie fished a five-dollar bill out of the pocket of her jeans and handed it over. "Ian makes everyone want a family. He's perfect."

144

"I'm not saying I want a family." I scrunched up my face, and leaned against the table. "At least, not yet. Oh, hell. I don't know what I want. I just know that something in my life needs to change. I need more purpose. Or some sort of meaningful crap like that."

Candace tilted her head at me. "Well, is Demo that purpose?"

Heat flushed my face. I hated being so…so *vulnerable* in front of everyone. Couldn't we just go back to Brian calling me a whore all the time, and me insulting his manhood? Yeesh, ever since Fletcher and Lexie took the vows, I acted like I was on a permanent hormonal road trip, and I was ready to get the hell off of this bus.

Lexie looked at Candace. "It was that kiss. It's got her twitterpated."

Candace nodded. "I know. She's never felt like that after one kiss before. Not even with Fletcher. No offense."

Fletcher shrugged. "Whaddaya gonna do?"

"Mar's going soft." Brian snorted.

"I can't wait to see you pregnant. You'll be hilarious." Lexie covered her mouth to hide her grin. "You made fun of my cankles so much."

"Ugh. Can it. All of you. No more discussing my love life." I pushed myself away from the table, and handed another loaf of bread to Lexie. "Go. Take your filthy children down to the bird poop infested water and feed the already overweight ducks. I hope one explodes all over you."

"Ahhh. There she is. She never disappoints." Brian refilled his plate of potato salad and called to the kids. "All right, goofballs. Let's go feed some birds."

"Don't you give my salad to the damn ducks," I scolded as they walked away.

I took another whiff of the salmon, and gazed across the park at the kids running down the hill like little maniacs. They really were cute little buggers. Fletcher and Lexie's daughter, Martha, was super smart and constantly schooling me on random facts. For instance, last time we all ate dinner together, she informed me that cows can smell aromas from six miles away, *and* that one of those One Direction boy-banders had an Arabic tattoo on his chest. I didn't even want to know how she found that out, but the cow fact was interesting.

And Martha's little brother, Ian? Well, let's just say that up until that kid popped out, I thought all babies were messy, smelly, loud little bottom feeders. Now every time I saw that drooling little bundle of blue, my stomach ached. At first I thought the kid had given me an ulcer. But then I realized I felt that way because he was so damn cute. It never occurred to me that I had a maternal instinct. I assumed I'd been born without one.

Candace and Brian's kids took cute to a new level. Since Brian was Asian American, and Candace was an all-American blonde with blue eyes, the mix of the two gene pools created children so gorgeous, I was almost certain they were aliens. And oddly enough, the little aliens were starting to grow on me. If I listened to them, rather than tuning them out like I usually did, they were pretty darn funny. The other day Quentin told Brian that his nose hairs looked like a forest. *That's funny.*

"Guess what? Guess what? Guess what? LookwhatIcandobecauseI'msograceful!"

I looked down at Ellie, Candace's almost six-and-a-half-year old daughter, who was the oldest of the Chang children and usually the ringleader in their trail of destruction. She bounced on one foot right by the grill. "Be careful," I warned, putting down my tongs and gently moving her away from the sizzling grill. "You might fall and burn your face off. And then you'd never get a boyfriend, would you?"

Ellie stopped jumping and stared up at me, her face grave. "Mommy says real beauty is on the inside."

I cringed. Yikes. My maternal instinct may have kicked on recently, but that didn't stop me from saying the wrong thing. My humor wasn't exactly kid friendly. But I was learning. Sometimes potty humor could translate seamlessly between a thirty-two-year-old and someone who's six.

"She's right," I said quickly. "Sorry. What I meant was, if you fall and hit the grill, you could get burned. And then who would stand around doing all that terrific jumping?"

Ellie's face softened. "I can jump twenty-three times in a row."

"Impressive." I smiled at her. Those eight reality TV kids had nothing on Ellie. Her little almond eyes were lighter than her dad's and she had her mother's button nose, the lucky little punk. I planned on shaving another centimeter or two off of my own schnoz as soon as I could find the time off. "What other kinds of tricks can you do?"

Ellie started spinning. "See? I can spin! Seeee?"

"You sure can. Good thing I made you move away from the grill. When you fall over, try to aim for that grass, so you'll have a soft landing."

Ellie cracked up and stopped spinning. She swayed in place. "I won't fall."

"Right. You look about as steady as Auntie Marisol at Madison's on a Saturday night." Whoops. Bringing up my favorite martini bar downtown was probably a bad idea. Once again, I cringed, adding, "I mean, because I'm tired. Just…beat."

Ellie tipped over and landed on her back in the thick grass. "Oof!"

"Told ya." I turned a piece of salmon on the grill, and turned off the flame. "Are you ready to eat some food that is *muy deliciosa*?"

Ellie looked up at me from the ground. "Are you 'peaking 'panish again?"

"Yes. That's Spanish." I held out my hands and tugged her to her feet. When she let go, my hands were covered in something sticky. "Let's call everybody over to eat, shall we?"

A shrill cry rang out, and I noticed that Ian's stroller was wiggling in its spot next to the table. "Oh, crap," I muttered, shielding my eyes from the sun and scanning the park for Fletcher and Lexie.

Ellie looked up at me. "That's a naughty word."

"*Crap* is?" I looked down at her. "You've got to be kidding." *That was my edited version.*

"My mom says *stinky feet.*"

"Yeah, well, your mom's a freak."

Ellie frowned. "That's not nice."

"Right. Sorry." Ian screamed again, and I sighed. "For what it's worth, it was *your* mom who taught me how to do a beer bong."

"What's a beer bong?"

"It's a…" I spotted everyone else down the hill by the duck pond, at least a football field's length away. "A toy. A toy for college kids."

Ellie resumed her bouncing. "That sounds like fun."

"Eh. It's sort of sloppy." I waved my arms at my group of friends throwing bread into the pond. "Hey! HEY GUYS! Woo hoo, over here!" Ian's crying was getting persistent, and I knew my, ahem, *plumbing* wasn't going to satisfy his needs. Lexie still breastfed him like a Pioneer woman, even though he was a year old. "Oh, good Lord," I muttered, stomping over to the stroller. "Sure. Just leave me here to cook all the food *and* watch the baby, too. Why not leave your car for me to wash, too?"

Ian's wails increased and Ellie tugged on the hem of my sundress. "You better give him a bottle or something."

"Yeah, yeah. Thanks for the tip." Casting a frustrated glance at Lexie, who was playfully throwing crumbs at a mallard duck with her back turned to me, I pulled back the hood on Ian's stroller. And my breath caught.

149

Ian pale white skin practically glowed in the sunshine, and a dusting of pale freckles decorated his cheeks, which were also painted a bright pink since he'd been crying. His eyes, the lightest ice blue I'd ever seen, were wide and lined with thick lashes. And his head was covered in round, orange curls that Lexie and Fletcher refused to cut. As soon as I peered in at him, he put his hands out and grinned so wide, half a cup of drool dribbled out.

I picked him up and cradled him to my shoulder, relishing in the way it felt as Ian nuzzled into my neck. "You're not so bad, are you?" I whispered to his curly head, automatically starting to sway back and forth in place, like some sort of insta-mom. "Don't tell your mommy I said so, though, mmm'kay?" He cooed his reply, and soaked my shirt with warm drool. "Hey, easy now. That was expensive."

But I didn't move him. Instead, I pressed my nose to his hair and drew in a long, deep breath of his baby-cookie-slobbery aroma.

My favorite scents used to be expensive men's cologne and beluga caviar. Now a days, I craved the scent of baby Ian, pizza served out of a box, and surly, unshaven mechanics. In no particular order.

"That baby likes you," Ellie told me, stopping her bouncing and staring up at me. "You should be a mommy someday."

"Cool it, kid," I said down at her with a contented smile. "I haven't even got a boyfriend."

She seemed to think about that for a minute, and I ignored it as everyone down by the pond stopped what they were doing and watched in wonder as I comforted Lexie's baby. Good grief, they acted like they saw a unicorn.

Ellie stuck a finger in the air proudly. "Then go get one at the store!"

Snorting, I rubbed circles on Ian's back. *If only it were that simple…*

Chapter Twelve

I lifted a dolma out of the pan with painstaking gentleness and examined it. The grape leaf had held up beautifully while I simmered it, and now there was nary a fleck of rice or lamb sticking out of its perfectly tucked envelope. Drawing in a long inhale of the aroma, I smiled. Lemon, cinnamon, pine nuts, cardamom. The salty, briny scent of grape leaves. Perfection.

This was it. The batch that would prove my superior ethnic food cooking skills. I couldn't wait to call Lexie at home to brag about it.

"Looks like I didn't need to seduce Demo Antonopolous after all." I muttered to myself, blowing on the dolma. "He can suck it."

Okay, so I was bitter. It had been a week since my little pow wow with Yiayia, and I still hadn't heard from Demo. And sure, I could call him myself. God knew I'd never been afraid to pursue a man. I was probably a little more adept at that than what was socially acceptable.

But not when it came to Demo. He was different. He threw me off of my game, made me self-conscious in ways I'd not been since puberty, and he made me feel the ultimate worst way any woman could ever feel: *vulnerable.*

Shuddering, I turned off the burner and slid the pot of dolmades off the heat. The Eats & Treats kitchen was empty, and the late evening sun poured through the windows, which was how I preferred it when I tried new recipes. It was no fun to screw up a recipe with a hungry coworker standing there, waiting to be fed.

Hopping onto the stainless steel table, I gathered my hair into a messy bun on top of my head and un-tied the strings of my apron. When I tugged it off, chunks of parsley and rice fell from the front of my shirt. I'd been cooking all day and most of my makeup had melted off while I sautéed shitake mushrooms in red wine earlier. I was pretty sure I looked and smelled like a drunken lesbian. Not that there was anything wrong with that.

There was a knock on the glass door at the front of the shop, and I rolled my eyes. The neighboring music store employees were infamous for coming over to score free food off of us, but I wasn't in the mood. I'd been rolling these dolmades for two hours, and I wanted to be left alone to relish in my accomplishment.

"We're closed!" I hollered, before gazing lovingly at the dolma. "Here goes nothing, my pretty," I whispered, taking a big bite.

As soon as my teeth cut into the grape leaf, it disintegrated, and the contents—which were mushy and clumped into on giant wad of what tasted like Greek bubble gum—rolled down the front of my black shirt, leaving greasy spots of olive oil in its wake. The consistency of the bite in my mouth was what

153

I was pretty sure would happen if Elmer's Glue and wet paper towels had a baby. It was gross. Super gross.

"Shit. Double shit." I muttered, throwing the remaining grape leaf into the nearby sink. "*Nunca voy a conseguir este derecho!*"

A deep, gravelly voice interrupted my pity party. "Oh, I'm sure you'll get the hang of it."

"GAH!" I turned around with a jerk to find Demo leaning against the kitchen doorway, his arms folded across his chest. He was wearing his trademark torn up jeans, a dark grey tee shirt that had seen better days, and a smirk. "What the hell are you doing in here?"

"Your work address was on your business card." He shrugged. "I drove by on a tow job and saw that the light was still on."

I scowled at him. "You scared me. What's wrong with you? I could have shot you!"

He laughed, the sound rumbly and undeniably *masculine.* "With what?"

I looked around, and grabbed a fork. "With this. Or... a gun. I have a gun, you know."

"So you said. You know, you don't seem like the gun-toting type."

Gritting my teeth together, I marched over to where my Hermes purse was buried underneath a pile of aprons, towels, and Bon Appetite magazines. After a twenty-second search to the bottom of the bag, I emerged, holding up my Smith & Wesson .38 special, air weight. I bought it a couple of years before,

when a woman in Spokane had been sexually assaulted in the park near Eats &
Treats. Better safe than sorry, right?

Too bad I perpetually left my purse at work and in the car. And still
hadn't found the time, or the desire, to let Brian teach me how to shoot it.

Oh, well. I had it now. "Ta da," I sang.

"Holy hell!" Demo ducked, and held his hands up. "Good Lord, put
that thing away. You could've killed me."

"That's what I was trying to say!" I yelled, making sure the safety was
on and tucking it back into the handbag. "I wish I would've had my purse handy
when you tried breaking in the other night. Then you wouldn't have made fun of
Agnes's skillet."

When Demo stood back upright, his eyes were wide. "Why in the
world do you have that thing?"

"A single woman can't be too careful," I said smartly.

"Well you sure didn't have it handy on the night of Greg, did you?" I
pressed my lips together. It figured Demo would bring that up. Upon seeing my
expression, he added, "Or like you said, the night I scared you and your
neighbor."

I peered over his shoulder. "How did you get in here? We're closed."

"So you said." Demo leaned against a table casually. "The door was
unlocked."

I slapped my forehead. "I can't even tell you how many times I
reminded Lexie to lock the door on her way out."

"Lexie?"

"My business partner. And friend."

"That the blonde who dropped you off at the shop that day?"

Shaking my head, I leaned against the table a few feet apart from Demo. "No. That was Candace. She's another friend."

"You got a lot of friends," he commented.

I raised an eyebrow at him. "You don't?"

Demo offered a halfhearted shrug. "Got a few. Don't really need many. Got a big family."

"My friends *are* my family." As soon as I said it, I surprised myself. I deliberately kept Candace and Lexie and their families at arms' length. I could still hear my dad swirling his glass of single malt scotch, saying, *better to stay unattached.* But the truth was… I was very attached.

Suddenly I craved scotch. "I would've assumed you don't have very many friends because you're so cranky all the time."

"I'm not cranky." He frowned. "At least not with everyone."

Time to get my flirt on. "Oh, am I special?"

His expression softened. Just a little. "Maybe."

My insides started to twist up like a Cirque Du Soliel performance. *Be cool,* I reminded myself. *He's just a guy, like any other. You've got the upper hand here, just—*

"Really?" I blurted, my voice cracking.

Well, crap.

Demo's smile returned.

I cut him off before he could make some biting remark. "Special enough to jam your tongue down my throat, then ignore me for a week. Right?" I folded my arms across my chest and waited for his answer.

He mirrored my pose. "You don't strike me as the type of gal who needs a call the next morning after a single kiss."

Well, he had me there.

"What if Agnes hadn't been there." I swallowed, and avoided looking directly at that crooked smile. "What if more had happened between us? Would you have called?"

His eyes narrowed. "No."

"No?" Okay, now I was ticked. I was usually so good at reading men, I could predict not only *that* their shirts would hit my bedroom floor, but *when* during the date it would, right down to the minute. When men wanted me, I could tell. When men were turned on by me, I knew long before their bodies, *ahem*, showed it. I knew ancient Egyptian ways of using my tongue on a man that were illegal in three states.

So why was it that I couldn't read Demo at all?

I glared at him. "Now, listen here—"

"Whoa. Take a breath." He put his hands out. "Let me finish."

"Has anybody ever told you that you're bipolar?" I hissed.

Demo nodded. "Once or twice. Can I finish, please?"

"Fine."

He took a step closer to me. "I wouldn't have called the next day, because I wouldn't have gone to bed with you."

I opened my mouth. Then shut it. Then opened it again. And shut it. My words had apparently abandoned me for the first time in… say, ever. Embarrassment flushed my cheeks with heat.

Demo's eyes bored into mine, a wrinkle forming between his brows. I couldn't tell if he was irritated or just intense. "And I wouldn't have gone to bed with you, because you're different."

Hope sprouted inside of my chest like a seed. "Different?" I asked hoarsely. "Is that supposed to sweep me off my feet?"

One of his eyebrows ticked upward. "Did it?"

"No."

"You see? That's what makes you different." Demo rubbed his whiskers thoughtfully, creating a scratching sound that made goose bumps pique on my arms. "Most of the time, you seem so unaffected by me."

Well, that was interesting. I allowed myself to smile. Just a little. "And you're used to women usually being *affected* by you."

He shook his head. "Don't put it that way. That makes it sound cocky."

"Well, isn't it?" I laughed.

"Yeah, but you feel the same way about men." When my smile dropped, Demo took another step closer. "Don't you?"

I tightened my grip around myself. "What makes you say that?"

"You seemed surprised that I didn't fall at your feet the first day we met." He swallowed, and his Adam's apple bobbed. "You're confident. Way more confident than a lot of the women I know."

I shrugged. "Maybe."

He narrowed his eyes, just a little. "You know that can be intimidating for a guy, right?"

Smiling despite myself, I chuckled. "I'm counting on it. But you're confident, too. That's why you're so aloof. You don't feel the need to impress anyone. Am I right?"

Demo stood up straighter. "Why should I? People usually love me or hate me, and it isn't because of anything I do or don't do. Usually I have nothing to do with it."

"Seems we're cut from the same cloth, Mr. Antonopolous." I took a deep breath, then released it slowly. "I find that men like me long before they get to know me. It's when they get to know me that they're heading for the door. And most of the time, I'm fine with them leaving."

His lips tugged upward. "Women do that with me all the time. They love me, and want to marry me, and want to have my babies... until I talk. Then they're on to the next prospect. Well, most of them, anyhow. There are the occasional stragglers."

"Cocky, much?" I teased.

"Nah. Just honest to a fault." He looked around the room, his cheeks coloring. "So you're a single woman in her late twenties—"

"Thirties." When he looked down at me with those dark eyes, I added, "I'm thirty-two. But nice use of subtle compliments. Well played, sir."

He grinned. "Thought you'd appreciate that. So, you're divorced? Never married? What?"

"Never married. Never wanted to. Yet." I cringed inwardly when I added that.

Demo tapped one of his callused fingers on the stainless steel tabletop. "And you're a business owner."

"A *successful* business owner," I said quickly.

"That's what I meant." He smiled. "And you own a nice house in a really nice neighborhood."

"So?" I poked him in the chest. It was solid. *Very solid.* "What's your point?"

Demo brought his eyes back to mine. There was something behind his usual conceited smirk. Tenderness in his eyes that I'd not seen before, and it looked great on him. "You're not the kind of woman a guy like me goes to bed with."

I wasn't sure whether to be flattered or insulted, so I decided to be both. "Um, thanks. Or, rather, what?"

"You're not a roll in the hay kind of girl," Demo explained, dropping his hands at his sides, where they hung limply. "I don't know how to explain it."

The excitement of being this close to him fizzled, and the heavy weight of the truth pushed down on my shoulders. In an instant, my arms hung at my own sides the same way. "Honestly, Demo? I *am* a roll in the hay kind of girl."

When one of his eyebrows rose, I swatted at his middle. "Don't get too excited

there, chief. It's not an invitation. It's more of a… confession."

"You Catholic?" he asked.

"Not unless you count dressing up like a slutty nun for Halloween last

year," I said sadly. "Demo, I've never been in a serious relationship. I go from

man to man, and adventure to adventure, because I'm too chicken shit to

commit."

He nodded, his eyes wide. "I'm the exact same way. My brother calls

me a serial dater, and I don't even care. I haven't cared in ten years. The way I

see it, if there's no commitment, there's no—"

"Heartache," I finished for him. We stood there in silence for a beat,

the weight of our words dangling between us like thread. I finally took a breath.

"The problem is… eventually everyone you know grows up and gets married."

Demo's mouth pulled into a frown. "I've been a groomsman in eleven

weddings over the past six years."

"Most of my friends have kids now, too." Nodding, I tucked a stray

strand of hair back into my messy bun. A flash of self-consciousness rippled

through me. I never hung out with a man looking like this. If I wasn't dressed to

the nines, I was naked. I was neither dressed up, nor dressed completely down,

and felt utterly exposed. "Nothing to make you more aware of your expiration

date than watching everyone you love walk around with a baby on their hip."

He nodded. "I have eighteen nieces and nephews, half of which came from my younger siblings."

"*Eighteen*?" I gaped at him. "You could have a show on TLC."

"We're not that interesting." Demo stepped closer to me, and my pulse spiked. "Do you see my point now?"

I swallowed. "I think I lost the point about five minutes ago."

A line formed between his dark eyebrows. "I wouldn't just go to bed with you, because you're different."

"Kind of sounds like we're one in the same."

He leaned forward, completely invading my bubble. Not that I minded. "Did you not feel something, I don't know, *huge* when we kissed?"

I choked back some laughter, and another chunk of hair slipped out of my hair band. "We weren't *that close*, Demo. Now you're just bragging."

"Come on." He rolled his eyes and chuckled. "Don't jerk my chain."

I lowered my eyelids. "Baby, you won't ask me to stop when *I'm* jerking anything."

His hand raked through his hair, making it stand on end. "Knock it off."

"Sorry." I blinked a few times. "Old habits die hard."

"Did you?"

"Did I what?"

His eyes searched mine. "Don't make me beg, Marisol. Did you feel something that night? In front of your neighbor? The kiss and all that?"

162

My stomach whirled at the memory. "If by the *kiss and all that*, you meant did I feel like I was going to pass out cold, or explode into a trillion tiny pieces, or maybe both?" He nodded once, and I said, "Then, yes. I felt something."

He moved closer. His chest brushed against mine, and it made me want to purr like Concinero. "Me, too," he said quietly.

Suddenly the air in the Eats & Treats kitchen was entirely too hot, and it was hard to breathe. I tried to think of something witty to say. Something to cut the tension in the room. But the only phrases that popped into my mind were different ways of asking Demo to hump me silly all over the stainless steel table.

Which would not only have defeated the purpose of the very conversation we were having, but would also have broken some health codes.

"You make me want more," Demo said, his voice rough.

I leaned against his chest, closing the space between us. "More what?"

"Time with you. I want things." Demo clenched his teeth, as if it pained him to admit this. "Stability. One woman in my bed every night. Dinners around a table. Picket fences and swing sets in the yard. Garbage like that."

My breath hitched in the back of my throat. Never in thirty-two years had I ever want to hear a man say those kinds of things to me. Usually I ran from this kind of talk. But for the first time, I wanted to hear more. I *craved* more. "I'm starting to think I want those things, too."

I raised a shaking hand and tried to tuck my hair back into its pony, but Demo's hand on my wrist stopped me. His touch scalded my skin, but instead of pulling away, I turned my hand so that his rough fingers could lace themselves with mine.

"Don't." His breath tickled my face. "Leave it alone."

"I'm a mess, I—"

"I like you this way. I like the way you look when you're dressed down." Demo cupped my face, gently dragging his thumb across my lower lip. A fire started to crackle and pop in my belly. "You're even more beautiful when you're not trying so hard. I didn't think it was possible, but you are."

"I... I..." Words eluded me. I don't know why. I'd been called beautiful before, but never when wearing grubby clothes covered in debunked dolmades.

He grinned. "Just say thank you."

"Thank you." I bit my lip. I hadn't bitten my lip around a man since I was in a training bra. "Listen, are you gonna kiss me anytime soon, because I'm ready to climb a wall here."

Demo's nose brushed the end of mine, and my spine melted into goo. His thumb did another sweep across my lower lip before he leaned in and nipped at it. Though the touch was gentle, it sent a shockwave twirling down my spine, then back up again. When his lips opened, and the silky warmth of his tongue slid against mine, I wrapped my arms around his neck and tangled my hands in his dark hair.

Demo's rough hands glided down my arms to my ribcage, squeezing my waist before slipping to my backside and lifting me up. When I gasped against his mouth, he rested me on top of the table before settling in between my knees. Latching my ankles behind his back, I tilted my head to the side and deepened our kiss, wanting more, more, more—my mind begging for the moment not to end. I could feel Demo's heart thudding against my chest as we leaned back against the cold steel, and my own heart matched its rhythm perfectly.

Maybe those health codes will *get broken after all.*

Frantically, I tugged at the hem of Demo's tee shirt with trembling fingers. His mouth began a trail across my jaw and down the side of my neck. "We should lock the door," I whispered.

Demo's head popped up, and he looked at me with wide eyes. "No," he said breathlessly.

"No?" I giggled lowly. "That's very risqué of you, Mr. Antonopolous."

He nipped at the skin just above my collarbone, then shook his head. "No."

"Whatever, Captain Morality, I won't tell the health inspector." Tugging on his neck, I brought our mouths colliding together again, earning an appreciative growl from the back of Demo's throat.

"Wait," he mumbled against my lips. Finally, after another two—okay, *four*—minutes of making out, his hands came down on the table top with a slam, and I fell backwards onto the metal.

"Oof," I grunted, pushing myself up onto my elbows. "Um… what the hell?"

Demo stood upright and backed away from me like I was a lit firecracker. "This..." He gestured between the two of us. "Is not happening tonight."

My head flopped backward. "If I had balls, Demo, they'd be—"

"If you say blue, I'm out of here." When I lifted my head and looked at him, he adjusted the front of his jeans. "I think I've got that covered here, okay?"

"Fine," I growled. "What's your problem now, Demo? I mean, wasn't it humiliating enough to admit that I'm like every other woman in the world, looking for the nuclear family, and praying for a Tiffany engagement ring?"

"It isn't that I don't want this, I..." He stopped speaking and stared at me. "Tiffany engagement ring? Aren't those like ten grand?"

I sat up and shrugged. "For the small ones."

"Listen." Demo drug his hand down his face. "I'm not nailing you on a metal table." I opened my mouth to say something rhetorical, but he cut me off. "I'm not nailing you until..."

I waited for his announcement, so that I could mark it on my calendar. In red ink. Circled twice. "Well?"

Demo stood up straight, and smoothed down the front of his tee shirt. "My grandmother is never gonna get off of my back if I don't take you on a date."

Slumping over, I gaped at him. "That was the worst pick up line I've ever heard in my life."

He laughed. "Sorry."

"Try again," I ordered.

"Ugh. Fine." He stepped closer, and put his hands on the table on either side of me. Once again his breath tickled my face, and I had to bite my lip to keep from wiggling in place. "Will you go out with me, Marisol?"

I paused. It was a completely, utterly deliberate pause, and I could tell by the way a wrinkle formed between his eyebrows that Demo was annoyed by it.

Good.

Finally he scowled at me. "All right, if all you're gonna do is mess with me, I—"

"Yes, I'll go out with you." I laughed, then pressed another kiss to his mouth. "Now can I have the recipe for dolmades?"

Demo grinned. "Nope," he replied, before plastering his mouth on mine again.

Chapter Thirteen

When I saw the headlights in my driveway, a hysterical squeal escaped my lips, and nearly dropped the phone.

"Holy Hannah, did you just *squee* in my ear?" Lexie asked. "This is historic. Hey, Fletcher! Mark the calendar—Marisol is acting like a teenager with a crush."

I heard Fletcher laughing in the background and winced. "Don't tease me. Remember the time your boobs leaked at an event, and you had to stuff your bra with coffee filters."

Lexie's giggling stopped. "You said you'd never bring that up."

"I lied." Looking down, I picked at invisible lint on my skirt. "Come on. Focus. Do you think I picked the right dress?"

"The red one with the halter top, right?" She popped something into her mouth and crunched down on it. "And the black strappy heels, right?"

"Uh huh." I nodded even though she couldn't see me.

"You look fabulous, and you know it," Lexie told me. "Relax. Demo will take one look at you and ravage you."

"I don't want to be ravaged." I surprised myself when I said it. "Well, maybe a little. But it's our first date. No ravaging. Mostly I want him to *want* to ravage me."

"Well, I think that's already been established," she said. "Which is why I had to sanitize that table twice, I'll have you know."

"I told you all of our clothes stayed on." The doorbell rang, and I jumped half a foot into the air. "Holy balls, he's here!"

"Shhhh. He'll hear you." Lexie started to laugh again. "Take a deep breath, hang up the phone, and answer the door."

"Okay."

"Oh, and call me later to fill me in."

"Got it."

"And don't forget to be a lady. Order a salad and all that."

"You're joking."

"You're right. Get the lobster."

I scoffed. "Shut up. I've got to go."

"Fine." She sighed happily. "My little girl's going out on her first date that won't end in a one-night stand. I'm so proud."

Snorting, I pressed end and dropped my phone into my purse. Where yes, my gun was in the bottom, too. The last thing I needed was to forget either one. *Again.* The doorbell rang a second time, and I suppressed an excited scream as I turned the doorknob. "Get a grip, Vargas," I hissed, before opening the door and flashing my twenty-tooth grin at Demo. "Well, hello. You're early."

He was as handsome as ever, but the obvious effort he'd put into himself made the whole package even that much more delectable. Instead of his usual torn, dirty Levis, Demo was wearing dark wash jeans and a button down shirt that was white enough to look fresh and clean, but just wrinkled enough to reinforce his casual attitude. *What, me? Nervous for a date? Pssshh. Pass me a Heineken.*

Demo grinned at me, and I noticed he was clean-shaven. For the first time since meeting Demo I realized his roguish good looks, whiskers, and disheveled locks were all hiding a boyish face.

"You look like a million bucks," he said.

I struck a pose. "Oh, this old thing?"

"You're gonna look pretty out of place in my tow truck." He shoved his hands into his pockets and rocked back on his heels self-consciously. "Not that I'm complaining."

For the briefest of moments, I was mortified that I would be driving around in a tow truck all night, and I could practically hear my mother's inevitable groan of disapproval from clear down in California.

But as quickly as those thoughts came, the image of my huge, empty house waiting for me when I got home pushed them aside. Followed quickly by the empty right side of my bed, and the not two, not three, but *four* empty bedrooms that sat unused upstairs. Sure, my last date had been with a real estate developer who drove a Ferrari, but the date was dead in the water before we'd even finished our salads.

Of course, I didn't tell Candace and Lexie that the next day—the version I'd told them ended with mad, passionate lovemaking that blew his mind.

It was time to stop acting like some sort of unattached sex kitten. I wanted different things now. And Demo was just that. *Different*. Different was good.

I offered him a warm smile. "I think it's your tow truck that'll make me look good."

Demo's lips twitched. "This nice side of you is kind of pleasant. You know that?"

"Likewise," I told him, holding out my hand. "Ready to go?"

He took my hand, lacing his rough fingers with mine. Giving me a tug, he pulled me over the threshold, and I yanked my door shut with a click. "Ready as I'll ever be."

"So where are we going?" I asked, enjoying the warm evening sunshine on my shoulders as we walked over to his truck. The bright white paint was decorated in cobalt blue script, aptly the same color scheme as the Greek flag, and a cartoon of three men with curly dark hair and wide smiles lined the doors. I pointed one of my freshly-painted nails at the picture. "Looks just like you."

"Ha, ha, ha. My niece painted that." He walked to the driver's side door. "It's my grandfather, my father, and myself."

"You all look the same." I touched the smile on one of the faces.

"We did in real life, too. Wait 'til you meet my family."

A funnel cloud of excitement whirled through me. He wanted me to meet his family? In twenty years of interactions with people of the male persuasion, I'd only been invited to meet a man's family three times. Once when I was sixteen, and that was only because his mom wanted pictures of us before the prom. The second time was when I was twenty and his mother immediately hated me because I asked for something stronger to drink with her meatloaf than lemonade—whoops. And the last time was when I was around twenty-eight, and he introduced me to his family because I showed up at the same restaurant where they were dining. Alas, I'd been on a date with another man that night, and we broke up via text message by the next morning.

I decided many moons ago that meeting the family wasn't for me, and therefore avoided it like one avoids head lice.

Not anymore.

"If your family is as nice as your Yiayia, I can't wait," I told him happily, waiting by my door. Come on. A girl's got to have some standards.

Demo winced. "Oh, yeah. Sorry. Forgot about that." With a sheepish grin, he lumbered around the truck and tugged my door open. It creaked loudly, and he snickered. "Your chariot."

"Wow. Be still my heart." I was teasing, but in all reality, my heart thudded like a base drum with Demo so close to me.

He leaned in, his still damp hair flopping across his forehead. I could smell the scent of whatever soap he lathered up in. "Thanks for going out with me tonight, Marisol," he whispered, his minty fresh breath dancing across my cheek.

Dear God, I promise to be a good girl and stop acting like a tramp if you make him kiss me right now. I also promise to give a bunch of money to charity, and go to church with Lexie and Candace once in a while, even though Lexie's mom makes me want to poke myself in the eye with a pickle fork. Amen.

Thank heaven for answered prayers, because Demo's mouth met mine with the reverential gentleness of a fifteen-year-old kissing a girl for the first time. But the passion behind his lips was definitely full-grown man. Because when his hands met my hips, and he walked me backward until my back pressed against the cool metal side of the truck, his tongue brushed mine in a way that hinted of things to come.

Good things. *Ravaging* sorts of things. Uh huh.

When he pulled away, staring down at me with heavy-lidded eyes and a hand on either side of me, trapping me against the vehicle, I said, "I thought you were supposed to kiss me at the end of the date."

"Guess I forgot." He licked his lips. "You taste good."

Sweet Jesus, thank you for listening to my prayers. My check to the Red Cross will be in the mail first thing tomorrow morning. Amen.

I cleared my throat, and sat down in the cab. "What do I taste like?"

"Candy." He shut the door and took his time sauntering back to the other side. He knew I was watching him. Cocky bastard.

"So where are you taking me?" I asked as he climbed in and started the engine. There were a handful of new restaurants that had opened up downtown that I'd been dying to try out, and I was dressed for a night of three courses and expensive wine, if I did say so myself.

Demo looked at me and winked. "It's a surprise. We'll start with dinner."

"All right then. Let's do it." I sat back in my seat and buckled my belt. "Let the shock and awe begin."

We drove along High Drive with the windows down, the May breeze bringing the scent of fresh lilacs into the cab as we talked. On one side of the road there were huge brick houses, palatial structures that'd been there for a hundred years, and on the other side was a cliff overlooking Latah Creek. The view was incredible—the sky rich with pinks and oranges as the sun set—and the conversation was even better.

Turns out, Demo was a giant softie. When he was fifteen, he rescued a neighborhood kid from drowning in the Spokane River, and then spent every day after school for the next two months reading to him until he could return to school. His nieces and nephews—all eighteen of them—called him "Uncle Bobo," and he gave each and every one of them a crisp two-dollar bill in their birthday cards every year.

But what was weird was the information Demo pulled out of me—and the fact that he still seemed to like me after I said it all. He was now the one person in the world who knew that I slept with one of my father's dress shirts wrapped around my bed pillow for two years after he left, and still had it tucked underneath the corner of my mattress. And Demo didn't bat an eye when I told him that I lost my virginity to a camp counselor my ninth grade year simply because I caught my mother flirting with him while I dropped my suitcases off in my cabin.

We talked like old friends as Demo's tow truck rumbled down the hill into downtown, then crossed the Spokane River toward the north side of town, I looked around curiously. "Didn't you want to stop?"

He gave me a sideways glance. "Nope."

"But downtown's where all the good restaurants are." As soon as the words left my mouth, I felt stupid. Here I was, trying to show Demo how *not* snobby I was, and what I'd just said was, in fact, completely snobby. "What I meant is, I haven't heard of any new places up here. Where are we going?"

"Who says we're going to a restaurant?"

I opened my mouth, then closed it. After a beat, I smiled sheepishly. "Touché."

He grinned. "You're not used to not being in control, are you?"

"How'd you guess?" I laughed as the tow truck turned toward the city courthouse. We left the cosmopolitan part of town, leaving behind the mirrored high-rise buildings and ornate brick structures overlooking the white waters of the Spokane River, and now we were idling through the rougher neighborhoods. Dilapidated brownstones with sagging front stoops lined the road on either side of the palatial courthouse, and tiny mom and pop cafés and greasy spoon diners

175

filled the spaces between buildings. People were sitting on their stoops to beat the late spring heat, and a group of men outside a corner market with barred windows were sharing a forty-ounce bottle of cheap beer. Their eyes locked on the tow truck as we idled by, narrowed and suspicious.

In the years I lived in Spokane, I'd only been in this neighborhood once or twice, to file for our small business licenses and stuff like that. And judging by the amount of broken-down cars lining the sides of the road, and the presence of sweaty wife-beater shirts, I could tell why. Had I been by myself, I'd have pressed the lock button inside my Beemer, and headed back to my gated neighborhood. But Demo seemed unaffected by the ghetto we were rolling through, a mild smile on his face, his elbow hanging out his open window in the sun.

"Okay, Princess, I want you to have an open mind, all right?" he asked as we pulled into a cracked parking lot outside a seedy looking bar. The lettering above the door said "Yokey's Watering Hole," but several of the letters were flickering, so that when the sun went down, it probably said "Yo terin Ho".

"I...uh..." I swallowed. How to put this delicately and *not* come across as a class A bitch? Annoyance flushed my face. Had Demo told me we were hitting the local dive, I would've picked a more appropriate outfit. Jeans, a tee shirt, a visible thong to hang out of the back of my pants. Something more appropriate for this 'hood, if you will. "I just... I think I'm overdressed."

Demo surveyed my dress. "No matter. I'll have the hottest date at the truck."

Truck? I frowned at him. "Hottest date at the what?"

Demo jerked his head in the direction of the street. "Miguel's. He comes to me for all his oil changes. His empanadas are out of this world. His paella is so good, Yiayia actually asked *him* for a recipe. He calls it Spanish-Latin American fusion, or some nonsense that would probably make sense to you." He softened the words with a lopsided grin.

I followed his line of sight until I spotted the bright red and yellow food truck. A crowd of people stood around its window, and several little kids danced to the mariachi music being pumped from the rusted speakers on top of the roof.

"A food truck?" A tentative smile spread across my face. We weren't going to the dive bar, after all. I could do *this*. Hell, my dress matched the truck.

Demo opened his door and took my hand. "You too upper crust for mobile tacos, Princess?"

Narrowing my eyes at him, I slid across the seat to exit on his side of the cab. "Don't tick me off, Mr. Bipolar, or I might leave you for one of those guys sharing the forty over there."

He laughed and helped me out of the tow truck, pulling me close against his chest. My heart stuttered inside my chest and I held my breath. Was he going to kiss me again? Good Lord, I hadn't been this excited by mere kisses in nearly twenty years.

"You really do like slumming it, don't you?" he so quietly only I could hear.

I looped my arms around Demo's neck and dug my hands into his still damp hair. I could smell his shampoo, and so help me God, it was like an aphrodisiac. "Only with hot mechanics who comp my auto repairs."

One of his dark eyebrows pricked upward. "Oh, so you're using me now?"

"What do you mean *now*?" I laughed. "I've been using you the whole time."

He didn't need to know that my interest in him had evolved from pursuing his affection purely to prove that I could score his yiayia's dolmades recipe. Besides, my physical magnetic pull toward Demo had been alive and well the whole time. The man was gorgeous. It wasn't until recently I figured out that he was gorgeous on the inside, too.

Lucky me.

Demo's kiss took my breath away. His lips on mine were just forceful enough to suck all of the air out of my lungs, but gentle enough to make my spine go weak. His arms held me against the length of his body as he coaxed my lips open and sent a shock of electricity whirling through my body to my toes. Having Demo's mouth on mine was a thousand times better than any sexcapade I'd had over the past five years. Okay, ten.

When he pulled away, I nearly cried. "The owner of the food truck is laughing at us," Demo whispered.

"Let him." I tugged his face back to mine, but he ducked his head so that I missed. "Are you trying to kill me?"

178

"Maybe. We're in the right neighborhood for it." He grinned, and wrinkles appeared on either side of his dark chocolate eyes.

"Shut up and buy me something horribly fattening."

"Your wish is my command." Demo took my hand and led me to the food truck. "Hey, Mike! *Dos platos de nachos por favor.*"

I elbowed him. "I can order for myself, Prince Charming."

Demo snickered and rubbed his side. "Point taken."

A Hispanic man in his late twenties leaned out the window with a smug grin. His dark hair was dampened around his neckline, but his wide, white smile was friendly and relaxed. Dimples played across his face, and, if I hadn't been with Demo, I might have been tempted to have a go at him. He looked like a movie star in his white chef's jacket.

I cast a sideways glance at Demo. Yeah, he eclipsed anyone, even Mr. Movie Star here. Apparently, I had it bad for Demo, if I couldn't even find the will to flirt with someone as attractive as Mike.

"Never gonna figure out how to win over the ladies, are you Demo?" He winked at me. "Got yourself a charmer here."

Demo grinned and shook Mike's hand. "Mike, this is Marisol. Marisol, this is Mike. Or Miguel, if you want to get technical. No Janine?"

"She took the night off. On Food Truck Friday. Go figure." Mike held out his hand to me. "Chef extraordinaire."

I shook the chef's hand. When I pulled away, my hand smelled like onions and cilantro. "Pleasure to meet you."

"Marisol is a chef, too." Demo explained, leaning against the truck and waving at a group of little girls giggling at him. "She runs a catering company."

"Awesome." Mike grinned. "Maybe we can trade recipes."

"That would be something. I keep bugging Demo's grandmother for her recipes." I nudged my date, and he rolled his eyes. His arm was warm when it slipped around my shoulders. "But she's a locked vault."

"Yiayia?" Mike shook his head. "Man, I've been working on her for a few years now, and she won't tell me anything, even when I offered to trade. She says I have to be part of the family."

"That seems to be her prerequisite," I agreed.

Mike winked at us. "Looks like you're already halfway there, eh?"

Demo squeezed my arm. "Why don't you let us get through our first date, would you?"

"First date?" Mike's eyebrows rose on his forehead. "I think he'll keep you around, Marisol. I'm definitely picking up a vibe from you two."

"Who says I'll keep him around?" I joked, pretending that my stomach didn't squeeze when he said that.

Demo's fingers started tracing circles on the side of my shoulder. "You will if you want those recipes."

I shuddered happily. I wasn't sure if I cared about the damned recipes anymore. I mean, sure. The upcoming Greek wedding was Eats & Treat's biggest event of the year, and we stood to make twice as much as we'd made on all of last year's weddings. But now that I was finding myself fantasizing about

180

Demo and me sitting on a porch, swinging while a bunch of Latino-Greek hybrid children rolled around in the grass at our feet... my focus had shifted

I was going soft. And I wasn't sure whether to laugh or cry about it.

Demo nudged me. "What are you hungry for tonight, Marisol?"

Besides you? I cleared my throat. "Um, I think I'll try the tilapia tacos with cilantro."

"Wise choice." Demo pulled out his wallet. "You won't be disappointed. Try not to screw up the fish, I'm trying to impress the lady."

Mike switched the mariachi music to some fifties tunes, and set off to make our food. "You got it, chief." As he dropped the fish into the fryer, his voice was strong and deep as he sang along to an old Elvis love song.

The food was incredible, to say the least. Fish so tender it melted in my mouth, and vegetables so fresh I could still taste the sunshine that grew them. If I'd not been sitting on the hood of the Triple D's tow truck while eating it, I'd not have believed it'd been prepared in a truck. Now all I needed was to get Miguel's to park outside Eats & Treats at lunchtime once or twice a week.

And to think, I refused to eat out of a food truck until then. Oh, the food I'd been missing out on...

"Okay..." I wiped my mouth and hands on a paper napkin after polishing off my second—yes, I made Demo go buy me a second—taco. "Now that my belly is full, and I'm too fat for this dress, what are you going to do with me?"

Surely the date wasn't over yet? The sun was setting beyond the spires of the courthouse, and the streetlights blinked on. I wasn't ready for the evening to end. Especially now that I was chalk full of finger-licking good Latin food. I felt like salsa dancing. Or attacking Demo in the cab of his truck. Probably both.

"I've got big plans." He slid off of the truck, and gathering up our trash. "Time to show you what a good time looks like, Princess."

Ooooh, maybe we were *going salsa dancing.* I hopped off of the hood and started to reapply my lipstick in the side view mirror. "Dancing? The new martini bar downtown?" I asked excitedly. "Or maybe a show? I heard the touring company of *Wicked* is in town."

Demo stared at me, deadpanned. "Do I look like a guy who wants to see a musical?"

"Maybe not." Giggling, I opened my door. "Hey, I know where we're going. That cigar bar in the Audubon Park area. I've heard good things."

He just shook his head. "Not even close. Hey, stop that. Wait for me." Charging around the side of the truck, Demo tugged the door handle away from me. "There you go."

"Well, thank you." I said, climbing in. "You know, I like this nice guy routine you're pulling. You should consider being friendly all the time."

"No way." Demo crossed around the front of the truck and climbed behind the wheel. "That would ruin my bad boy image."

"Almost as much as taking me to the theater would."

"Exactly." He put the truck into gear and waved at Mike. "Besides, as much as I want to impress you—"

"Whatever." I snorted and shifted uncomfortably in my dress. I really should've worn a more forgiving fabric. "You're not interested in impressing me, are you? You don't strike me as the kind of guy who sets out to impress anybody."

Demo looked at me, and for the first time since I'd met him, his eyes were wide and vulnerable. "I've wanted to impress you since the day I met you. That's why I was such a jerk."

I almost laughed. "That's not a quick way to sweep a woman off of her feet."

"I know." He hung his head, and fingered the steering wheel. "You just seemed so... so..."

"Bitchy?" I offered.

He brought his eyes back to mine. "Out of my league."

A weight pressed against my chest, so I reached out and took Demo's hand. "That's probably my fault. I..." I took a deep breath, then blew it out slowly. This whole honesty thing was new to me. I preferred keeping men under the guise that I was unnaturally perfect, and most likely an alien. "I wanted you to want me. I set out to make you desire me."

He thought about that for a minute, the wrinkles on the sides of his eyes returning. "Well, you did a hell of a job."

Pride spread through me like warm sunshine. "But you don't have to impress me, Demo. I mean, you may have a week ago, but now? I don't know. Things are different. I think I've changed." I blinked at him, shocked at my own admission. "There's something about seeing everyone you love find their other half. It makes you want things that are out of your norm."

He nodded, and stared at the road. "Agreed."

"So don't try to impress me." I tucked my hair behind my ears. "I don't need to be impressed anymore."

Demo waved a hand. "Of course you do. You're a woman." I opened my mouth to argue, but he cut me off. "But not with extravagant restaurants and the hottest clubs. You've already seen all that. Been there, done that. Am I right?"

I nodded. "Well, I don't know if I'd go that far." When Demo raised one eyebrow at me, I sighed. "Fine. You're right."

Demo turned the tow truck into a crowded neighborhood with a thin, car-lined street. "I want to impress you with things you've never seen before. Show you how the other half lives." He winked at me, and my stomach twirled. "I want to teach you how to eat in hole in the wall diners, score free orchestra concerts in the local parks, and go camping in the woods."

A year ago, or maybe even a few months ago, and I would've scoffed at the notion of such things. But now? Maybe cuddling in a sleeping bag under the stars with Demo wrapped around me and risking tetanus to eat at some local greasy burger joint was better than meaningless sex with some noncommittal

CEO in town for the weekend. Hell, simply *holding Demo's hand* felt better than waking up with someone whose name I couldn't remember.

I gave him a sly look. "Is this you asking me to go camping?"

"Maybe." Demo grinned as we rounded a corner and pulled up next to a park filled with huge maple trees and apple trees covered in pink blossoms. "This is Audubon Park. Have you been here before?"

I shook my head. "I've only ever driven past it."

"Snob." He turned off the truck, and tucked a strand of hair behind my ear.

Smiling, I enjoyed the tickle of excitement his fingers created on the cuff of my ear. "Shut up."

"My family lives nearby," Demo told me. "My house is only a few blocks north. We spend a lot of time in the park."

I looked around. So this was Demo's hood? That made sense. The craftsman houses were all older, decades older than my own, and most of them had wide porches with pitched roofs. Mature trees hung lazily over the streets, where kids chased each other with popsicles in the twilight. Wives sat on their front steps watching the kids, while their husbands bent under the hoods of their beat up trucks, wielding a wrench while sweat soaked the underarms on their shirts.

This was definitely Demo's type of neighborhood. It was like a picture out of a modern-day Norman Rockwell painting—if Norman Rockwell paintings had featured kids on rollerblades with iPod buds in their ears.

A crowd had gathered around a cement stage just beyond the playground. "What's happening there?"

Demo reached up and plucked a bright orange flyer from behind his visor. "Shakespeare festival. Spokane Youth Theater. My niece, Eleni, is playing Helena in A Mid… summer… something or another."

I looked at the flyer. "*A Mid Summer Night's Dream*, oh cultured one. Candace made me see this play in college. She was always dragging Brian, and Lexie, and me to these types of things. Your niece is one of the leads? How old is she?"

"She's fifteen." Demo turned off the truck.

"Wow. When I was fifteen, I was too obsessed with designer handbags and sucking face with boys to focus on Shakespeare."

He looked at me through the corner of his eye. "Don't tell me that. I don't want to have to kick a teenager's ass today."

Snickering, I went to open my door. "So you brought me to see your niece in a play?"

"Yup. Hey, wait. Lemme get that." He got out and crossed around the front of the truck to open my door. Holding his hand out to take mine, Demo explained, "My family is a huge part of my life. Almost everything I do is centered around my family. Always has been."

A pang of jealousy tightened my chest. "That's the exact opposite of my family. Almost everything I do has absolutely nothing to do with either of my parents at all. It's always been that way."

His eyes softened. "That's really sad."

I half shrugged, and let him pull me out of the cab. "I survived."

Demo's arms enveloped me. "Nobody deserves to grow up without a family." He pressed a kiss to my temple, then pulled apart, keeping his arm around my shoulder. "I like you, Marisol. A lot."

I grinned up at him. "I like you, too."

"Then you should get used to spending time with a family." He waved to someone, and led me to an empty bench at the edge of the crowd. "Because my yiayia already loves you, and as soon as the rest of my clan finds out I'm dating someone, they're gonna be on you like white on rice."

I settled down next to Demo, and squeezed his thigh suggestively. "Oh, so we're *dating* now?"

He tried not to smile. "I dunno. Maybe."

"All this and we haven't even slept together yet?"

He put a finger to his lips. "Shhh, my sister's right over there."

"Well, I'm serious." I giggled. "Did you pass me a love note in second period that I missed? Did it say to check yes or no?"

"Stop bustin' my chops." Demo nodded at someone who settled down next to us, while a smile tickled the corners of his mouth. Good Lord, he was gorgeous.

"Fine." I lowered my voice as music started to pipe over the rickety speakers set up on either side of the stage. A girl who had to be Demo's niece— because her dark hair and deep chocolate eyes were clearly a family trait—

peeked around the edge of the curtain to scan the crowd. "So after this play…
are you going to take me home with you?"

Eleni spotted Demo and waved excitedly. His grin widened, and he
waved. "Nope," he said quietly.

I got closer to his ear, electricity buzzing through my body. "Then are
we going back to *my* place?"

The curtains opened and the park crowd started to applaud. Demo
leaned in close—close enough to kiss me—but remained a centimeter apart from
my lips. "Nope."

"What? Why?" I swallowed back the urge to jam my tongue down his
throat. Neither the place, nor the time, no matter how much I wanted Demo. And
believe me, *I wanted him.*

The music died down, and a spotlight focused on center stage. Demo
cupped my chin, and gently made me face him. His dark eyes were warm and
crinkled at the edges. "Because you, Marisol, are worth more than that."

Chapter Fourteen

"Ta da!"

I looked up from the cookbook I was flipping through—rather violently, if I did say so myself—to find Lexie standing before me with a dolma in her hand.

"Tried again, eh?" I asked, slamming the book shut and shoving it across the stainless steel table. "I don't know why we promised that family an authentic Greek feast. We can't even pull off cheap Americanized gyros. We suck."

Lexie's shoulders drooped. "Whoa there, Negative Nancy. What's with the 'tude?"

"I don't have a 'tude."

She stuck the stuffed grape leaf under my nose. "Yes, you do. Here. Take a bite."

"Fine." I huffed and took a bite, chewing for a good long while before swallowing and looking up at her. "The cinnamon tastes great. And is that a hint of mustard powder I detect?"

She nodded happily. "I think I may have nailed it."

"Maybe—" I stopped talking as soon as I saw that the leaf itself was rubbing off on Lexie's fingertips. "Aw, hell. I think you overcooked them."

"What?" She looked down. "I was afraid of that. It's what I do every time."

"I've tried shortening the cooking time, but then the rice is tough." I chewed my lip. "But when I precook the rice, it turns out sticky and mushy."

"Blech." Lexie made a face. "We need yoyo's help. Seriously."

"Who?" Snickering despite myself, I polished off the last of the mushy dolma. Once I'd finished chewing, I asked, "You mean Yiayia?"

"That's the one." Lexie tossed the rest of her grape leaves in the trash. "I think you need to appeal for her help."

"Again?" I rubbed my eyes. We'd done prep work for a tea party all day, and if I made one more finger sandwich—without seeing a call or a text pop up on my iPhone soon—I would put my head in the blender. "Lex, I've already explained this to you. Until Yiayia considers me part of her family, I'm not getting a single recipe."

"Well, weren't you out sucking face all over town with her grandson just last weekend?"

I closed my eyes. Holy sexual frustration, yes I had been. After the play, we wound up walking along the trail next to the river until midnight, stopping only to kiss until we were dizzy. When I asked Demo—again—to come into my house for a nightcap (a "nightcap" meaning crazy jungle sex in at least three of the rooms in my house) he politely declined, then drove off into the darkness.

That was four days ago. I'd not heard from him since. And I was *pissed* about it.

"I highly doubt making out with her thirty-eight-year-old grandson justifies earning Yiayia's three-hundred-year-old family recipes." I stomped over to the sink to wash the green mush off of my fingers. "Besides, even if it did, I wouldn't feel right about taking them anyway. Not after being ditched by Demo."

"Ditched?" Lexie followed me to the sink. "Wait, wait, wait. You said that he wanted a relationship with you. You said that you guys were…" She made imaginary quotation marks in the air. "Going steady now."

My cheeks scalded. It was more humiliating to care about a man I'd never seen naked than it was to be caught getting freaky in a broom closet at a Bar Mitzvah we were catering. And yes. That happened. Once. Maybe twice, but I digress…

"Screw going steady," I snapped. "The bottom line is I'm not going to screw some poor old lady out of her family recipes because she's got some pipe dream that I'm going to make an honest man out of her grandson."

Lexie shook her head. "You're going soft."

"I am not," I grumbled, avoiding her eyes.

191

"Baloney!" She barked, turning off the water, then grabbing my shoulders. She forced me to look at her. "A year ago... hell, even a month ago, and you would have screwed Yiayia and the entire Antonopolous family out of not only their recipes, but possibly even their virtue, too. What gives?"

I pressed my lips together as tears pricked the backs of my eyes. When Candace cried as we watched the last Twilight movie, I threw popcorn at her and proclaimed she reached an all-time personal low. When Lexie had baby Ian and proceeded to cry every time someone looked at her because of her surging hormones, I threatened her with a restraining order and told her to go on *Dr. Phil.*

I wasn't exactly a crier. No. *I never cried.*

Lexie's eyes widened, and her grip on my arms loosened. "Mar? Are you crying right now?"

I shook my head, and a few tears spilled over. "No."

Lexie froze. "Ohmigosh. I had no idea. I mean, I knew you liked Demo and his family, but I didn't know you... you know, *liked* them."

"Well, the jokes on me." I wiped my eyes on a nearby towel. "Because he hasn't called me since our date."

"Now, a month ago, you would've called that the perfect out." She tilted her head at me. "But now you're sad?"

Nodding, I wriggled away from her hands. "I know, I know. I'm a total loser. The next thing you know, I'll be collecting cats, cross stitching pictures of Wills and Kate, and planning my imaginary wedding to Gerard Butler."

"Oh, so you're planning on becoming Aunt Dory?" Lexie grinned, referring to her aunt—Candace's mom. Her mom and Lexie's were as crazy as they came. "As long as you aren't wearing wedding dresses all the time like Mrs. Havisham, I think you're okay." She folded her arms across her chest. "Listen, maybe Demo has a perfectly relevant reason for not calling you. Maybe he knows you're a recovering commitment-phobe and wanted to give you some adequate space between dates."

I threw the towel in the air. "It's taken me thirty-two years to actually want a commitment from someone. The last thing I need right now is space."

"Well, then, why don't you call him?" She looked down at a plate of macaroons I made for the tea party. "Or better yet, why don't you go see him? You can take these. You know, a way to a man's heart is through his—"

"Yeah, yeah, yeah. I've heard it before. Through his stomach." I stared down at the pistachio macaroons with a frown. "You know the only route I've ever taken in the past is through his zipper."

"Super classy." She picked up the plate and covered it in plastic wrap. "Listen... trust me on this. Show up at Triple D's with these and tell him that you missed him. He'll take one look at you in that dress and melt in your hands."

I looked down at my sundress. It was hot pink and covered in black polka dots. Very fifties' housewife, with a naughty twist thanks to the scooped neckline. "Well, there's no arguing with you there." I took the plate of cookies from her. "What about tomorrow? Will we have enough for the tea party?"

She dismissed me with the wave of her hand. "Forget about it. I'll stay late and make another batch. Fletcher's going to some sort of charity golf tournament with Brian in a couple days, so he owes me a night off."

"Golf, huh?" I raised an eyebrow at her. "Is this what I have to look forward to? Does monogamy and domesticity mean letting my man golf all day while I work? Sounds pretty sexist to me."

Lexie snorted. "I'm no deprived housewife, Mar. My man will be carrying Ian around in a chest pack all night while he helps Martha with her science project. Then when I get home, I'll devour him. It works for both of us."

"Now you're starting to sound like me!" I laughed.

"Like the *old* you. Before you went soft." She looked up at the clock. "Now, go. It's already four-thirty, and you need to get to Triple D's before Demo leaves for the day."

"Ha," I scoffed. "Please. The man lives underneath the hood of cars. Not like your husband, mind you, who spends his days under a different hood altogether." I waggled my eyebrows at Lexie to remind her that her husband is a gynecologist. You know, in case she forgot.

"Ugh. Shut up." She made a face. "Do you know how many times I've wished Fletcher's job was a little bit more benign?"

Snorting, I hiked my purse up on my elbow, then walked towards the door. "Like Brian? Optometry isn't nearly as exciting as staring at vaginas all day."

Lexie shrugged. "I dunno. Candace says Brian has been pretty tired lately. Maybe being an eye doctor is more taxing than we presume."

"Whatever. Brian's a wuss."

"Leave it to me to finally please my mother by marrying a doctor, and I marry an OB/GYN." She closed her eyes and pinched the bridge of her nose. Lexie's mom was, how do you say, extremely difficult to please. "If I had another nickel for how many times she's reminded me that Fletcher sees other women's private parts all the time—"

"You would have a butt load of nickels by now." I winked at her. "Okay. I'm out of here. I'll see you tomorrow morning, bright and early."

"Hey!" She plucked my phone off of the table. "Seriously. You forget this thing all the time. Take it with you. Then you can text me after you finally talk Demo into bed."

"Ha!" I took it from her, and pulled the door open. "Like that will happen. I'm pretty sure he's taken a vow of chastity and joining a monastery."

"Give it time, Mar. He wants you. But he respects you. You're not used to that."

Respect? I thought to myself as I walked to my car. As much as I hated to admit it, Lexie was right. Demo and I were so different from each other. He was respectful; I was crass. He was a family person; I'd been alone for as long as I could remember. He was beat up cars and greasy spoon diners; I was filet mignon and caviar. Demo was apples; I was oranges.

I hoped we could make some decent fruit salad someday.

When I pulled up in front of Triple D's, it was hopping. There were cars—old and new—parked in the garage, and outside the doors, and Trey spoke with a customer in the sunshine by the front door.

"Oh… hey, Marisol! How are you?" he squeaked as I approached. Excusing himself from the customers, he approached me with a nervous smile. "What are you doing here? Was Uncle Demo expecting you?"

I held up the plate of macaroons. "It's a surprise. Is he here?"

"Well, uh, yeah." Trey scratched his head, making his dark curls tumble across his sweaty brow. "I'll find him for you."

"No, that's okay." I patted him on the shoulder. "Get back to work. I'll find Demo."

"Wait." He grabbed my arm, smearing grease on my skin. "Yiayia is here. She'd love to see you. Why don't you wait in the office?"

I looked down at the black smudge. "Trey, you're acting weird. *And* you just got me dirty. I'm starting to get irritated, and irritated Marisol is never good."

Trey snickered. "Did you just refer to yourself in the third person?"

"Maybe." I sniffed indignantly, and stepped around the gangly teenager. "Is Demo in the garage?"

"No." Trey reached for my arm again, but saw my warning glare, and put his hands up defensively. "Look, why don't you head to the office, and I'll send him right in?"

Narrowing my eyes, I balanced the plate of cookies on one hand and put the other on my hip. "What gives, Trey?"

His face paled. "Nothin'."

Okay, I'd seen that look a thousand times before. It didn't matter if it was Candace's five-year-old son, Quentin, a teenager like Trey, or a grown man in his thirties making it... it meant trouble was brewing. I'd seen it on my father's face more times than I could count. The look reeked of guilt, and I loathed guilty men.

"You've got to be kidding me," I muttered, my hand dropping off of my hip. "Where is he? Just tell me."

"Thanks a bunch, Trey!" A man called from inside a Hyundai that resembled a tic tac with wheels. "Tell your yiayia hi for me."

Trey peeled his eyes away from mine long enough to give him a nod before he fired up his engine and pulled out of the parking lot. As soon as the mobile breath mint moved, it revealed two people caught in an embrace at the far end of the garage.

Demo and Stacia.

His hands were on her overly-tanned shoulders, and her fingers were tangled in his dark hair. Their mouths mashed together in in a kiss that was as frantic as it was passionate, the sound of moaning and damp lip smacking ringing out over the sound of the passing traffic.

Anger filled my body like a pitcher, hot and bubbly like lava. "What. The. *Hell?*" I snarled, pulling my arm back and launching the plate of cookies at the two of them.

"Oh, snap!" Trey said behind me.

When the plate landed with a deafening shatter at their feet, Demo's open eyes landed on me.

"Marisol!" He croaked, pushing Stacia away and stepping towards me. His boots crackled on the shards of broken glass. "This isn't what it looks like."

"Oh, no you don't." I held up a finger and wagged it at Demo. "Don't use a line like that on me. I *invented* that line, do you understand me?"

Stacia turned around and surveyed all of the glass. "Crazy bitch."

Swallowing back my tears, I forced myself to throw my head back and laugh. "Honey, you have no idea."

Demo approached me like a tiger about to pounce. His hands out, his posture crouched and cautious. "Listen, Marisol, *she* was kissing *me*. Not the other way around. I was trying to make her leave."

"With your tongue down her throat?" I leveled a glare at him. "Really, Demo?"

"Demo, stop playing games with the poor woman," Stacia said, putting her hands on her bony hips. "Tell her about us."

"Shut up, Stacia." He pointed to a bright red car parked down the block. "Go home."

Stacia seethed in her spot, steam practically pouring out her nostrils. "Are you kidding me?"

"No. Go." Demo turned back to me, his eyes wide and apologetic. "Listen, Marisol, let's go into the office, and talk—"

I reached into my purse and pulled out my keys. "No need." Walking backwards away from him, I nudged my head in Trey's direction, who was still standing there with arms raised like I'd been holding up the shop. "But do yourself a favor next time, Demo. Don't put your nephew in charge of recon. He sucks at it."

"Recon? What?" He glowered at Trey. "That isn't what he was doing."

"Whatever." I turned and stalked back to where my car was parked. I could hear his heavy footsteps following me. "Honestly, it doesn't even matter. Because it's not like we were exclusive, or anything."

"In my eyes, we were," he growled.

I turned around and rested a hand on the car roof casually. Stacia gave me the finger behind Demo's back. "It sure didn't look exclusive to me. And frankly, I think your friend over there thinks differently."

"*She* kissed *me*." He laced his fingers around the back of his neck and started to pace. "I told you that I had a past, and that I dated Stacia. She's having a hard time letting go, that's all."

"It's hard to let go when the man is dry humping you in the parking lot of his work," I said flatly.

"I wasn't dry—" Demo drug a hand down his face. "She threw herself at me. I was just trying to—"

"If you say let her down easy, I'm going to vomit. Seriously." I unlocked my car, and threw my purse inside. Yanking my sunglasses off of the dashboard, I shoved them onto my face, practically knocking myself out in the process. Anything to hide the emotion that clogged my throat and liquefied my eyes. The last thing I needed was for him to see how crushed I felt. "Listen to me, Demo. See whomever you want. Kiss whomever you want. Screw whomever you want. I don't care. We were just having fun acting like two chaste little teenagers. But I get it. An adult man has *needs*. I've heard it all before. And the truth is, an adult woman has needs, too. Which is why… I've got a date… tomorrow."

The lie fell out of my mouth and bounced on the pavement at Demo's feet. His mouth dropped open, and he gaped at me. "You're going on a date?"

The wheels on Stacia's car squealed as she peeled away from the curb, and I laughed bitterly. "Yeah." I shrugged, pretending to be nonchalant even though I wanted to lie down in the backseat of my car to weep and suck my thumb for a while. "After the Rosewood Bridge Club tea party tomorrow I'm going out with a business associate. He's an ad exec in town for the week. We're old friends, if you know what I'm saying." I paused dramatically. "You're not upset, are you?"

Silence stretched out between us, the only sound filling the space was the air compressor in the garage, which I was pretty sure Trey was doing on

200

purpose. Finally, after about a minute-long stare down, Demo straightened his shoulders and wiped sweat off of his tanned brow.

"Nope," he said finally. "Have a good time, Marisol."

Chapter Fifteen

I popped a flower shaped cucumber sandwich into my mouth and chewed thoughtfully. Thanks to Yiayia's baklava—and the tacos from Miguel/Mike's truck—I spent more time on the treadmill at the gym than in my own bed at night. The white bread lathered in cream cheese I chewed on wasn't going to help the situation, but I didn't care. I'd been dumped. And I wasn't taking it well.

Every time I saw my friends with their husbands, I mourned the absence of such a relationship in my life. Take Candace and Brian, for instance. They'd been mad for each other for since they were nineteen, and from what Candace told me, the passion was as hot as it had been when they'd lost their virginity to each other. Their life—the house, the kids, the matching ugly Christmas sweater holiday photo cards they sent out every year—was like the gold ring on the carousel I desperately wanted to grab. But kept falling short.

I really thought I found it in Demo.

He was different. He occupied all my thoughts, and I felt his presence around me even when we were apart. It didn't matter to me how much of an A hole he acted like, because I knew there was a caring, family-oriented man deep down inside, underneath his crusty mechanic exterior. The idea of merely kissing him made my skin warm and sweat prick at my hairline. He made me fantasize—not about being tied up with silk scarves or having sex in an elevator, like I used to wonder about—but about waking up to the sound of Saturday cartoons playing downstairs, or the chaos that an Antonopolous family Christmas dinner would bring into my otherwise empty home.

The truth was… I was starting to think I—gulp—loved him.

Shoving another cucumber sandwich into my mouth, I tried to bury my unrequited feelings beneath a blanket of cream cheese.

After all these years, and all those men, I'd finally fallen. At the feet of a mechanic. With a giant Greek family. And a girlfriend named Stacia.

THUD. I bent at the waist, and my head hit the wooden tabletop. I whimpered.

"Oh, dear," Lexie said as she and Candace came into the kitchen to find me bent at the waist and hunched over the table. "It's taken a turn for the worse."

They spent the bulk of the tea party correcting my mistakes. When I placed the petit fours on the tables before serving the scones, Candace swooped in to replace the silver platter. When I served rose bush tea instead of Earl Grey, Lexie apologized for my faux pas and won over the room of old ladies with a story about baby Ian. After over a decade of friendship that (mostly) involved me acting superior and confident, I'd been reduced to a weepy, red-nosed, lovesick sap.

If this was love, I was done. This crap was for the birds.

Candace put her arms around me, and lifted me back into a standing position. "Mar? Come on. Pull it together. We need you."

"I want to go home." I sniffled and wiped my nose on a crumpled napkin. "You two can handle the tea party. It's practically over now. We can all split. They won't even miss us. Pack up the trays."

"They haven't even paid us yet." Lexie pointed out. "You need to find Mrs. Harrison and ask for final payment. She still owes a hundred and sixty-four dollars."

"You can get it," I whined. I usually collected final payment from our clients. But my no-nonsense attitude had been replaced by Eeyore's pitiful poor me gig. And it hurt even more that I actually knew—thanks to Candace's kids— who Eeyore was.

Candace rubbed my arms. "Come on. Perk up for me."

"I can't…" I wiped my eyes. "I don't want to."

"Well, you have to," she said, smiling gently. "There's someone—"

"It's so easy for the two of you." I wriggled away from my friends and went to grab a couple more cucumber sandwiches. "You're both happily married to *doctors,* for hell's sake. You've got kids and carpools, and I've got an empty house and an annoying, pissed off cat—"

"I told you not to get that thing," Lexie interrupted.

"I love Cocinero!" I bellowed, before dissolving into tears again. Lexie put their fingers to her lips, and Candace put an arm around my shoulders as I dropped my voice down lower. "But honestly. Look at you two. It's so easy for you to tell me to perk up. You've both got the perfect lives. Your husbands are best friends, and your families barbeque together every weekend. Aren't they golfing together tomorrow?"

They nodded in unison. "What does that have to do with anything?" Lexie asked.

Candace elbowed her. "Marisol wants what we have."

Part of me wanted to argue with her. Point out the fact that fifty percent of all marriages wound up in divorce, and that they'd spend the rest of their lives screwing the same man. But I knew it was a moot point. Because now all I wanted was to spend the rest of my own life screwing the same man.

Didn't see that one coming.

Too bad I lied to him and told him I had a hot date with an imaginary businessman.

Lexie took one of my hands in hers. "Listen, Mar. I know you're feeling awful right now, but all is not lost. What you're feeling... it's called *love.* And I know you're scared, because it's such a big feeling, and everything. But it's *normal.* And if you tell Demo how you're feeling, I'm almost certain he'll say he's feeling it, too. That's how it works, you see."

"Stop talking to me like I'm eight years old," I snapped, blowing my nose. "I know what love is."

"But you admit you've never felt it before," Candace said gently.

"Well, not for a man. Hell, I don't even know if I love my own parents." I looked up at my friends, the only people in the world I'd ever cared about more than myself. "I've only ever loved you guys. And that stupid cat."

Candace and Lexie froze, their eyes wide.

After about five seconds, Lexie blinked. "I'm sorry. Um… what?"

I gestured at the two of them. "You guys. I love you guys. You're like the only family I've ever known. Don't you know that?"

Candace pressed a hand to her chest. "I feel like we're having a breakthrough here."

"Me too, right?" Lexie wiped the corner of her eyes. "I mean, I always knew you cared about us. Why on earth would you choose Spokane of all places to settle down?"

"It's because you guys, and your husbands and kids, are everything." Another fresh crop of tears filled my eyes. "Wherever you guys are, that's home."

Lexie sniffled and put her arm around Candace. "We love you, too, Marisol."

Candace reached out and wiped a tear off the end of my chin. "Come on, let's get you cleaned up, okay?"

"What for?" I reluctantly let her tug me towards a nearby sink. "I just had an emotional breakthrough. Shouldn't that make me exempt from work for the rest of the night?"

"Under normal circumstances, yes." Lexie turned on the cold water, dunked her hands, and started patting my puffy face. "But tonight you have something to do."

"What?" I grumbled. "I've already lost love and professed love in one night."

"True." Candace tugged my hair out of its ponytail and ran her hands through it. "But there's someone here to see you."

My insides froze. "Excuse me?"

Lexie beamed like a proud mother. "Your face isn't red anymore. Except your nose. That'll go away in a while."

I grabbed her shoulders. "Who's here?"

"Well, go outside and see for yourself," she giggled.

Sure enough, outside the back kitchen door stood Demo, with a bouquet of purple and white lilacs in his arms. Once again, he'd recently showered and shaved, as his face was soft and devoid of all whiskers, and his hair had been combed and gelled into submission. He wore wrinkled cargo khakis—I would have bet money that those were his nicest pair of pants—and a light grey tee shirt.

"Um, hi?" he said as I approached.

I prayed he couldn't see my red nose in the dwindling sunlight. "What are you doing here?"

"Stopping you from going on a date with another guy." Demo handed me the bouquet. "These are from my yard. I've got more than I can stand, so when they die, I'll bring you some more."

I smelled them. They were so fragrant and sweet, I sighed blissfully. "They're great. Thank you."

Demo's gaze intensified. "I'll bring you fresh ones every single day, if I have to. I'm sorry, Marisol."

I looked up at him and bit the insides of my cheeks to keep from tearing up. Again. "I'm sorry, too."

"I should have called after our date, and I know it." He shook his head. "It's just that I didn't want to scare you away. You keep telling me that you've never stayed in a relationship, so I didn't want to come across too strong."

I winced. Lexie was right. I hated it when that happened. "I know. And I could have called, too."

"What I think is happening here," he said with a smile. "Is a case of two people who have no idea *how* to be in a relationship *want* to be in a relationship."

I couldn't help but laugh. "You're probably right."

"Listen, Stacia and me... we're not dating." Demo shook his head, frowning. "We went out a handful of times a couple of months ago. We met at a bar, and fooled around. I..." He pressed his lips together, and his face reddened. "I slept with her a few times. That's why she's having a hard time letting go. I

208

never promised her anything. I was always honest with her and told her I didn't want a relationship. But I think she thought I'd come around."

This story was all too familiar. I lost count of how many times I slithered out of someone's bed, knowing he wanted a commitment I would never deliver on. "And you didn't?" I sighed.

"No." He shook his head. "She keeps coming to my place and to Triple D's. She shows up and talks to Yiayia, who can't stand her. Yesterday she just lunged at me. I was pushing her away when you saw us. I wasn't kissing her back, Marisol. I swear it."

I smiled. "I knew I liked Yiayia for a good reason."

Demo sighed. "That's why I've been moving slow with you. I don't want to go too far, too fast. I'm trying to make this last, because…" His words petered out, and he shrugged. "I don't know. I just feel more for you."

"I know." I reached out and laced my fingers with his. "I feel more, too."

Tell him you love him.

No. Too fast. Don't scare him away.

Tell him!

I opened my mouth at the same time he spoke again.

"Can I take you somewhere?" Demo asked softly. "Somewhere important?"

"Sure." I beamed, tugging him towards his tow truck parked on the street. "Whisk me away, Mr. Apple."

"Apple?" He looked at me quizzically, but I just laughed.

***

"Holy crap," I breathed as soon as we pulled onto Lincoln Lane. We were a few blocks north of the park where we watched the play, only it had been transformed into a gorgeous block party that took over the whole street. Lights twinkled and paper lanterns hung between the telephone poles; multicolored flags strung along rectangular tables that bore every kind of food imaginable (mostly Greek, of course); and a deejay played fifties' music while couples, old and young, danced. It was magical.

My mouth dropped open. "What is this? What's going on?"

"Block party." Demo smiled proudly, and waved to someone on the sidewalk. "Which ultimately means an Antonopolous family reunion, with a couple of other families thrown in for good measure."

"You all live here?" I craned my neck to search the crowd. Sure enough, most of the people had Demo's dark, wavy hair and deep chocolate eyes.

"Lots of us do, yeah." He winked at me. "I told you my family was pretty tight. We tend to see each other every day, and touch bases with each other all the time. We all know what's going on in everyone else's life, and eat at each other's houses every night." Demo chuckled to himself. "Oh wait, that's

210

me. I make the rounds and eat at everyone else's house, and if play my cards right, I only have to cook for myself like once a week."

I stared at him. "I eat meals with my parents once every two years."

"Well, that's got to change," Demo said with a nod.

After parking at the barricades at end of the street, Demo opened my door and took my hand. "This is my mother's house," he said, pointing to a grey house with white shutters on the corner. "And the brick house right next to it is my Aunt Vesna and Uncle Stavros' home."

A group of kids zipped by on bikes, waving. "Hi, Uncle Bobo!" one of the kids called.

"Hey guys." Demo waved. "Two of those kids are my nephews. Nick and Steven. They belong to my sister, Cressida."

"Is that Eleni's mom?"

He shook his head. "No, that's my other sister, Athena. She lives in the other brick house with the red door."

I peered down the street. "Which one is yours?"

"The blue and white one." He pointed to a house in the middle of the block, where a man grilled steaks in the front yard on the biggest iron grill I'd ever seen. "I'm sandwiched in between my Uncle Miles and Mr. Polbert, who is not a relative, but a former postman who has made each of us nifty handcrafted welcome signs to hang above our doors."

"I see." I noticed a woman holding a baby watching us with a grin, and nudged Demo. "Who's that?"

211

"That's Eleni's mother, and the baby she's holding is her youngest, Christopher." He took me by the elbow and led me over. "Hey, sis. This is my new friend, Marisol. Marisol, this is my sister, Athena."

She reached out a hand for me to shake, and the baby released a scream. "Ugh. Sorry. He's sort of a clingy baby. It's nice to meet you, Marisol. I've heard a lot about you."

Glancing at Demo, I shook the three free fingers on her left hand. "It's nice to meet you, too. I didn't realize Demo had told anybody in his family about me."

"Oh, he hasn't. He's been trying to keep you a secret." She winked at her brother, who just rolled his eyes. "It's my grandmother I've been hearing all about you from."

"Oh, really?" I chuckled. "I have to say, I really dig your yiayia."

"We all do. What's not to like?" Athena started to bounce the baby on her shoulder. "She seems to think you and my brother are dating. Is that true?"

"I think so," I said. "But it's new, so don't go picking out china patterns yet."

Athena laughed. "You got it. I like you. Demo, why haven't you brought her around before now? She's got sass. I like sass."

"Did you hear that?" I looked up at Demo. "She likes my sass."

Demo rubbed his eyes. "Don't encourage her."

"Who?" Athena and I said in unison, making Christopher wail again.

"This one cries all the time," Athena explained, holding the wriggling baby out to me. "I've got to go get a bottle. Would you mind?"

"What? Me?" I blurted, looking around for someone—anyone—else more capable of holding the drooling baby. "Oh, I don't think—"

"He should be fine for a minute." Ahtena gave me an encouraging nod. "He's not nearly as whiney as Demo was when he was a kid. Is he, Demo?"

"Athena..." he warned.

"Whoa. Okay." I grasped Christopher as Athena dropped him in my arms and grinned. "I, uh, don't have that much experience with babies. My friends have kids, but—" I shut up as soon as the baby started to wail again.

"Demo was always crying about something." She rolled her eyes as her brother turned red as a beet next to me. "I can't find my GI Joe doll. Mom said I could have two sodas today. Where's my Superman cape? Day in, day out with the incessant whining. Makes Christopher here seem like a monk with a vow of silence."

I felt Demo's hand on my shoulder. "Thanks for the trip down memory lane, sis. That was great."

She grinned, looking just like Demo and Yiayia all at once. "Shall I tell her about how you wet the bed until you were thirteen?"

Demo's mouth pulled into a defiant line. "I was *twelve*."

"Touchy." Athena patted my other shoulder. "I'll be right back with the bottle. Take my brother over to the food and make him eat something. He gets a little cranky when he's hungry."

Snorting, I turned towards the smoking grill in front of Demo's house. "You fast often, I presume."

"Har, har. Come on, I smell goat." Demo made a beeline for his front yard.

"I, uh, what?" I had to walk quickly to keep up with him. He was a man on a mission, as he plucked two paper plates off of a table and started loading them with meat. "Did you say goat?"

Demo nodded, a proud smile splayed on his face. "Marisol, this is my cousin, Pirro. He's the best cook in the whole family."

The balding man wielding a giant pair of tongs waved. "Don't tell Yiayia he said that."

Demo shook his head. "She'll kill me."

"It's true," his cousin agreed.

"It's nice to meet you." I watched as Demo filled my plate with more Greek delicacies than I ever realized existed. Dolmades, feta, mousakka, taziki, souvlaki. All piled high and dripping over the edges. "Whoa. Slow down. I'm not going in the electric chair."

Demo nudged Pirro. "What do we think of women who refuse to eat, cousin?"

Pirro waved his hand. "No good. Find a woman who will eat with you. Nothing's sexier than a woman who eats."

A laugh bubbled up in the back of my throat. I could get used to that kind of attitude. "Well, then throw another baklava on. Did Yiayia make those?" They both nodded. "Make it two."

"Atta girl," Pirro said.

Demo looked at me with a wide, happy gaze. "You're really somethin', aren't you?"

"That's what they tell me." I winked.

We ate. And ate, and ate, and ate. Athena brought me a bottle for Christopher about halfway into the amazing food, and I fed him until he fell asleep on my shoulder, with a string of drool dripping into my hair.

I didn't care. Demo and I danced to the music until the moon was high in the sky, with Christopher between us. Every few minutes or so, we were interrupted as a relative came over for an introduction. I stepped back to allow Demo to dance with his mother and Yiayia a time or two. But I didn't mind. It was great to watch him in his element. With his family around, Demo was witty and fun, smiley and jovial. He played with his young nieces and nephews, giving them horsey rides on his back on the grass, and chased the older ones on the dance floor until they were adequately humiliated doing the jitterbug with him.

And as far as Demo's family went? Well, I was sunk.

They were by far some of the nicest people I'd ever met. Each and every relative at the block party—I lost count after thirty-eight—came up to me, hugged me, and welcomed me into the fold. Many of them said they were relieved to see Demo had finally stopped acting like a middle-aged playboy. I didn't share the fact that until I kissed Demo, I'd been quite the player myself. They didn't need to know that. Or the fact that my uterus contracted every time Demo bent down to press a kiss to Christopher's head, making his now messy brown hair tickle the side of my face.

I wanted him. And not just in the usual *do me against a wall and make me scream obscenities in Spanish* sort of way (though I *did* want Demo that way, too.) But rather, in a *when can I move onto Lincoln Lane and wake up next to you every morning* way. And I couldn't keep it to myself anymore. I felt like a teapot filled with boiling water, on the verge of blowing the whistle. I wanted to tell Demo what I felt. No, I actually *had* to tell him, otherwise I was going to burst... and leave a giant mess all over the pavement.

"Hey," I said, pulling Demo's neck to bring his face closer to me as we danced to a slow song. The night was winding down, and most of the neighbors and family members had gone home to put their kids to bed. Athena had taken Christopher inside, leaving Demo and I to dance closely for the last few songs before the deejay packed it up for the night. "I need to tell you something."

Demo looked at me, the wrinkles on either side of his eyes deepening. "Want to go inside my house?"

Mother of God, YES. Pressing my lips together, I smiled coyly. "Sure."

He led me up the walk and into the front of his house. It was decorated exactly like I expected it to be. Not much color, minimal furniture, and a giant flat screen the size of a ping pong tabletop hanging on the wall. But the dark

216

woodwork shone, and the floors creaked delightfully underneath our feet as Demo led me from room to room.

"And this is my bedroom." He flicked on a light, illuminating a large room with French doors that led out to the backyard. His bed was big, and covered in a thick blue and white quilt I was pretty sure had been designed to resemble the Greek flag. Demo shrugged embarrassedly. "Yiayia makes them for each of her grandkids."

I suppressed a smile. "I see." Walking over to the bed, I perched demurely on the side and put my hands on my knees. "Come and sit with me."

Demo stared at me with eyes that could only be described as hungry. He shoved his hands in his pockets, and furrowed his brow. "Are you sure?"

Grinning, I patted the quilt next to me. "Come on. I won't bite."

He tilted his chin upward, his stature defiant. "What if I want you to?"

I swallowed. Hard. "Then you wouldn't have to ask twice."

"I want you, Marisol." His voice was rough around the edges. "Make no mistake of that."

Demo was so beautiful, standing there in the doorway with a narrow strip of light running across his face. I had to remind myself to blink. I didn't know what to do with myself. Sit. Stand. Fold my arms. Tear off my shirt?

I used to say things so bold and crass, men almost swallowed their tongues. Now I couldn't get the simplest of terms out.

Finally, I cleared my throat. "I want you, too, Demetrious."

217

"I want to make this right," he told me, his chocolate brown eyes shining. "I should be honest with you."

The cloud of sexual tension thickened between us as straightened my back and faced him. "Okay. Hit me."

"I want to stay on this street, near my family. Forever. My mother's getting older, and needs us kids around. And Yiayia—"

"It's fine," I interrupted him. "They're amazing. I... I wouldn't want to leave them, either."

He smiled. A small, tiny smile that lit his face up like Christmas morning. "I want kids." When I raised my eyebrows, he added, "Someday. I mean, I know I'm going to be an older parent, but I don't care. I've always wanted them. And I don't care if they're mine or somebody else's. I just want to raise a family someday."

My eyes filled. "I do, too. I mean..." I sniffled. "I don't want a family band, or anything. I don't want to have a whole soccer team. My vagina's not a clown car. But one. Or two... would be nice."

Demo laughed. "Has anybody told you that you've got a way with words?"

One of my shoulders rose and fell. "Maybe. Once or twice."

"I was engaged once." His mouth turned down in the corners. "She left me the night before the wedding. I beat a guy up and went to jail."

"Yiayia told me." I stood up and stepped closer to him. "My father left my mom and me when I was a little girl. I was raised by nannies after that. That's why I'm such a cold bitch."

Demo reached out and stroked my cheek. "Not so cold to me."

I shuddered when he touched me. But holy crap, Demo's touch was otherworldly. "I have another confession."

"What's that?"

Here goes nothing.

"I think I'm falling in love with you."

He didn't say anything for a moment. It felt like ten minutes, but in all actuality, it was probably closer to ten seconds. But when Demo drew a long breath, then let it out slowly, I prepared myself for the worst.

I was moving too fast. This is why he dumped the ever-available Stacia. Soon it would be me throwing myself at him in the Triple D's parking lot.

"I love you, too, Marisol."

I released the breath I'd been holding. "Gah! Oh, thank God, because I was afraid you were going to tell me to buzz off. Do you know I've never said that to a man before? Well, my father, I suppose. But I'm not even sure I meant it. Because I've been infatuated with a man before, but I've never wanted to, like, *give myself* to someone before. You know? Inside and out, you know? I don't—"

"Marisol, shut up."

219

I looked up at him and blinked. "I, uh, okay."

His gaze was heavy. "I've haven't said that to anyone since Belinda."

"Do you mean it?" I gulped, suddenly insecure. "You're not just trying to—you know—get into my pants?"

Demo shook his head. "No. Are you trying to get into mine?"

Giggling, I leaned back onto my elbows. "Baby, I've been trying to get into your pants since I met you."

"Well, then I'm out of here."

He turned to leave the room, and I jumped to grab his arm. "Come on, Demo, don't leave me now. I'm just getting started with this whole opening up thing—"

In a flash, he turned around, swept me off of my feet, and placed me down on his Greek flag quilt. Once his shirt had been peeled up over his head—and dear heaven, he was every bit as glorious beneath his shirt as he was from the neck up, and you can take that fact right to the bank—he started to pepper the skin on my neck and collarbone with kisses.

I dug my hands into his hair as he started to unbutton my blouse. "Demo?"

"Hmmm?" He lifted his head and gave me a heavy-lidded gaze. I could feel his heart thudding through his chest, and his fingertips left a trail of heat across my ribcage underneath the thin silk of my shirt.

"Thank you," I whispered. "For bringing me to life."

"I think you're the one who brought me to life, Mar." He brought his mouth back to mine, opening my lips with a warm swipe of his tongue.

Closing my eyes, I let the sensation take over my body, setting it on fire and lifting me off of the bed. The only sound in the room now was our baited breath, our bodies moving across the worn quilt, and our hearts thrumming in unison.

Maybe we'd brought *each other* to life?

Chapter Sixteen

When Demo brought me home early the next morning, my feet didn't touch the front walk as I wandered into my house. In fact, I don't think they touched the floor as I fed Cocinero, watered my plants, walked upstairs, or started to fill the bathtub.

Yup. I was in love. And walking on air.

"I can't believe this is happening," I said out loud to Cocinero as I undressed. All these years avoiding falling for someone, avoiding commitment like the flu, and sidestepping any man that had deeper feelings for me than the desire to screw. I'd been missing out.

Going to bed to someone you love is so much better. There's connection on levels that I hadn't realized existed. Being with Demo was like coming home after years and years of travelling. And waking up that morning, wrapped in his arms? The safest place in the world.

And the sex?

A hysterical giggle burst from my throat, and Cocinero meowed.

"Shush," I scolded him, covering my mouth and leaning against the counter. Images scrolled through my mind, the night before playing out like a vividly colored, slow motion film. Arms, legs, eyes, lips, skin, sweat… too much to process again. I felt weak.

The sex was amazing. *Ah. Maze. Ing.*

I looked at my reflection in the mirror above the sink. My lips were still swollen from hours and hours of kissing. The skin on my neck was pinked and raw from Demo's early morning whiskers. And my hands? My hands still smelled like him. Gasoline, soap, and… something so undeniably *male,* it made me dizzy.

You have no idea, Marisol…

Standing up straight, I touched my lips and stared at my reflection with wide eyes.

When a man loves you, it's the most incredible feeling in the world…

Gasping, I stepped away from the mirror and ducked into the shower. I looked just like my mother twenty years ago. Before all of her plastic surgeries. Before all of her marriages. Before she became the bitter, money-hungry, plastic shell of a woman that she is now.

I remembered the day she said that to me like it was yesterday.

It was eleven in the morning, and I'd been torn away from Saturday morning cartoons by the sound of the front door slamming. When I crept into the foyer and looked out the window, a man wearing dress slacks, and carrying his shirt in his hands walked down our driveway to a waiting cab.

I went up to my mother's bedroom, which was usually off-limits, but that morning her double doors were wide open. I wandered in to find my mother laying on the bed with a dazed grin on her face. The sheets and blankets were everywhere, twisted and sweaty, and a lamp had been knocked over. Gasping, I ran to her.

"Mommy, are you all right?" I asked, climbing onto the bed next to her.

She rolled over, and I realized she was naked under the corner of her sheet. "Good morning, Marisol," she said lazily. Her hair was loose and wild, tumbling over the pillows in thick waves; and her lips were red and swollen. "How are you this morning?"

"I'm fine," I said, looking away. It embarrassed me that she didn't have one of her fancy nightgowns on. "How are you?"

"Perfect," she purred, reaching out and playing with my hair. "Oh, kiddo, just you wait."

"Just wait for what?" I asked, bringing my eyes back to hers. She looked so pretty that morning. So much prettier than when she wore makeup and fancy clothes. I wished I could see her like that more often—except maybe with clothes on.

"Oh, Marisol, you have no idea." She sat up and looked at me intensely. The sheet was barely covering her top half now. "Just wait until a man loves you. And wants only you."

"Loves me?" I squeaked. I knew about boys and girls. One of my nannies had brought her boyfriend over one night, and I'd watched them making out for hours before they made me go to bed. And some of the girls in my class already liked boys. As for me? I wasn't really sure what I thought about them.

"Uh huh," she said excitedly. "When a man loves you, it's the most incredible feeling in the world."

"Daddy loves me." I smiled at her. I wasn't sure if it was true, because he never called me anymore. But before he left he told me he loved me. So I hoped it was true.

My mother's face dropped. "That's not what I mean. I'm talking about when a man is in love with you. When he wants to take you to bed with him, and can't get enough of you. That's the most incredible feeling in the world."

I thought for a moment, looking around the room. There was an empty wine bottle in the trash, and a man's tie hanging from the curtain rod. I remembered the last time I'd seen this room in a state like this, and nodded. "Like the way Daddy wanted Nanny Hanna."

My mother's face paled, and she looked around the room like she'd just woken up. Blinking, she pulled the sheet tighter around her body, and gave me a push. "Go," she ordered. "Go on. Go find something to do. Leave me alone."

"What did I do?" I asked, sliding off of the side of the bed. "I'm sorry, Mommy. I didn't mean to talk about Daddy."

Her face crumpled. "Daddy never loved me. Or you. He left us, didn't he?"

"Yes, but—"

"Shut up!" She yelled, her tears taking her mascara down her face with them. "Get out of here, Marisol. Do as I tell you. I am your mother."

I wanted to spend time with my mom. I wanted her to tell me what it felt like to be wanted by a man some more. And why it was so wonderful. I didn't want our time together to be over yet. "But I want to talk about love some more," I begged. "Please? I'll be good. I'll just listen. Please?"

My mother stood up, tugging the sheet with her. Patting me on the bottom, she moved me closer to her bedroom door. "There's nothing to talk about, Marisol. Love is just something men say when they're screwing you silly."

Her door closed in my face before I could ask her what she meant. Two months later, I got my first stepfather, and the rest came on average every four years after that.

I let the scalding hot water soak my hair and run down my face. When Demo said he loved me, he meant it. I knew it. I could *feel* it right down into my soul. There was no way I was going to let the bitter words of my dysfunctional mother under my skin now. Not when I'd finally let myself fall for someone so perfect.

I heard a buzzing sound coming from my bedroom and chuckled to myself. It was probably either Candace or Lexie, calling to see how my date with Demo went. And as much as I wanted to share all the details—every... single... one—I wanted just a few more minutes to keep it to myself. It felt too personal. Too deep to change into coffee talk while their kids played in the next room.

Cocinero meowed outside the shower stall when the buzzing sound returned. "Persistent, aren't they?" I called to him as I scrubbed my hair. I was going to wear it down today. Demo said he liked it loose.

Sigh.

I finally understood what Lexie and Candace were talking about when they said they were best friends with their hubbies. Demo and I had spent the night talking and laughing about everything under the sun. We made omelets at three o'clock in the morning, wearing nothing but our smiles as we sat across the table from each other, swapping embarrassing high school stories.

I knew now how Candace felt when Brian walked into a room and she sighed to herself because of how much she loved him, and how much he loved her. I used to mock her for being so whipped, and now? Now I was the one sighing. What a strange turn of events.

The buzz sounded again, and I rolled my eyes.

"Well, they can just wait. Can't they, Cocinero?" I said, letting the water flush down my back. He yowled as I started to sing a Buddy Holly song from the night before. The ringer on my home phone rang out, making me jump a foot in the air. "Geez. They're downright pushy today."

I climbed out of the shower and wrapped a towel around myself as I shuffled to my bedroom. Sure enough, when I picked it up off of the base, it was Lexie's cell number flashing on the screen. I wiped my ear off with the corner of the towel, then answered. "Fine, you pushy bitch, you. But I'm not telling all of the sordid details, because they're mine. All mine. Do you understand me?"

There was a pause, and then a choking sound. "M-mar?"

My blood ran cold. "Lex? Are you hurt?"

"Mar, we need you," She sobbed. "Right now."

I was already in my closet, yanking clothes off of hangers. "Where are you?"

"South Spokane General," she cried. "It's… it's Brian."

"Brian?" I pulled a shirt over my head. "Oh, God. What happened?"

There was a pause, and I could hear the sound of a loudspeaker in the background, paging a Doctor Smith. "He's…"

"Lex? Lex, are you there? What happened to Brian?"

Her voice wavered, as she struggled to get the words out. "He's *gone*, Mar."

Chapter Seventeen

When I was fourteen years old, I snuck out of my mother's house and went to a party with friends. On the way home, we T-boned a Cadillac and were all rushed to a hospital in Hollywood. For over eight hours, I sat in the waiting room with twenty stitches on my head, waiting for my mother to answer her phone and come pick me up.

All of the other kids had left. I sat with a hospital social worker who was on the verge of taking me to a foster home when my mother finally stumbled in. She wore a skimpy, sequined party dress and smelled like whatever club she spent the night in, and hadn't even noticed that I was missing until her stylist checked her voicemail.

When I walked into the South Spokane General that afternoon after Lexie's call, it made that excruciating night in a California hospital seem like a walk in the park. My teenage embarrassment and pain paled in comparison to the grief I witnessed when I ran into the waiting room with still wet, uncombed hair to find Lexie holding Candace her arms as she huddled on the floor, wailing with grief.

Brian had gotten to the fifth hole of the gold tournament before dropping to his knees from a heart attack. Fletcher performed CPR until the paramedics arrived, and he crashed in the ambulance during transport. By the time Candace and Lexie met them in the hospital parking lot, he was gone.

At thirty-five years old, he dropped dead on a sunny golf course with his best friend watching. They had no indication of heart issues, no warning signs of impending heart failure. To look at Brian, there was no hint that he was going to drop dead and leave a wife and three kids behind.

It was unthinkable. Unimaginable.

I tried to talk to Candace, but there was nothing I could say to soothe her distress. She was hysterical. Inconsolable. So much so that the ER doc prescribed her a sedative and sent her home with her parents.

Lexie and I spent the rest of the afternoon with Brian and Candace's kids. Crying, rocking, and comforting Ellie as she sobbed for the loss of her father; and explaining and re-explaining to five-year-old Quentin what'd happened to his daddy. I lost count of how many hours I logged sitting in Candace's creaky wooden rocking chair, brushing two-and-a-half-year-old Aubrey's hair back from her sweaty head as she keened for her mommy, completely perplexed by the mayhem around us.

But no amount of comfort would be enough for those kids. They lost their father. Their mother was a wreck. And Candace had lost the love of her life.

Reminders of their love were all over their house. Black and white photographs from their wedding; framed snapshots of the two of them on scattered vacations; pictures of an ecstatic Brian holding each of his newborn children. A framed love letter written to Candace by a very drunk Brian during a frat party his junior year of college. The preserved calla lilies that Candace carried on their wedding day.

When she met Brian the first time, Candace had charged into my dorm room with her blonde hair flying in all directions, her blue eyes shining. "I've met him!" she cried, throwing herself onto her bunk and kicking the air wildly.

"Met who?" I asked from my perch, hanging halfway out the window, where I snuck a smoke. We'd known each other for three months, and while I tried very hard to hate her for being so all-American and peppy, she won me over, and I already adored her.

She sat up and beamed at me. Her cheeks were pink, and she clasped her hands beneath her chin. "My future husband. I met him. And I love him."

"Love him?" I laughed. "Do you even know him?"

Tears filled her eyes. "No. But it doesn't matter. I looked in his eyes and just knew. I knew, Marisol. Do you understand?"

Dissolving into tears for the hundredth time, I pressed a kiss to the now snoring Aubrey's damp head. I hadn't understood what Candace meant that day

231

in my dorm, but I understood now. And I was finally ready to listen to what she'd been telling me for ten years.

"Lex?" I called, standing up carefully so as not to wake Aubrey. I came around the corner to find Lexie and Fletcher sitting at Candace's dining room table, going through photo albums.

"She finally passed out?" she asked, her voice hoarse. I noticed that one of her hands covered Fletcher's on the table top, and my heart tightened. Fletcher looked horrible, dark circles shadowed his eyes, and I hadn't heard him utter a word in hours.

"Yeah." I walked over to a playpen set up nearby and slowly lowered Aubrey onto the mat. "Listen, I need to go home to grab my phone charger and some clothes for tomorrow."

She wiped her eyes. "Yeah. Okay. Are you coming back?"

I nodded. "Give me an hour or so. When I get back, you two can go home to your own kids. Okay?"

Fletcher looked up at me, his eyes shining with tears. "Thank you for being here, Marisol."

I tried to take a breath, but it felt like a large animal sat across my chest. I had to get out of that house. I needed air. I needed Demo. "You're welcome," I said quickly. I wanted to say so much more.

I'm sorry you lost your best friend today. I'm sorry your CPR didn't work. I'm sorry you had to watch Brian die right in front of you.

But nothing I could say would make anything better. And for once in my life, no crass joke was going to cut the tension.

"I…" I opened and closed my mouth a few times before waving. "I'll be back."

I didn't drive to my house. Instead, I drove through downtown and over the river to the Audubon Park area. It was late—after nine—so the neighborhood was quiet as I pulled up in front of Demo's house. There was a light on in the living room, so I knew he was awake. Maybe waiting for me. He'd called and texted several times earlier in the day, but I'd not yet responded. What the hell was I going to say?

Hey, sorry I haven't gotten back to you. My best friend's husband kicked the bucket today, and I've cried so much that I look like my mother, post plastic surgery. Thanks for the mind blowing sex last night. Talk to you later.

Yeah. Not so much.

Making a beeline for his front door, I didn't look at, or even think about, anything besides getting into that house, and feeling Demo's arms around me. I'd finally found the one man in the entire world I loved, and come hell or high water, I was going to hold on to him for the rest of my life—

The front door swung open. "Marisol?"

I smiled weakly, my finger still poised over the doorbell. "Hi."

"I haven't heard from you all day. I was worried." He stepped out of the door, pulling it shut behind his back.

Well, that was weird.

"I, um, something came up." My voice shook and I reached for him. "I'm sorry I scared you."

For a split second, his arms went around me as naturally as taking a breath. They felt warm, safe, perfect. And then he stiffened. "Something came up around here, too."

My shoulders shook as I pictured Candace on a gurney in the hospital, a needle in her arm as the nurses sedated her. "Let me go first," I whimpered, my tears soaking the front of his black tee shirt. "Please… if I don't tell you now, I don't know if I can get it out."

Demo held me at arms' length. "Hey, are you crying?" He used his thumb to swipe away the moisture on my face. "What's wrong?"

I told him everything. How my best friend lost her husband and now she was a widow with three small children. How she spent the bulk of her adulthood devoted to the one man who fit in her life, completing it, like a puzzle piece. How I loved him more than I even knew how to articulate, and that I never intended to let him go. That if I had a chance to have a tenth of what Candace and Brian had had, I never wanted to be without him again.

"Oh no," Demo said, pulling me close and resting his chin on top of my head. He rocked me back and forth as I cried. "Oh, no, no, no, no. Shit. Oh, shit."

Hiccupping, I pulled back and looked up at him. "Are you all right?"

His face was different. Gone were the crinkles on either side of his eyes, and his dark brows were knit close together. "Marisol, we have to talk."

The curtains on the living room window shifted, and a chill ran through me. Blonde hair. I saw blonde hair. I backed away from him slowly. "Demo, please tell me nobody's inside your house."

He grit his teeth together. "I… yes, there is."

Grief and pain were quickly replaced with rage. "Please tell me that isn't Stacia who just glared at me through your window."

Demo took a step closer to me. "Listen, I can—"

He didn't get to finish his sentence, because the door opened with a shrill creak. Stacia appeared in the doorway wearing a tight black dress and a smug smile. "Demo? Are you coming back in?"

"You have *got* to be kidding me." I stepped out of Demo's reach and backed down the stairs. "Okay, I really need to hear you say that she wasn't invited here tonight, Demo. I need to hear that she showed up, and you don't want her here." When he stood there saying nothing, my voice rose to an embarrassingly loud level. "Listen. I don't think you're understanding what I'm needing to hear right now, okay? *Please tell me she's not welcome here, Demo.*"

"Why wouldn't I be welcome here?" Stacia stepped forward, one hand on her flat stomach.

Holy hell.

"Marisol, Stacia stopped by tonight to tell me something." Demo followed me down the steps, but I backed away from him. He dragged a hand through his hair. "Dammit. I'm still processing it all myself."

My eyes flicked from his face, to Stacia's hand rubbing her middle, and then back to Demo. "It all? What does *it all* actually entail? Because from where I stand, it's not looking so good."

Stacia looped her arm through Demo's. He moved to the side, but her grip on his elbow remained strong. "You should tell her," she whispered. "It's not fair to keep her in the dark. We're all adults here. We can handle ourselves."

"You're giving me entirely too much credit, my dear." I clenched my hands at my sides, and turned my focus back to Demo. "Please. Just tell me what's going on. I've..." My breath halted, and I had to take a second to compose myself. "I've had such a horrific day."

Demo's face was pale. "Marisol, Stacia is pregnant."

My heart screeched to a halt, and I stooped over like I'd taken a punch to the gut. "This is real," I told myself, wiping my sweaty hands on my legs. "This is really happening."

Demo stepped out of Stacias' grip. "Mar, let's talk about—"

I put up my hands. "No. Let's not talk." Yanking my keys out of my pocket, I forced myself to smile, despite the fact that my heart was completely annihilated. "Listen, congrats. To both of you. Demo, you said you wanted a family." My voice cracked, and I cleared my throat. "Well... here you go."

He called my name, but I could barely hear it over the buzzing inside my ears. Thankfully, I got into my car and drove it a few blocks away before I had to pull over because I was so blinded by tears.

Chapter Eighteen

Speaking at funerals wasn't my bag, baby.

Okay, jokes were highly inappropriate, but that was all I had. Too many emotions pushed to the surface. Too many terrified thoughts. Too many worries. Too much anguish had been witnessed. And I felt entirely too much pain for my own good. If the old saying was *when it rains, it pours,* then it was a freaking tsunami in the middle of monsoon season in my life.

When Candace asked me to stand up and say a few words at the end of Brian's funeral, I thought she'd officially lost it. It was time to put her in a padded room with corks on her forks, the whole nine yards. She'd lost it. After all, Brian and I spent most of our time poking fun at each other and arguing.

But the more I thought about it, the clearer it became. Candace could see what I always ignored, which was that her husband and I had become good friends over the years. He filled the space left empty by my parents when neither of them had any other children. He was, for all intents and purposes, my brother.

And so, with shaking knees and more sweat underneath my arms than a real lady would admit—but hey, I wasn't a lady... and I was sweating like a damn cow—I stood up and recalled one of my best Brian memories.

It happened during our senior year of college. He was planning on proposing soon, and I was the only one who knew about it. Candace had dragged us to one of her stupid plays, and he and I were bored out of our gourds and whispering back and forth in the darkened theater...

"Good Lord," he hissed to me during an especially long stretch of undecipherable dialogue. "I'd so rather be watching ATTACK OF THE LIVING DEAD HOOKER FROM OUTERSPACE."

I snickered. "Or watching paint dry."

He grinned. "Or cutting my toenails."

I laughed, and slapped a hand over my mouth when Candace shot me a glare. "What?" I whispered from behind my fingers. "You don't simply adore this version of Much Ado About Nothing *as seen through the lens of the Victorian age? But it's so character driven, and the costumes..." I sighed melodramatically, just as Candace had a moment before, "...are divine."*

Brian looked over at Candace, and the love in his eyes made my chest hurt, just a little. "Oh, hell no. It's zombie movies all the way."

"Good luck getting Candace to go to those."

"Yeah," he said. Then he moaned loudly. "Brains!"

Candace shushed us, and I sank down lower in my seat. "Looking for one?"

He moaned again, softer this time. "Oh hey, sounds like your dorm room last night. Only if they're moaning brains *they're in the wrong room. I guess you're safe from the zombie apocalypse."*

I hit him on the shoulder, but I laughed, because I never could help it when Brian was around. "You're disgusting."

"You wouldn't have me any other way," he said. "Can, on the other hand, would love to see me more refined."

I looked at my blonde friend, watching the stage with her lower lip between her teeth. "Nah. She might like you to act human once in a while, but she loves you just the way you are." I paused and Brian just looked at me. "You know, because her standards are so low."

"Right." He smirked. "But you know what?"

"Hmm?"

"I'd do just about anything for her." He slid his hand over hers in the darkness. "She's worth it. We're *worth it, you know?"*

I just nodded. In typical, know-it-all Brian fashion, he was right. But then, he was ALWAYS right.

I don't think Brian ever got Candace to watch zombie movies with him. But I can't even count the number of times they went to see Shakespeare. Every year, he'd go, and, as far as I knew, he never once tried to weasel out of it. Because that's how much he loved her—he'd do anything to make her happy.

Because for Brian, spending three hours with Candace, even if it was at one of those super boring snoozefests that she enjoyed so much, was three hours well spent.

And at the end of the day, isn't that what we all want?

Later, after the service, I looked at Candace's red, splotchy face, and forced myself to smile. "Why don't you go upstairs to lay down, and I'll bring you a cup of tea or something to sip on." She didn't move, didn't blink, didn't register a thing I said. So I squeezed her shoulder, making her jump. "Candace?"

"Yes?" She focused on me, and blinked a few times. "What?"

My stomach dropped. She'd been like this for days. Six, to be exact. The funeral had taken the last shred of strength I had. Between speaking, the music, slide shows and shared memories, I had more crumpled tissues at the bottom of my purse than I'd even thought possible. At one point, I actually thought I was going to be sick from crying so much. All those years of barely shedding a tear, and now I couldn't seem to stop.

But Candace? Candace was *beyond…*

Her grief was palpable, like you could reach into the air surrounding her and grab a handful of it. She'd lost ten pounds already—that's what happened when you refused to consume anything but coffee—and her black dress hung on her bones like a coat rack. Her hair, which I had to force her to wash this morning, hung in a limp ponytail down her back, and the circles around her eyes resembled soot.

I brought her home after the funeral and reception, in the hopes that being alone with her kids would perk her up. Candace's parents were too busy taking care of the funeral arrangements—and Candace herself—to watch them. And Brian's mother, Mama Chang, was drowning in her own grief. Sitting at home with three small children was impossible for her, as well. Lexie had two kids of her own to care for, plus she was struggling to help Fletcher cope, and it wasn't going so well.

I watched as Candace looked past my shoulder at her kids watching a video in the darkened family room. She'd hardly touched Ellie, Quentin, and Aubrey since the day Brian died, and they were climbing the walls, desperate for Mom's attention. Ellie and Quentin were now sleeping under Quentin's bunk bed together at night, and had wet their pants at least twice a day, every day this past week. I'd done more laundry recently than I'd ever done in my adult life, and I had no idea how to help them stop regressing. Aubrey also refused to sleep unless she was resting on my shoulder, so I spent the last few nights sitting upright, so she would sleep. My back was killing me, and I couldn't turn my head to the left at all.

I'd been thrust into full time motherhood in the blink of an eye, and there was no damn instruction manual for these kids. I was flying blind, and it sucked. But what else could I do? They needed me. And honestly… I needed them.

Since leaving him outside his house that night, Demo called my phone eleven times, and left three notes and two bouquets of lilacs on my doorstep.

He'd even left notes for me at Eats & Treats, but since Lexie and I had cancelled a week's worth of events, and I'd been sleeping at Candace's house, I managed to avoid Demo pretty well.

Oh, I knew what he wanted. His voicemails were clear enough.

"Listen, Marisol, I know this is bad. I'm not gonna lie, I'm freaking out, too. But we can get through this. I know we can. I love you. I don't love her, and I never did. People co-parent without being together all the time. There's no reason I can't do that with Stacia. We just need to talk this out. Call me."

But I didn't call back. I'm not sure why. I mean, he was right. We *could* co-parent with that Stacia chick. And we both wanted kids someday. Well, now we had that chance.

So why was I ignoring Demo?

Because watching Candace's grief rack and shake her body, lay her out for days on end, and suck every drop of life out of her heart and soul… was an eye-opening experience. She was so consumed by sadness she couldn't even *hug her children*. She ceased existing. I didn't want that kind of agony in my life. Living alone and coming home to an empty house every day was depressing, yes, but not nearly as excruciating as burying the love of your life. And I knew this to be a fact, as I watched my best friend do it.

I didn't need Demo to have kids. If I really wanted one, I could adopt one. Hell, Angelina Jolie adopted ten of them. I could do that, too. I had the money. And the space.

Besides… if I did it alone, I would never have to worry about Demo hurting me again. Or knocking somebody up. Or keeling over on a golf course.

No love—no loss. It was the perfect plan.

"Go." I turned Candace by the shoulders, and shooed her in the direction of the stairs. "Go lay down for a while, because I'm making you read your kids a bedtime story tonight. No exceptions."

"I… oh… all right," she mumbled, starting up the stairs.

"I'll bring you some tea," I called after her.

She disappeared around the corner. "Coffee."

"Right." I sighed. "I forgot you only drink black death."

Picking up a sponge, I started to wipe down the already spotless countertops. I'd already scrubbed Candace's kitchen twice that day, but a third time never hurt. With all of the people coming in and out of the house, and all of the casseroles being dropped off from neighbors, the last thing I needed was for one of these kids to get sick. I was barely keeping them alive as it was, add in a bad case of influenza, and I was going to wind up killing someone.

Okay. Bad timing on the killing joke. Told you I was bad at this.

I dropped the sponge and covered my face. What the hell was I doing? Helping a friend? Playing house with her kids? *Hiding*? My shoulders started to shake as I started to cry, and I leaned forward to rest my forehead on the cool granite countertop.

"I would give anything to go back in time one week," I whispered to the empty kitchen. "Just one week back… before everything turned to garbage and everyone's lives were ruined."

The doorbell chimed and I sat straight upright. "Great," I muttered, tossing the sponge into the sink, and wiping my hands on my black skirt. More neighbors with more inedible casseroles. I'd eaten more chicken and Bisquick in the past six days than I ever wanted to consume again.

"Who is it, Auntie Marisol?" Ellie asked, peeking through the family room door. The lower half of her little dress was wet. She'd peed again.

"Probably just another person stopping to say hi." I bent down and pressed a kiss to her head. "Go change your clothes, sweetie. But wake don't your mama up, okay?"

"I want my moooooomy," she whined, leaning into me.

"I know," I said softly. "She'll feel better soon. I promise."

Sniffling, Ellie stomped up the stairs. I sighed and walked to the door. I didn't want to talk to another neighbor. I didn't know if I had it in me to sit through another fifteen-minute conversation about how shocking Brian's death was. I already knew it. We all did. Good Lord, I was pretty sure that people three counties overheard Candace screaming about it that first day.

Pulling the door open, I plastered a fake smile on my face. "Hello…" I stopped speaking, and all of the air drained out of my lungs in a long, noisy whoosh.

Demo stood with his hands in his pockets and a frown on his face. The warm weather streak had broken and rain poured from the heavens, soaking his oil-streaked coveralls, and separating his brown hair into wet clumps across his forehead.

"Hey," he said, his voice low and gravelly like the first time we met.

"What are you doing here?"

"You weren't answering my calls." The line between his eyebrows deepened. "Did you see the letters I left at your house and at your shop?"

I nodded. "Yes, I saw them."

His mouth pulled into a line. "And you still didn't call?"

"I was busy. My family needed me."

"I thought you said you didn't have a family."

My eyes stung. "I was wrong."

"Yiayia has been asking about you," he said, his voice soft. "She's angry with me right now."

I imagined poor Yiayia's face when he announced that he'd impregnated the sleazy girl from a bar he'd been banging. Not exactly a pleasant conversation to share over a plate of baklava.

"I don't blame her," I replied, wrapping my arms around myself.

His face tightened. "I deserved that."

"Yup. You did. So Demo, I'll ask again. Why are you here?" My voice cracked, and pressed a hand to my chest. "I mean how did you find me?"

He looked down at his boot, and scuffed it across the welcome mat. "I saw the obituary in the paper, and went to the church after the service. I told a woman cleaning up that I was a friend of the family, and she told me where I could find you."

I wasn't sure whether to slap him and call him a stalker—or bury my face in his chest and say how desperately I missed him. Because I had. I ached for him.

I just tightened my arms around myself. "Well, that was inventive. What is it you want?"

He lifted his chin. I could tell he was getting emotional, as his dark chocolate eyes were damp, and the end of his nose was red. "I'm so sorry you lost your friend."

Jutting my chin out at him, I said, "Thank you. But it isn't me you should feel sorry for. Feel sorry for his wife and kids."

"That's a damn shame. That's just awful." He dragged a hand across the back of his neck, sending droplets of rain in all directions. "Are *you* doing okay, Marisol?"

Tell him the truth. Tell him that he's all you think about when the fog of grief clears, and you can see past Candace's pain. Tell him that you can't go another day without him in your life. Tell him he's your Brian.

"I'm fine," I lied. He nodded, and the pause stretched out into uncomfortable territory. Finally, I groaned. "Listen, is that all you came for?

Because I've got three little kids to make dinner for, and another ten thousand loads of laundry to do, and I'm letting all the cold air—"

"I never meant to hurt you." He reached for me, but I ducked from his touch. "I never meant for this to happen. I never meant for Stacia to get pregnant, and I never meant to ask you to accept me and a baby with another woman. That was never the plan. And I'm not proud of what's happened."

I bit the insides of my cheeks to keep from crying. Or swearing.

He went on. "When I said that I loved you, I meant it. I still mean it. I don't think I'll ever stop loving you. You've been under my skin since that day you showed up in my garage with a broken shoe. When I close my eyes, you're there. When I lay in my bed, I can smell your shampoo on the pillow. You're everything, Marisol, and I would do anything to make it work with you."

My eyes filled. "*She's* having *your baby*, Demo."

"Yes. She is. And I refuse to turn my back on my child." He grimaced. "But Stacia doesn't have me. She has my support as a co-parent only. Do you understand that? I belong to you. And only you. She knows that. I've told her that. Again, and again, and again. And I'll keep telling Stacia that. Forever, if I have to. Because I only want you."

I wanted to tell Demo that we could make it work. That I didn't mind co-parenting, even with someone like Stacia if it meant being with him forever.

At that moment, Ellie came back down the stairs, wearing a new dress. Most of her hair had escaped its bow, and was now standing in all directions. She slid her tiny hand in mine and stared up at Demo. "Who's this?"

"It's a friend." I grabbed the door handle. "I've got to go, I—"

Demo's expression softened, and the line between his eyebrows disappeared. "Well, hi," he said gently, crouching down and holding out his hand. "My name's Demetrious. What's yours?"

Ellie shook his hand. "Ellie. Are you Marisol's boyfriend?"

"Not anymore." Demo shook his head. "Maybe you can help me change her mind."

My heart squeezed inside of my chest, and I swallowed the lump forming in my throat. "I have to feed the kids now. I'll... I'll call you later, Demo."

He looked up at me, his eyebrows raised. "You will?"

"My daddy used to be my mommy's boyfriend," Ellie announced solemnly. When Demo turned his attention back to her, she nodded. "And then he became her husband. That's when I came. And my brother and sister, too."

Demo smiled kindly, and I caught a glimpse of those wrinkles at the corners of his eyes. "I see."

Ellie's eyes widened. "Now my daddy is in heaven. He went there on Sunday. Now Mommy cries all the time."

I put my arm around her. "Okay, kiddo. Let's go make some quesadillas, shall we?"

Demo stood upright and took my hand. "Wait. Marisol, please. Will you call me later? There's so much to talk about."

Ellie reached up to me. "I miss my daddy, Marisol."

"I know, hon. I know." Scooping her up, I pressed a kiss to the side of her head and looked at Demo. He was so handsome, and so strong, but with such a kind, genuine heart underneath his rough, callused exterior. His family was huge and busy and nosey, and they all loved each other with the intensity of a speeding mac truck. He wasn't a CEO and didn't have an impressive bank account statement, but he was more loyal, loving, and devoted than all the men I'd been with put together. In a nutshell, Demo was perfect.

And I couldn't risk losing him someday. The pain would be too difficult. Too crippling. I wasn't as strong as Candace was.

So I would beat it to the punch.

Straightening my shoulders, I stepped back into the foyer and started to close the door. "Sorry, Demo. But I can't do this."

He stared at me, open-mouthed. "What? Why?"

"Because I can't!" I snapped. "Don't you get it? It's always been *me*. Just me. I get being alone. I've done it long enough. So why are you here? What do you want from me?"

Demo's Adam's apple bobbed. "I don't know. All I know is that I love you, Marisol."

I swallowed hard. "I can't do this with you. Not now, not ever. I tried, and it's not worth this."

Demo's shoulders dropped. "Not worth *what*?"

249

"This. This pain. This heartache. If loving someone causes this much pain, then I don't want any of it. Better for me to be alone, because *this*, losing *this*, would break me. And I refuse to be broken like that."

"Marisol..." Demo whispered, and the agony in that single word made my heart cough and twist, and sent a shockwave of pain through my entire body. I locked my legs in the upright position so I wouldn't tip over and land face down on the tile floor—because I wasn't sure I would ever get myself up again.

"It's over, Demo," I said, my voice raspy. "Go home now."

And then I shut the door before he could say another word.

A few minutes later, as I stood at the stovetop, flipping tortillas in a hot pan, I heard a shuffle and a scraping noise coming from the front hall. I peeked around the corner to find a yellowed note card had been shoved through the mail slot in the door. It was damp, splattered with food, and the words were written in long, curvy cursive writing.

At the top of the card, it read: *Antonopolous Family Dolmades Recipe, yields 48 dolmas.*

Chapter Nineteen

Two weeks had passed since the funeral, and Lexie and I were back to work getting ready for the Greek wedding that would pay the rest of our overhead for the year. We avoided it for as long as we could, but we had mortgages to pay, and it was time to finally get back to real life. Lexie and Fletcher had taken a trip down south to see some of his relatives, and regroup before he went back to work, and by the grace of God, Candace was up and moving again. Not happily, mind you, but she eventually came out of the grief fog enough to notice her kids needed her.

It stank to high hell to admit it, but I missed those little buggers. My neck was steadily recovering from sleeping upright for a week and a half, and I finally removed the stench of urine from my nicest pair of Adriano Goldschmeid jeans. But sleeping alone in my bed every night was depressing as hell, and Cocinero wasn't helping.

I missed him.

No, not my cat.

Demo. Every day I missed him more. Every day I drove past Triple D's on my way home from work—even though it was six miles in the opposite direction—and craned my neck for a glimpse of his grey coveralls. My heart longed for him in the same way I watched Lexie longing for Fletcher before they finally got together, and even though I considered her to be acting like a lovesick freak... I finally understood where she'd been coming from.

Because *I* was the lovesick freak.

But that didn't mean I regretted my choice. No love = no pain. There was a reason Annalise was the bitter, botoxed-to-high-hell train wreck that she was. It was because she loved and lost entirely too many times. She hadn'tprotected herself from the agony that came with adoring someone so much that when they leave, they take half of you with them...

And I was *never* going to be that woman.

"Okay, the dolmades are finished, and believe me when I say, they are perfection." Lexie adjusted the bandana holding her short red hair back from her face. "I made five batches, which means we've got two hundred forty of those bad boys to please the crowd."

I smiled at her. "Wonderful. Thank you."

She held one up. "Are you sure you won't try one? You always say serving food you didn't taste first is a one-way ticket to bankruptcy."

"No. I trust you."

I made Lexie prepare the dolmades. It hadn't felt right to use Yiayia's recipe, not when I hadn't become a part of the Antonopolous family. Plus, Greek food tasted bad now. Maybe because I was slowly filling up with bitterness, like my mother. I couldn't be sure. "I finished the cashew fingers and put them in the walk-in cooler a few minutes ago."

"Great." She pulled off her apron and brushed rice off of her front. "I'll pick up the tee shirts on the way home tonight."

"Ten, right?" I said. Since we weren't going to have Candace's help for the event, we hired a handful of culinary students from the local community college to fill the gap. I hadn't seen her in a few days, and it'd been even longer for Lexie.

"Right." Lexie leaned against the table and released a long breath. "Are you going to go check on her tonight?"

"I don't know." I took my own apron off and started to tug my hair loose from its bun. "I think she thinks I'm hovering."

"That's because you *are* hovering."

Lexie and I both turned to the door. There was Candace, her face pale and sallow, her clothes hanging off of her like an anorexic. "Can!" Lexie squealed, charging at her cousin and pulling her into a bear hug. "I'm so glad to see you. How are you? How are the kids?"

Candace's face tightened and she pulled away. "My husband's dead, Lex. How do you think I'm doing?"

Lexie winced. "I didn't mean—"

"It's okay. Sorry. That was bitchy." Candace shook her head. "I just… I just came to see how everything was going for the wedding."

253

"It's fine." I showed her the list of dishes we prepped. "We've got three quarters of it prepped and ready to go. The rest we'll do tomorrow morning."

"Do you have, um…" She rubbed her eyes. "Wait staff? Enough to handle a crowd that big?"

Lexie nodded. "We hired some from the college."

"Oh. Right." Candace's mouth pulled into a tight line. "Good."

I touched her arm. "Listen, I know you're sick of everyone asking how you're doing. So I won't say it. But I've been thinking about you."

"I know." She nodded stiffly, her eyes flicking between Lexie and me. She seemed ice cold, like a statue. Such a far cry from the bouncy, affectionate woman she'd always been. "Thank you. Both of you."

"How are the kids?" Lexie asked.

Candace shrugged her bony shoulders. "As good as can be expected. Quentin is back in pull ups at night, so that's a new development."

"Yeah, he fire hosed everything in his bedroom one night." I laughed uneasily. "I learned pretty fast that a good washer and dryer is key to motherhood."

Lexie snorted. "I have a hard time picturing you washing wet Bob the Builder sheets."

Nudging her, I smiled at Candace. "I learned fast. And they were Spongebob, anyway. I hate to admit it, but I miss them."

"They're great," Candace agreed, looking around the room. Her blue eyes suddenly filled, and she started to blink. "I just… I just… maybe I shouldn't have stopped by. I should go."

Lexie and I both blurted, "No!"

Candace put her hand over her mouth, and gasped. "It's just that… I keep trying to get back to normal, and… he's everywhere."

I can relate.

I silently scolded myself for even thinking I had an inkling of what Candace was going through. Brian was *dead*. Demo was perfectly alive and well; I'd just sent him packing.

"It's okay, Candace," I said gently, putting my arm around her and letting her melt against my side. "It will take time. You shouldn't rush yourself."

"We were so good together, you know?" she whimpered. "We just fit together like puzzle pieces. He *fit*, you know? I just don't know how to be me… without him."

Lexie moved to Candace's other side, and put her head on her cousin's shoulder. "You and Brian had the kind of love most people dream about. It will take a while before you learn how to be yourself without your other half."

My heart tugged and I rubbed at my chest absently. All this work to protect my heart, and it still hurt. Go figure.

Tears streamed down Candace's face. "It's not right. People shouldn't have to face life without the person they love the most. It's impossible to face another day, let alone a year or the rest of my life, without Brian." She lifted her head and stared at me, wild eyed. "I don't want to be alone forever. I never have. Why did this happen? Why me? Why us?"

"I..." I swallowed. "I don't know. But I'm so, so sorry."

"Shhh." Lexie smoothed down Candace's hair as she cried, and the three of us sank to the cold tile floor. "You won't be alone. We're with you. You know that."

Candace shook her head, tears dripping off of the end of her nose. "No. You've got Fletcher... and Marisol's got Demo. You've got people to live for and to love you for the rest of your lives. You don't understand how damned lucky you really are to have found your soul mate."

I bit my lip so hard, I could taste blood. This wasn't the time or place to bring up my debunked attempt at a relationship. This was Candace's moment.

Lexie rested her head on Candace's shoulder. "I understand."

"You guys have to..." Candace hiccupped. "You have to hold on to them. Fletcher and Demo. You found them, now make every moment count. Hold on to them and soak up every single drop of every single moment. Savor every second with them. Because for all you know... poof!" She wiped her nose on the end of her shirtsleeve. "Gone. Just... gone."

"We will," Lexie whispered, dabbing at her own eyes. "Right, Mar?"

I opened my mouth. Then closed it, and pressed my lips together tightly.

I hadn't told a soul—save for Cocinero—that I broke things off with Demo. Partly because the right moment hadn't presented itself. I mean, how does one bring up the fact that they've broken up with the man she'd barely started dating… when her friend was mourning the death of her husband of ten years? I worked too hard at quashing my self-absorbed ways to backslide now.

And I also kept it to myself because I wasn't sure I wanted to hear Lexie and Candace's disapproval. There was no way I was going to be able to explain why I gave up a life with my soul mate. The fact that he was expecting a baby with someone else wouldn't phase Lexie at all. Hell, she met and fell in love with Fletcher while pregnant, and Candace supported her the whole time. They would support me if I decided to remain in a relationship with Demo, and co-parent his baby with Stacia. But they wouldn't support my dumping him because I never wanted to face losing him.

They would have called that move childish.

I grimaced. Maybe they would be right.

Candace used the end of her sleeve to wipe her eyes again, and I noticed how sallow her cheeks looked. I wonder how much weight she'd lost. Pain seeped from her like carbon dioxide as she sat there. I could practically see it in the air around her, wavering and blurring like heat waves.

I couldn't go through that. I wouldn't make it. She was so much stronger than I was.

"Right," I said finally. Tucking my hair behind my ears, I smiled as widely as I could. "Absolutely."

"I'm sorry I fell apart." Candace pushed herself to her feet, and laced her shaking fingers together. "I thought I was ready to get out of the house, but I think I was wrong."

"No, you're fine. It was so nice to see you." Lexie stood up and wrapped her arms around her cousin, and I watched as Candace stiffened.

That was unusual for her. Usually Candace was all over both Lexie and me, hugging us and showering us with compliments and smothering us with affection.

"Do you want me to come home with you?" I asked, following her to the door as soon as she wriggled out of Lexie's grip. "I can make the kids dinner while you take a nap or something?" Candace just shook her head, not looking at us. "Okay, I'll be honest. I miss your kids."

Lexie scoffed. "Whatever."

"No, I'm serious." I laughed. "They've grown on me."

"No, thank you." Candace fingered the door handle. "You've got a life. Go have fun. Don't worry about me."

Lexie and I exchanged a nervous look. "It's no big deal. I'd be happy to."

"No." Candace's voice was sharp. Her blue eyes rose and she forced a smile. "Sorry. I'm just fine. I don't need your help."

I nudged Lexie, so she stepped forward and touched Candace's arm. "What about me? Need a little cousin time?"

Candace jumped away from her hand like it was on fire. "I said no."

Lexie's face dropped. "Oh, okay."

"I'll see you guys later," Candace said, pulling the door open, and looking at us with damp eyes. "Good luck on the wedding tomorrow. And... and remember what I said, okay?"

As soon as the door shut, Lexie turned to me. "She's not okay."

"I know." I nodded, a sick feeling roiling in my stomach.

"Why wouldn't she want us to be with her?" Lexie's voice started to waver. "Why would she want to be alone?"

"She *is* alone now, Lex." I rubbed my eyes. "I don't think she wants us around because we're not. We have someone in our lives. Or, did." Lexie looked at me strangely, so I added, "Loneliness can do a real number on a person."

"I can't stand the fact that she feels this way." Lexie wrapped her arms around herself and leaned against the table. "It breaks my heart."

"I know. Mine, too." I started putting dirty bowls into the stainless steel sink. "I'll go over to her house after we're done here."

Lexie bit her lip. "But Candace said not to."

"Well, she needs to know she's not alone." Releasing a long, guttural sigh, I turned on the hot water and poured some dish soap into the sink. "Besides, it's not like I have anything better to do."

Lexie looked at me quizzically. "Where's Demo tonight?"

"I don't know," I said quietly, tears pricking at the back of my eyes.

She leaned closer. "What is going on with you?"

"Nothing."

"Knock it off. Something's wrong." I glared at her, and she shook her head. "I mean, besides the obvious. Spill it."

I avoided her eyes and started to wash a bowl. "We're all stressed out. With the funeral, and worrying about Candace, and the wedding tomorrow. I… I'm just tired."

"We're *all* tired." She moved closer to me. "Is everything going all right with Demo?"

"Everything…" I gulped, swallowing down the growing lump in my throat. "Everything's fine."

"Did he dump you?" she whispered.

I scrubbed harder. "I said everything is *fine*."

"That's bull crap," Lexie said, touching my arm. "Mar, stop cleaning and talk to me."

The lump morphed into a cactus, and it prickled and jabbed me from the inside out. I wanted to tell her so badly. I wanted to tell somebody, *anybody,* who cared. I needed to get it out in the open, because the secret was rotting inside of me.

When I turned to Lexie, hot tears spilled over the edge of my eyes and rolled down my cheeks. "Oh, Lex…" I whimpered, falling forward against her shoulder.

"It's okay," she told me, rubbing circles on my back. "It's okay. It's okay…"

And then I told her *everything.*

Chapter Twenty

Taking a deep breath of the garlic and lemon-scented air, I uncovered the silver chafing dish filled to the top with dolmades. There they sat, perfectly rolled and shaped into small, bite sized bundles of Mediterranean goodness—the literal representation of my short-lived relationship with Demo Antonopolous.

Lexie had gone above and beyond bringing Yiayia's recipe to life. They were picture perfect and culinary magazine spread worthy. Every employee we hired for the day had raved about their flavor and texture, including one young man who came from a Greek family who prided himself on eating authentic recipes. When we put them on the buffet line, they were the first dish to disappear, and I overheard the bride telling the groom that they were "orgasm inducing."

Overall, after all the test recipes, the worrying, and the planning, the dolmades wound up being a *slam-freaking-dunk*.

I was just sad I couldn't go thank Yiayia for the recipe.

"Hey, Marisol, can you grab some more tahini sauce from the kitchen?" Lexie asked, whisking past me with an empty platter. "And ask the wait staff to start refilling the red wine glasses at the head table. They're drinking like fish out there."

"You got it." I checked to make sure that the flames underneath the dish were still glowing, and plucked a few crumbs off of the crisp white tablecloth.

I spent an hour talking to Lexie the night before. It wasn't easy. Upon hearing that Demo was expecting a baby with someone else, she immediately started fishing through her purse for her keys so she could go to Triple D's to use a battery recharger on his face. But the further I went into my feelings, and why I walked away from our relationship, she quieted and eventually put her car keys away. In fact, by the time we turned off the lights and locked up Eats & Treats, I think she may have actually understood where I was coming from. After all, she had a man in her life she couldn't bear losing, too.

"Thanks, Mar." The sound of a plate breaking rang out, and Lexie charged into the kitchen with a scowl. "Friggin' great."

I glanced around to make sure nobody was looking, then plucked a dolma out of the chafing dish with one of my gloved hands. Though the thought of eating one of Yiayia's delicacies made my heart ache, I wanted to taste them for myself.

Hey, five hundred guests at a Greek wedding can't be wrong, right?

I popped it into my mouth and began to chew. "Oh, my gosh…" I moaned quietly, leaning against a nearby wall. The bride was right. These things *were* orgasmic. Almost as orgasmic as Demo making an omelet in nothing but his boxer briefs.

Demo.

My heart ached and I sucked in a sharp breath. Probably shouldn't have thought about him. Every time I did, it made my insides twist and spasm, and usually left me breathless and in need of a good cry sesh. And crying in the middle of this wedding was *not* an option.

I used the corner of my apron to dab my eyes. "Pull it together, Vargas."

"Was it really *that* good?" A deep, rough voice asked.

Excitement danced up my spine, and I turned in time to see Demo emerging through the kitchen door. He wore a pair of dark jeans and a clean plaid shirt, but there was an endearing streak of oil mixed with the dark whiskers on his chin. He stood out like a nun at a runway show amongst all of the white tuxes and brightly dressed guests that filled the hotel ballroom.

"Demo!" My voice squeaked, so I pressed a hand to my throat. "What are you doing here?"

He hung close to the kitchen door. "My mother said there was a wedding at the Orthodox church this afternoon. I figured it was the one you were catering, so I asked around to find out where the reception was."

"Your stalking skills have taken new heights," I said wryly, ignoring the way my heart had started thumping *Ode To Joy* as soon as he walked in. I wanted to throw myself at him, and press my face to his neck, but refrained.

I heard my dad's voice in my mind: *What's done is done. Move on.*

I pushed myself off the wall and folded my arms across my chest. If I didn't get Demo out of here, I would start backtracking, and that would lead to more hurting. And frankly, I'd met my hurt quota for the quarter. "First Candace's house and now this. Can't you take a hint?"

He frowned. "I tried. I really did."

Irritation bubbled in my gut. This wasn't helping. Not one bit. My heart was breaking, and I was barely keeping myself together without turning into a bitter lush. If Demo insisted on showing up where I *worked*, I may as well sign my half of the business over to Lexie right here and now.

"Well, this is a wedding and you weren't invited," I hissed, grabbing his arm and dragging him into the kitchen. The hustle and bustle of the wait staff stopped as soon as I walked in. "Get back to work!" I snapped.

Demo nodded at them as they lifted their trays onto their shoulders and hustled off. "You're right. I wasn't invited. But as it turns out, Yiayia was, and she couldn't be here today. So I came in her place. Problem solved."

Rubbing my forehead, I closed my eyes. "You can't ambush me at work, Demo. I made my decision, now it's your job to respect that."

He put his hands on my shoulders. "I know. And I'm sorry. But… you need to know how I feel."

"I already know how you feel." I nearly melted under his touch. "What we had was nice. Super nice. But I'm not the type to settle down. My life is

264

better when it's just me. It's less complicated, less…" I searched for the words but nothing came to mind. Damn Demo and his magic hands.

"You want the same things I want," he said, leaning close so that I could hear his voice over the clatter of some pans. Lexie was sautéing garlic a few feet away, and if she knew Demo was here, she would lose it. "You told me so."

"So what?" I pulled away from his touch, immediately missing it. "I changed my mind."

"You changed your mind?" He scoffed. "You're chicken shit. That's what you are."

The irritation in my gut quickly morphed into rage. "Excuse me?"

His face pulled down in a scowl. "I didn't stutter."

"*¡Eres una basura!*" Clenching my hands at my sides, I shoved past Demo. "Get out of here. I've got work to do."

He followed me to a rack of pastries, where I started to slam sheet after sheet onto the counter. "You think calling me a piece of garbage is going to scare me away?"

"I can say something worse if you like." My chest throbbed. I wanted to crawl into the nearby walk in cooler and sob for an hour or two. "Since you're not taking the hint."

"You love me." He grabbed my elbow. "*I know you do.*"

"Go away."

"You're just afraid! You're scared that if you have a life with me, it won't be all champagne and flowers every day." He tried to turn me so that I would face him. "You're scared that there may be some hard times. That we may fight and yell at each other. That raising my kid might be tough from time to time, or that raising the kids we have together won't be a walk in the park."

"Go to hell," I barked over my shoulder. His words hurt. They stung like a sunburn, leaving scars on my heart. Demo was right. Every last word was dead on.

"And what's worst of all…" Demo put his hands up on the rack, one on either side of me, so I couldn't move. "You're so afraid of losing the people you love, you won't even let yourself love them. Not really. And that, as I said, makes you chicken shit."

Spinning on my heel, I yelled a string of obscenities that would have made even the dirtiest biker rush to a confession booth.

The kitchen went silent. Every waiter stopped what they were doing—again—to peer at me. What made it worse was that I lost the battle against my tears, and now I was crying. Me. The woman who used to *never* cry. And now I couldn't seem to stop.

Awesome.

Demo touched my face, sending an electric shock through my skin down into my chest. "Marisol, don't cry."

I swatted at his hands. "Then go away!"

His thumbs swiped away my tears. "I love you." When I tried to bolt, he pressed his lips to my forehead. "Don't you understand that? I love you, Marisol Vargas. And I want—"

A pimple-faced waiter popped up right next to us, holding a silver tray of bite-sized pastries. "Ms. Vargas, what do you want me to do with the touloumbes?"

The look Demo gave him was positively lethal. "Give us a minute, kid."

It felt like all the oxygen had been sucked out of the kitchen, and I couldn't take a breath. Not being with Demo felt like it was going to kill me. But being with him meant taking on a world of stress and fear that made me want to curl up in a ball and suck my thumb. I avoided falling in love for thirty-two years. If this is how relationships felt, why did so many people want them, for hell's sake?

"I…" My eyes bounced between the waiter and Demo, looking for the answer. Waiting for someone—anyone—to tell me what the hell to do. Struggling to breathe, I pried Demo's hands away from my face.

Straightening my shoulders, I wiped my cheeks and looked Demo dead in the eyes. "I'm sorry, Demo. I can't do this."

Fisting my hands at my side, I turned and walked away.

"Ms. Vargas?" the waiter repeated. "The touloumbes?"

I gasped for air and pushed on the kitchen door. "*Bend over and I'll show you what to do with the touloumbes!*"

"What the hell is going on?" Lexie slammed a pan down and charged towards Demo. As soon as she rounded the corner of the rack and spotted him, her eyes narrowed. "You," she growled, pointing a greasy spoon at his face. "What in the world are you doing here?"

"I needed to see her." Demo put his hands out defensively. "Put the spoon down, would ya?"

"Make me!" Lexie snarled. "You wanna know why she's rejecting you?"

I closed my eyes and pushed through the door. I didn't need to hear Lexie reading Demo the riot act. Nothing she said would change the fact that I was in love with him… and totally unable to commit. Blame my mother, blame my father. Hell, let's get real, and blame *me*. But the bottom line was: I was forever stunted, and it was time to accept that.

The door swung closed behind me.

Chapter Twenty-one

"Just keep swimming, just keep swimming…" I stopped singing to myself and nodded at a groomsman who approached the buffet to grab a few more dolmades.

He gave me a smug grin. "Were you singing to me, beautiful?"

I would have laughed, had I not been singing to keep myself from weeping all over the food. That stupid song from the fish movie Candace's kids watched approximately eighteen *thousand* times a day kept rolling off my tongue as I refreshed all of the foods on the buffet and prepared to wheel out the wedding cake. It was all I could do to keep myself in one piece after I saw Demo leave the hotel, stomping back to his tow truck with his hands shoved in his pockets.

At first I wondered what Lexie said to him. Then I decided I didn't care. At least he was gone, and I could go back to being emotionally constipated again.

Wouldn't Annalise and my dad be proud?

"Tempting, but not today," I told the groomsman, who checked to make sure his fly was up. What a winner.

He leaned against the buffet table, making it shift slightly. So help me, if he knocked this food over...

"Hey, uh, did you know this ballroom is next to a hotel?" he asked, not-so-subtly, setting the beer bottle he was carrying down on the table.

"Please tell me you're kidding," I said flatly.

"No, really." He nodded. "It is. I'm staying there this weekend. I'm from Arizona."

I wasn't quite sure how to react. A few short months ago—okay, let's be honest, maybe a month ago—I would have asked him which room he was staying in, and then possibly enjoyed a lovely nightcap with an inebriated groomsman after the reception. After all, I could tell just by looking at him that he was wearing Gucci shoes and a Jack Spade watch. He was my type.

However, as I looked into his nice green eyes and caramel colored hair, all I longed for was Demo's heavy, grease-stained boots and his sweat-soaked brown curly hair in perpetual need of a haircut.

"Well then, I'm glad this place is next to a hotel." I forced a smile, knowing it came off like a grimace instead. "Otherwise you're going to be mighty uncomfortable tonight."

He laughed like I'd done an entire stand up set. "You're funny, has anyone ever told you that?"

I blinked at him. "Once or twice. Well, enjoy the food. Cake is coming up soon."

I started to walk away, but he reached across the table to touch my shoulder. The bottom hem of his suit coat brushed across a dish of tzatziki sauce, making me bristle. "Hey, wait—"

"No, *you* wait." Shaking off his hand, I pointed at his now soiled clothes. "First off, you need to learn how to take a hint. I'm not interested, okay chief?"

His eyes widened. "You got a boyfriend, or something?"

My hands went to my hips. "And second, if you drag your coat through my buffet again, I'm going to have to jump over this table to break your arm. That's just the kind of mood I'm in."

"Yikes. *Easy.*" He put out his hands. "Sorry to have ticked you off, beautiful. Just trying to have a good time."

"Yeah, well, go hit on one of them." I pointed across the ballroom where one of the bridesmaids was doing the worm on the dance floor, her peach satin dress flopping up over her ample bottom, revealing a lovely pair of black Spanx. "You've got a much better chance at one of those ladies."

He grimaced, and plucked his bottle of imported beer back off of the table. "Come on. That's just mean."

I sighed, and I felt my shoulders drop a few inches. "I'm not being mean. Listen, I'm sorry. What's your name?"

He flashed a grin. I waited to feel the spark of attraction flare inside of my gut, but instead there was... *nothing*. "James. James Koffer."

"Well, James-James Koffer, what do you do?"

"I'm a criminal defense lawyer."

I paused, waiting for my girl parts to start singing. But there was nothing. "Interesting," I said, shifting some baklava on a tray. "What do you do for fun, James-James?"

"I like waterskiing and spending time on my boat."

Again, I waited. Surely at any time my inner temptress would wake up after being dormant, and encourage me to hook up with this lawyer to get Demo out of my brain. After all, the best way to get over one man was to get into bed with another. At least that's what my mom told me.

James-James took a swig of beer, then tilted his head. "Come on. Why not?"

I watched wistfully as the bride and groom went to the center of the floor and started to laugh and dance together. "Because I like men who have dirt and grease underneath their nails. I like to eat tacos out of a truck, and I like men who smell like gasoline, and who live two houses down from their mother and grandmother so he can score free meals off them every night."

"Huh?" He made a face. "Please. I bought a house for my parents in Palm Springs so they'd get off my ass."

Sighing, I plucked a crumb off of the table. "You're just not my type. We're complete opposites."

"Don't be a snob." James-James waved his hand, sloshing beer. "Aren't opposites supposed to attract?"

"Not this time."

"Whatever... so we're different. Maybe we'll find out that we're like..." He looked up and down the buffet, then grinned and pointed to an elaborate fruit tray I made, complete with pineapple owl and a watermelon swan. "Apples and oranges. And what's to say that wouldn't make for a great hookup."

My mouth dropped and I stared at him. Had he really just said that?

James-James spoke again before I had a chance to react. "We might make a delicious fruit salad, huh?"

My stomach roiled, and a pain shot through my chest. "Excuse me, I've got to get out of here," I said, bolting for the kitchen door. I needed air. Lots of air. And maybe a stiff drink. A super stiff drink, with a stiffer drink chaser.

What the hell was I doing sending Demo away? He was everything I would ever want in a man—flaws and all—and by some sort of miraculous alignment of the planets, or a gift from *God* or something, he wanted me, flaws and all, right back. If Candace had known that Brian was going to drop dead of a heart attack on a golf course one day, would she have walked away from him at that frat party and never had a family with him?

Oh hell no.

So why in the crap did I send Demo packing at the mere notion of less-than-perfect times?

273

I had to get to him. I had to find Demo and tell him I loved him, too. That I wanted a life with him… and his kid… and his crazy family… and his little run-down house on Lincoln Lane. In fact, I could no longer imagine my life any other way.

Shoving on the door, I was met with a muted thud, and then an "Ooof!"

"Oh, damn," I muttered, peering around the edge of the door to find Lexie rubbing her forehead. "Sorry. Hey, I've got a ten-minute break coming. I've got to go."

Her eyes widened. "You never take breaks."

"I know." I peered at her head. "It's not swelling. Are you sure you're okay?"

"Yes." She gave her head a shake, then smoothed down the front of her apron. "But seriously, you can't go. Just go check the pastry table. Make sure they're still stocked."

Panic started to spread through me like a fog. "Lex, I'm sorry. But I've got to run. Most of the guests are done with the buffet. We just need to ask the wait staff to clear, then we can get the deejay to announce it's cake cutting time."

Lexie's brown eyes flashed. "Yes, exactly. There's so much to do. You can't leave now."

I used my eyes to plead with her. "I've got to go. I can't explain, but… but I promise I won't be long, okay?"

"No," she said flatly, her jaw twitching.

"Excuse me?" One of my eyebrows rose high on my forehead. Lexie never bossed me around. We were coworkers. Not boss-and-employee.

She squared her shoulders. "You're not going anywhere. I need you here."

"Actually…" I paused to suck in a deep breath and collect myself. Swearing at my best friend in Spanish would not help the situation right now. "I *am* going somewhere. In the state of Washington, where we reside, it is a mandated ten minute break every three hours. So I'm going to take my—"

"No. You're staying." Lexie bit her lip. I think she thought I was going to punch her. Maybe I would.

Gritting my molars together, I rocked back on my heels. "Listen, Lex, I'm not gonna lie. I need to go to Triple D's. I swear upon everything holy that I'll be back in ten minutes. If I'm not, you can take the entire commission for this wedding." I put my hands on her shoulders and looked her square in the eye, willing her to understand how important this was to me. "If I don't get to Demo now, I'm going to shatter into a million pieces, Lex."

She blinked at me a few times, and the music across the room stopped. "I'm sorry, Marisol. I need you right now. You… you can't leave. I mean it."

I tried to step around my friend, but she just moved so that I couldn't get through the door. My eyes blurred with tears. "Mother of God, Lexie. You are *really* pissing me off."

Lexie winced. "I don't care." She took my arm and turned me towards the buffet. "Go check the pastry table. *Now*."

275

"*Vete al infierno*," I hissed, stumbling over my own feet as I stomped away.

"Okay, everybody, if I could just get your attention turned this way for a few moments," the deejay said, his voice booming through the oversized speakers.

I glanced up at the head of the dance floor where flashing lights were rolling from ceiling to floor. Guests were gathered around the stage, some holding drinks, others with their arm around a loved one. The evening sky was visible through the floor to ceiling windows, the purplish sky streaked with orange, and it was gorgeous.

I wanted to be enjoying it from the comfort of Demo's arms. Not working while he thought I no longer wanted him. My heart ground inside of my chest.

Demo.

"We'll be getting to the cake cutting very soon, folks, I know you're all excited for that," the deejay's velvety deep voice announced. "But a friend of the groom's family has gotten special permission from our happy couple to make an announcement."

Cringing, I used the corner of my apron to dab at my eyes. This was my least favorite part of catering weddings. Listening to cheesy toasts and dedications made by sappy, inebriated guests. Ugh. Kill me now.

"So without further adieu, folks, please give family friend, Mr. Demetrious Ant... anton... an... anotoff..." My head snapped up in time to see Demo lumbering up to the deejay booth with a scowl.

I gasped out loud. "What the..."

"Antonopolous," Demo growled at the deejay.

"Yeah," the deejay said, clapping him on the back. "What he said. All right, buddy, do your thing."

Demo walked over to the microphone and cleared his throat. His dark eyes scanned the crowd looking for me, and when he found what he was looking for, they locked onto mine like a vice grip. Sweat stung my skin, and I felt like everyone in the joint was gaping at me—though they weren't. They were looking at Demo. But he didn't notice them. He only watched me. *Me.*

"Uh... hello, everyone. Congratulations..." He glanced at a paper in his hand. "Paul and Nikki, on your wedding and all that. As promised, I'm back with my Yiayia's award winning recipe for her Melomakarona. Those of you who know my family know that my grandmother's recipes are top secret. She only shares them with people she considers... *family.*"

A shiver rippled down my spine, and a clenched my hands at my side. I was considered part of that blessed family. Or had been. Once.

I gulped, but didn't break eye contact with him.

He acknowledged me with a nod. "And so, because what I need to say is so important, I went and begged Yiayia for the recipe, to give to the brides' mother as bribery. Apparently Yiayia's Melomakarona has beaten Mrs.

277

Katopokaus' recipe two years in a row, and she's ready for the streak to end. And because Yiayia knew how dire the situation was, she agreed to allow this. So, Mrs. Katopokaus, here you go. Use it wisely."

Demo held a tattered note card out and forced a smile. A titter went through the crowd, and a very satisfied-looking woman wearing a corsage the size of a hubcap stepped forward to collect it.

As soon as the ballroom went quiet again, Demo cleared his throat and wiped some sweat off of his brow. "So... uh... I'll make this quick. Because I'm not much for public speaking, and frankly, the woman I'm trying to speak *to* just told me to take a flying leap, so she could call security on me at any time. She's back by the dessert table... wearing an apron."

The wedding guests all chuckled and looked around, searching for me. My face started to scald, so I started walking back toward the kitchen door. A pair of small hands grabbed my shoulders from behind. "Oh, no you don't," Lexie whispered. "You get to stay out here and listen to every word he has to say."

I glanced over my shoulder. "You were in on this."

Her brown eyes filled, and she grinned at me. "I love you, Mar. Of course I was in on this."

"I... I love you, too." The words tumbled out of my mouth, and as soon as they were out in the open, I felt self-conscious. "I don't know what to say. I thought you were being a bitch, I—"

She gave me a squeeze, then pushed me forward. "Don't be so mushy, you big sap."

Demo's eyes met mine again, and he locked one of his hands on the microphone stand. "Look, I know everyone here is ready to cut into that cake, but here's the deal. I met the woman I love a few weeks ago, and she's been the only thing I could think about since. She's everything I never thought I wanted in a woman. She's sophisticated. She prefers fine dining over a cold beer and fishing. She's the opposite of me in every way, and yet—for some reason I don't understand, and may never understand—she is the perfect fit."

Suddenly there was no one else in the ballroom. Just Demo and me. Everyone else just faded into a blurry background image like a chalk drawing in the rain.

"The problem is, she's afraid to be with me, because her friend—er, her *family*—went through something traumatic recently." Demo's eyes softened, and the corners of his mouth pulled downward. "And between that, and a recent and, uh, unexpected turn of events in my life... she's scared to commit to me. She's afraid that if she gives in, and agrees to let me love her for the rest of her life, something will go wrong, and it won't be easy peasy anymore."

"Did he just say *easy peasy*?" Lexie whispered behind me.

I ignored her.

"The thing is, life isn't all about passion and romance and all that crap." Demo tugged a hand through his dark hair, making it flop across the forehead in the front, and stand adorably upright in the back. "It's about finding the person who will take the ride with you. It's about being with the same person through all the ebbs and flows, and the great things and the shitty days." His eyes widened. "Oh, sorry. I mean the *rough days*. My parents and grandparents all found their perfect mate, and so did my siblings. Paul and Muriel, you've found yours. Isn't that what it's all about? Finding that person who loves us even when we're a complete train wreck, but still doesn't want to get off at the next stop?"

Everyone laughed, but I couldn't. I couldn't even breathe. He wasn't giving me up without a fight, and I no longer wanted him too. I found my *one* person. The sweet apple to my acidic orange, and was I willing to give that up again?

Oh, hell to the no.

I started weaving my way through the crowd, sidestepping guests and members of the bridal party as Demo started to talk again.

"I knew as soon as I saw her that she was the one I was meant to take the ride with." His voice thickened and he pressed his lips together. "I haven't felt that way for a long time. Years. Maybe ever. But I've found her now, and I'm not willing to give that up again."

"I'm not either," I called, nearly stepping on the bride's train. "Oh, sorry."

She turned to me and smiled. "You'd better get up there."

Demo smiled, his white teeth gleaming and the wrinkles around his eyes out in full force. That smile was going to be my own personal kryptonite for the rest of my life. "I don't care what the future will bring. I don't care how great or not great our life will be. The only thing I care about is spending it with you, Marisol Vargas."

I emerged from the crowd and stood just a few feet from him, my heart pounding in my chest like a snare drum.

"I'm sorry," I said, my voice cracking. "I was wrong. I shouldn't have—"

"Shhh." Demo reached into the pocket of his coveralls. When his hand emerged with a little black velvet box, the crowd erupted into cheers. "I have a question to ask."

My heart screeched to a halt inside of my chest, and I froze. This was the very moment that I'd lived in fear of for twenty years. After watching my mother march down the aisle more times than most people cleaned their ovens, the idea of marriage had taken on a slightly unattractive feel.

Trapped. Tied down. Off the market. Taken.

Fight or flight! Get the hell out of Dodge!

But I remained standing. Even if my mind screamed at me, warning me of impending doom, I knew one thing for sure. I couldn't live without Demo any more than he could live without me. This was it. The moment I'd been dreading for more than half my life.

The moment I settled down.

"Marisol Vargas? Will you make me the happiest man in the world and marry me?"

The entire ballroom of people focused on me. Over a thousand eyes honing in on me to witness my reaction. Could I really do this? Could I really settle down and spend the rest of my life with a man who smelled like oil and sweat?

Why, yes. Yes, I could.

My face split into a grin I couldn't hide. "Of course I will."

The end.

Epilogue

Demo

"It's a girl!" Fletcher cheered happily, emerging from between Stacia's knees with a blood-covered screaming bundle. "Congrats, Demo. You're a father."

Flashes of light popped in my peripheral vision, and for a second, I was dizzy.

I was a father. *I* was a *father.* To a *girl,* no less.

I needed to buy a shotgun.

"Is she okay? Is she okay?" Stacia wept.

I looked down at the sweaty fingers laced with mine and realized I couldn't feel my hand anymore. "Yes," I told her, pulling my hand free and wiggling my fingers. "Yes, she looks fine."

"She's more than fine!" boomed the chubby nurse who was now wiping my daughter—my *daughter*—off on a warming bed. "Ten toes, ten fingers. And bellowing like a baby elephant. She's perfect."

Stacia beamed, collapsing back onto the bed with a relieved sigh. "Thank you." Tears rolled down her face as she looked up at me. "Thank you so much."

I bent down and pressed a kiss to her sweat-slicked forehead. "You're welcome. Thank *you*."

We gazed at each other. Pride, and joy, and terror, and elation all rolled into one sappy look between new parents. The air in the room felt different as I pulled it into my lungs. Cleaner, fresher, almost ethereal. Like all of the planets had aligned and earth stopped rotating for just a moment while we welcomed our child.

I was a father.

"And thank you." Stacia's voice was weak. She looked beyond exhausted as she turned and looked up to the person standing on the other side of the bed, holding her other hand. "Thank you so much."

My eyes rolled up to Marisol's face, which was pale as she stared, wide eyed, at the baby across the room.

"You okay, babe?" I asked.

She met my gaze and blinked. "That was un-freaking-believable."

I laughed. "It sure was."

"I'm glad it's over." Marisol focused on Stacia, her eyes still wide as half dollars. "I can't believe your body just did that. I can't believe you survived. Holy hell."

Fletcher looked up from whatever he was doing—I didn't even want to know—and said, "She did an amazing job. Just like you will someday."

Marisol narrowed her eyes at me, even though her mouth still pricked upward. "Don't get any ideas, Romeo."

She never ceased to amaze me. She was the only woman in the world who could watch something that clearly repulsed her, and still look like a Playboy model after. But that wasn't why I loved her as much as I did. I loved Marisol because she's everything I'm not. Creative, determined, confident. Every personality trait I lacked, she had in spades, and when we were together, we made one perfect entity.

"Why don't you let her get through the wedding first," Stacia peered around my shoulder to where the nurse was wrapping the baby in what looked like yards and yards of pink cotton. "Where's Toby? Is he all right?"

Toby, who wasn't a half bad guy, considering the fact that I fixed Stacia up with him, peeked from around his camcorder. "I'm all right. You did so good, sweetheart, it was incredible" He gave me a thumbs up. "Got it all on tape, Dad."

My stomach hurtled. Wasn't sure when I'd have the stomach to watch that movie. "Thanks. I think."

Toby dropped the camera onto a nearby chair and squeezed past me to envelop Stacia in a hug. Tears leaked from her eyes as they rocked. "When can I hold her?" she asked, sniffling.

"Now." The nurse brought the bundle to Stacia and gently rested it on her chest. Little eyes covered in clear gel blinked up at me, shooting a shock of emotion straight to my heart.

"Hello there," I whispered.

"My Gosh, she's incredible," Marisol said, her voice breaking. She bent down and pressed a kiss to Stacia's forehead, in the same spot where I kissed her. "Thank you for this gift. Thank you so very much."

Her engagement ring caught the bright light from above the bed, and my breath caught. Our wedding was in a month. We pushed it back long enough that our daughter would be old enough to attend, and so that Stacia and Toby could come, too. Marisol hadn't wanted a big wedding, but once her mother, Annalise, got wind of our engagement, she called Spokane's premier event planner, and it snowballed from there.

I didn't care. It didn't matter to me if we had a damn three-ring circus, so long as I got to dedicate myself to the woman I loved at the end of it all. Oh, and so long as Yiayia headed up the catering for the reception. Which, of course, she did, with Lexie as her sous chef.

Marisol fit right into my motley crew of a family, and moved into my house on Lincoln Lane three weeks after my proposal. We earned enough money from the sale of her fancy house in the gated neighborhood to fix up my old house pretty nicely, and even managed to do a few things around Yiayia's house, at the insistence of Mar, who said "living without central air is just plain barbaric."

My life used to be filled with anger and isolation. I never thought finding love was a possibility for me, because I rejected so many chances in the years since my debunked wedding to Belinda. I figured God was punishing me for kicking my best friend's ass in His church, and that I was destined to a life of mooching meals off of relatives, then suffering through heartburn alone. Now I was about to be married to a caterer who insisted on naked omelet Saturdays.

Score.

Add in the fact that Stacia had agreed to a 50/50 split on parenting duties, so we would raise our daughter in a very modern American—er, scratch that. Make it a Greek-Latino-American—family… and I was the happiest man alive.

Marisol looked at me, tears dragging her makeup down her face. "I can't believe you have a daughter."

"*We all* have a daughter," Stacia reminded her weepily.

I grinned. "It feels surreal."

"Surreal?" Marisol squeaked. "It feels out of this fracking world!" She put her hand on the baby's head, gently swiping her damp hair. "We're parents." She glanced at Stacia and Toby. "All of us. Holy hell. We're all *parents*."

I laughed and wiped tears from my eyes. Gazing at Marisol, I felt my heart tighten inside of my chest. She was so incredibly gorgeous, sometimes it hurt to look at her. It was like looking directly at the sun. Which fit, because there were no words to describe how much light she brought into my life. When I looked at her, I saw years—decades—into our future, surrounded by droves of children and grandchildren. I saw days spent arguing over the cable bill, and nights spend making up in each other's arms. I saw noisy family meals peppered with Greek and Spanish conversations, and impromptu make out sessions while weeding the flower gardens in the summer.

There were times when I wondered how I managed to go so many years without her in my life. Being without her felt like being void of oxygen.

I crossed around the bed and drew Marisol in my arms.

"I love you," I whispered into her sweet-smelling hair. "I love you so much."

Her tears soaked the skin on the side of my neck. "I love you, too."

Together we wept like any new parents would.

Of course we did. Hell, we just met our daughter.

Acknowlegements:

Marisol's story was born one afternoon when my beta reader said, "You're gonna write Marisol's story. Right? *Right?*"

It wasn't until that moment that I even considered making Baby & Bump a *series*. And thus the This & That Series was born. Marisol's story came to me fast and furiously, almost filling my brain faster than I could type. Which, if we are all being honest, is exactly Marisol's style, wouldn't you say? I have to say that I had so much fun writing it, and that Marisol will go down as one of my favorite characters of all time. Thank you, Marisol Vargas, for being you.

I have some of the most supportive friends and fellow writers in my community, and I am eternally grateful for each of them. Katie & Jess, you two are the best beta readers an author could ask for. Thank you so very much. And Jess, thank you from the bottom of my heart for the midday plotting sessions that usually consisted of me griping about my personal life more so than actual *work*. Thanks for never getting sick of me. Or at least not showing it when you were.

Special shout out to "The Itzel Library"....you know what you helped with, and I appreciate it. Very much.

At the risk of sounding over the top, I literally cannot take all of the credit for this book, or Baby & Bump, without throwing out homage to my CP and editor, Meggan Connors. This woman earns her keep, folks. She listens to my whining, accepts my moods—no matter how foul, and she literally turns my books into little works of silly, romantic art. Without her, my stories are just that… stories. Thank you, Meggan. *You are priceless.*

A special thanks goes to my family. They never make me feel bad when I am buying KFC—again—so that I can get back to writing. And they always tell me I'm pretty, even when I haven't showered for two days, and my hair looks like a lesbian logger (not that there's anything wrong with that.) My children are wonderful, chipper, funny little people who make me feel like I've done something right in this world, and my husband is truly the greatest gift I've ever received. Thank you.

As always, I've saved the best for last. To my readers: I will never be anything without each of you, no matter where you are, or what you look like. You're wonderful, you're supportive, you're perfect, and in my imagination you've all got most excellent hair. Thank you for making my career dreams come true. It is all because of you that I can say this adventure was a success. Thank you so very much.

And as always… stay tuned. There is always more to come.

Then & Now

Book 3 of the This & That Series

I blinked at the man sitting across the table from me, waiting for him to tell me he was kidding, but alas… he just sat there. Wiggling his eyebrows at me. I may have seen a bit of tongue poke out of his mouth, too, but I couldn't be sure, because the waiter approached our table with the check.

Thank you, God, for rescuing me from this pervert.

"How was dinner tonight? Good, eh?" The waiter beamed down at us like our steaks could've changed our lives.

Mine hadn't changed my life. It had, however, given me a rotten case of indigestion. Or maybe that was the company. The slick expensive suit and Mercedes Benz parked outside of the restaurant weren't enough to convince me this date was a good idea. In fact, I was pretty convinced that it was a completely, utterly bad idea.

This was the last time I let my friend, Marisol, fix me up. Six dates with a myriad of handsome, successful men, and not one of them had made my heart twitch. Or my girlie bits twitch… because that's what she said really mattered when you're a thirty-four year old widow. (Her opinion, not mine.)

As if Marisol's illicit track record as a serial dater—before she married a handsome Greek mechanic—weren't enough to convince me that I was better off alone, then the fact that I was getting more hot and bothered fantasizing about getting home and devouring my latest novel was. I could practically feel the thin cotton comfort of my favorite sweats on my legs, instead of the constrictive grey skirt I was wearing. And in the back of my mind, I imagined the way the worn pages turning would sound in my quiet bedroom.

I almost gasped. I had a babysitter back at home, which meant the kids were probably already asleep. And that meant I would be left alone to read in *peace.*

Hot damn! I could hardly contain my excitement. I had to get home. Now.

My eyes darted from the waiter's face, to my date's, who was staring at me like a teenager stares at the most dangerous ride at a theme park. Like a roller coaster he needed to conquer.

Sorry, buddy. There won't be any conquering tonight.

Suppressing a shudder, I smiled up at the waiter. "The steak was dry," I said sweetly. "And the asparagus tasted like gym socks. Could we get our check please?"

Okay, okay. So I was being kind of nasty. Usually that wasn't my style. Or, it wasn't before my husband dropped dead on a golf course, leaving me

292

alone with three small children to raise. In the twenty-two months, eight days, and five hours since, I'd become a bit callused. My friends and family tell me that they miss the "old me." That it's been nearly two years, and I need to perk up.

Hey, we can't help what grief does to us, right? At least that's what my therapist says. I consider that permission to be as bitchy and antisocial as I want. Hey, that's why I pay her the big bucks, right?

"That was, uh, *direct*." Irritation flashed in my date's—Rick, or Rich, or... oh, crap, I don't care, anyway—eyes. "You know, I had to pull some major strings to get us into this place without a reservation. It's the hottest restaurant in town."

"Oh, really? I wouldn't know." I fiddled with my earring, and looked at him coyly. "Thank you for the dinner, Rich."

"*Rob*," he hissed, adjusting his cufflinks.

Seriously, who cared?

"Right." I looked down at my hands and noticed the subtle indentation the third finger on my left hand still had. A sinking sensation filled my stomach, and I sucked in a sharp breath of air.

I'd only stopped wearing my wedding ring a few months ago. Around the same time Marisol convinced me to go on debunked date #1. Thom with a "th," who'd asked me if I wanted him to come to his place for some sex and won tons. Little did the poor schmuck know I'd given up both sex *and* won tons after my husband, Brian, died.

"Where are we headed next?" Rob asked me, smoothing down his tie. "How about some martini's at Madison's? Maybe that'll loosen you up."

I looked at him sharply. "Need loosening, do I?"

He scoffed. "Well, *yeah*. When Marisol Vargas called to tell me she had someone she wanted me to meet, I expected someone a little more…"

I knew where this was going. I'd had the same discussion with most of the other dates. When Rob paused, I folded my arms across my chest. "Promiscuous?"

"No!" He shook his head, then laughed and nodded. "Well, yes. Maybe. A little."

Good Lord, I hated dating. I'd hated it clear back in college when I'd met Brian at a frat party. "Sorry. Not my style."

Rob leaned forward, his elbows on the table making his roll plate tilt. "Marisol says you're a widow."

"Uh huh."

"I'm sorry to hear that."

No, he wasn't. They never were. If he hadn't died, we wouldn't be on this date. Duh.

"How long has he been gone?" Rob asked, tilting his head to the side.

Ah, the head tilt. The #1 way people expressed their sympathy without actually uttering the words, *my sympathies*.

"Nearly two years," I told him, my arms tightening around my middle.

He clicked his tongue. "That's awful. Just awful."

I didn't know what to say, so I decided on: "Yes."

"So, in those two years, you haven't… you know, *dated* anyone seriously?"

Aw, hell. I knew where this was going. Date #3—Patric-without-a-K— had gone there, too. The whole *you're a lonely widow, you must be so horny* thing. Oh, yeah. I'd heard that one before.

I shook my head. "No."

His eyelids lowered in what I could only assume was supposed to be a seductive gaze. "So…" He licked his lips. "In theory, you haven't been with a man in, like, *two years*. Right?" He said this like I'd actually refrained from something necessary for life. Like water. Or air. "I'll bet you're lonely."

"Listen, Rob, I—"

He didn't let me finish. "Listen, why don't we go back to my condo? I've got a hot tub, and maybe we can get to know each other better. Work off some of that sexual tension you must have pent up."

I rubbed my eyes. "Oh, good Lord."

The truth was, I'd only recently started to miss sex. In the months and years prior, I'd missed Brian's hands on my skin, or the way he laughed into my neck when we made love, or the scent of his cologne on my pillow in the morning. I still missed those things. But the all-consuming ache I felt for those moments had dulled. Now they were distant memories that made me wistful.

I no longer craved Brian's adept ability to satisfy me. Now I just craved the release. The explosion of sensation that made my mind go fuzzy and blank.

The split second of utter disconnect when I could forget how lonely I was, and the stress of being the only parent my kids had left. When the buzz filled my head and my toes curled and my body hummed. That's what I missed nowadays.

Not that I was going to admit that to Rob. I'd rather grow cobwebs in my woo-hoo than go to bed with the likes of him. Or any of the other losers I was being set up with. No thank you. Because as much as I missed the feel of someone else's hands on my body other than my four-and-a half year old's, having a friends with benefits relationship wasn't my style, and never would be.

I liked being a wife and mother. I was good at it. Too bad it had come to an abrupt end.

Then & Now: Book 3 of the This & That Series

Coming soon from Brooke Moss!

"I write because if I don't...my head will explode, and ruin the drapes." ♥

Brooke writes complex, character-driven stories about kismet, reunited lovers, first love, and the kind of romance that we should all have the chance at finding. She prefers her stories laced with some humor just for fun, and enough drama to keep her readers flipping the pages, and begging for more. When Brooke isn't spinning tales, she spends her time drawing/cartooning, reading, watching movies then comparing them to books, wrangling five kids, mugging on one hubby she lovingly refers to as her "nerd", and attempting to conquer the Mount Everest of laundry that is the bane of her existence. Brooke is also an avid Autism Awareness advocate, and a passionate foster/adoptive mother, who loves to share her experiences with anyone who will listen. Find Brooke elsewhere on the web at www.brookemoss.com

www.ingramcontent.com/pod-product-compliance
Lightning Source LLC
Chambersburg PA
CBHW060536180626
46817CB00002B/595